D0342985

"Stands out brightly above other thrillers for originality, ingenuity, local color and unputdownableness."—*Barbara Bray*

"Intricately plotted, convincingly written, David Downie's Paris City of Night is a fast-moving, atmospheric thriller. Best to start reading this one early in the evening...unless, that is, you don't mind losing a night's sleep!" —*David Hunt*

"A wild ride through the dark side of Paris with a writer who knows the city's streets and their secrets..." —*Diane Johnson*

DAVID DOWNIE lives in Paris. A journalist, he is the author of half a dozen nonfiction books, including *Paris, Paris: Journey into the City of Light.* Visit www.pariscityofnight.com and www.davidddownie.com.

PARIS CITY OF NIGHT

A NOVEL OF SUSPENSE

DAVID DOWNIE

Copyright © 2009 by David Downie

All rights reserved. No part of this book may be used or reproduced in any manner or form whatsoever without the written permission of the publisher, exception made in the case of brief quotations embodied in critical reviews and articles. For information contact MEP, Inc., 8124 N. Ridgeway Avenue, Skokie, IL 60076, USA, Tel: 800.277.4645, info@mep-inc.net.

Published by MEP, inc.
Skokie, IL

ISBN 978-1-60111-016-9

Printed in Canada

Jacket design by Jason Snyder.
Layout by Adam Hess.
Jacket photographs of Eiffel Tower copyright © 2009 by Alison Harris.

May 2009

For Alison

"Since love and fear can hardly exist together, if we must choose between them, it is far safer to be feared than loved."

—Niccolò Machiavelli, *The Prince*

PARIS CITY OF NIGHT

A NOVEL OF SUSPENSE

DAVID DOWNIE

PARIS CITY OF NIGHT

Paris, June 18, 1950

Watery silhouettes formed. First came a wharf and the sides of a gray ship. A wooden gangway strung with ropes appeared next. Two funnels welled up. A man leaned on the railing of the first-class deck, a newspaper rolled and held in his gloved right hand. He wore round eyeglasses, a raincoat and a panama hat.

The second-hand of the darkroom clock swept past 6:00am. Georges Henri removed the print from the solution and passed it from pan to pan.

The darkroom door led to a lavatory. Georges crossed the tiles and clipped the print to a line stretched over the claw-foot bathtub. Leaning on its edge, he closed his eyes. Summer was about to begin. But he felt cold. He shivered as he thought of the passenger with round glasses, and the things the passenger had done. His name was no longer Adolf Eichmann. Only he, MDL in Paris, Globke in Berlin, and Monsignor Petranovic in Genoa had seen the name in the new passport. Only they and Eichmann's escort knew the final destination of Signor Klemens. He was due to disembark in Buenos Aires in twenty-seven days.

Beyond the bathroom window, dawn forged the outlines of a city. The Eiffel Tower gave it away. Paris did not in any way resemble the port city in the print, a city whose church towers and hulking townhouses, and the jagged hills of the Italian Riviera, were coming into focus as the print dried.

The photograph had been taken from the deck of a freighter, Georges noted, preparing his report for MDL. It was anchored approximately one hundred yards away from the ship carrying Eichmann-Klemens. That would explain the elevated standpoint. Viewed with a magnifying loupe, the print and its negative would reveal other details. The approximate time yesterday when operative Grant took the picture could be calculated, for instance, and the ambient temperature. It was unusually cool for June in both Genoa and Paris. Eichmann's raincoat was beige, standard-issue, provided by CIC via the Red Cross. Three letters were visible in the name of the rolled newspaper. C-o-r. *Corriere della Sera* or *Corriere Mercantile*? Rolled inside was another newspaper, a German newspaper. The photograph was black-and-white. The three colors of the ship's flag were readable nonetheless. All that was required was familiarity with the gray scale.

Paris, December 26, 2007

Stop—stop it, stop!

The carriage jerked to a halt, the driver's words thickening from baritone to bass. Madeleine screamed herself awake in an unfamiliar bed. The coachman's face hovered over her. He wore white gloves.

Go away, Madeleine pleaded. Her voice startled her. It was the voice of an old woman, cracked and frail. She looked at her outstretched hands. But it was too dark. She couldn't see their age marks and knotted veins. She ran her fingers over pleats and pouches and whispered. This is the nightmare. I am the nightmare.

Madeleine fumbled for the light switch. It wasn't where it should be. Her hearing aid scuttled across the nightstand ahead of blunt fingers. *Go away*, she shouted again. The hallway floor creaked, the parquet wrestling in its grooves. Straining, Madeleine raised herself out of bed. She found her slippers and shuffled to the French windows, half expecting to see moonlight silhouetting the schooner shrouds and her grandfather's coachman. But the curtains were shut. She wondered why and pulled them open. Light bled in. There was no carriage, no coachman and no white sailing ship. A streetlight glowed beyond the shrubs bordering the garden. Hers was the last freestanding house left in the shadow of the Eiffel Tower. Old money. The world her grandparents had known. Her world. When she was gone they would build another of *those*. She stared at the marble-clad apartment building next door. I was born here. Ninety-three years ago. And I'll die here. Soon.

In the hallway Madeleine de Lafayette's grandparents frowned down at her from a gilt-framed photograph. Phaeton or landau, she asked herself. The daguerreotype on the shelf showed a phaeton with a schooner moored behind it. She lifted the daguerreotype and grappled with another memory, something about plates and numbers and a codebook. A voice whispered in her head, drawing her eyes toward the schooner's rigging. Sailors climbed up the ratlines into the shrouds on a winter day in 1915.

Madeleine didn't turn on the floorlamp. She knew the topography blindfolded. Christmas lights glowed on the small plastic tree. She wished it were a live fir tree. Perhaps they thought she wouldn't know the difference.

The Persian carpet in the living room had worn through. She felt it with her slippers. Threadbare. How had the Empire table separated itself from the Louis Philippe sofa? Somehow it had crossed the room, shedding its ship models and Degas bronze ballerina. She puzzled. Everything seemed to get up and move. Pictures. Sculptures. Books. Even furniture. Elves, she whispered to herself. Or rats.

"You're becoming absent-minded, Madame." That was

Mademoiselle Trichet's explanation. The nurse. "It's normal at your age. Take your medication. It's in your mind. There are no rats in the house, and no freighters or sailing ships in the garden."

Phaeton or landau, Madeleine asked herself again as she shuffled forward, hearing the gravel under the carriage's metal-rimmed wheels. It was pulling up to the wharf now where *La Liberté* awaited. A clock struck three. Beeswax. Dust. Who ever thought I would live to be so old?

The overstuffed armchair threw open its green upholstered wings. Madeleine sank into them, smelling the musty damask her mother had loved. She thought of her mother and humorless, mustachioed father. Grandfather hadn't approved of him. Grandfather hadn't approved of her, Madeleine, an only grandchild. Not a grandson and heir for a shipping dynasty. Later, years later, he'd scoffed at her again. Joining the Free French with General de Gaulle wasn't something a de Lafayette lady would do. Working for the Americans was worse.

But they were dead, she consoled herself. They and their world. None of it was any more real than a daguerreotype of a ship's shrouds and lines.

Angling the plate she caught the light off the Christmas tree. Madeleine scrutinized the daguerreotype. She remembered colors but saw only the plate's duochrome black-and-white. They'd scuttled *La Liberté* after 80 years of service. I wasn't yet ten. The road to the wharf was rough. That coachman was rash to drive so fast. The carriage was a phaeton, she muttered to herself. It was a phaeton. The ship had been square rigged. Why did the daguerreotype show an open landau coach and schooner rigging?

Madeleine peered as if into a looking glass, seeing her life reflected in the plate. She thought of Jay, her protégé. Jay Grant. She'd seen him in his crib. He'd bought the daguerreotype for her. *La Liberté: Study of Schooner Shrouds*, by Quincy Alphonse

Louis Thomas. Made in 1843. She couldn't help wondering why she had outlived Jay's parents, Marie-Anne and William. And her own son. No one is left, she whispered. No one but Jacqueline. Jacqueline visited once a week. But she was a decade younger so didn't count. Georges. Yes. Georges was still alive. But Georges was always so busy. And he'd scolded her, she couldn't remember why. The plates? Was that why Georges had asked her all those questions? Something about books and photographs, plates and numbers from the old days. With William. Something about rats and rigging and cargo ships.

Madeleine ran her fingers along the daguerreotype's metal edge. I never felt old until now. The medication wasn't working. Georges had sent in the rat-catchers. But the pills hadn't helped and the rats were still in the basement, looking for something. She would have to tell Georges again. Tell the nurse.

Light seeped through the French windows. The Christmas tree twinkled. Madeleine closed her eyes. Heat throbbed behind her temples. Horses reared up. The carriage flew over ruts and russet gravel, the ship's shrouds billowing above. She felt the coachman's hands on her shoulders again. A face welled up from the daguerreotype.

"Where is it Madeleine?" a voice wheedled. "Help us find it." Madeleine forced open her eyes. But the nightmare didn't stop. The silhouette shook her. Its gloved hands wrenched the daguerreotype from her fingers.

Stop it, she pleaded. *Stop.* Then a warm, scarlet curtain fell and all was dark and silent.

Paris, December 28, 2007

A tailwind had blown the Airbus 300C across the Atlantic. It felt to Jay like the wind was still behind him. He slipped his black oxfords on for the third time, repacked his briefcase and merged in the arrivals hall with other rumpled passengers from London and Milan. Why he had to submit to a shoe-check on the ground at Charles de Gaulle he couldn't figure out. But there was no point arguing. It only got you in trouble. Through the hall's outsized skylights his eyes tracked the Mirage fighter. Was it the same one that had escorted his flight? An orange alert had been announced the day before Christmas. According to the voice on the PA system it was still in effect. Orange wasn't red. And red wasn't black. But something had to be wrong.

"What's up?" Jay asked, watching his neighbor from business class crane her neck following the fighter's trajectory.

"Definitely something." Debra had a light southern accent. She'd said she was from Kentucky, an account executive now working in Paris. She held up the palm of her free hand. "Don't ask me what's going on. At least we got through Christmas without a bang."

"Bangs are for New Year's Eve, aren't they?"

Debra looked Jay in the eye. "I guess New Year's would be a good time for something unpleasant." She pointed to the sign overhead and the line of arriving passengers. "I'm non-EU," she sighed. She pronounced the European Union's acronym as if it were a disease. "See you again in Paris maybe?"

Jay took Debra's cappuccino-colored hand. He pecked her cheeks, smelling jasmine and toothpaste. "Absolutely," he said, unsure of what he was feeling. "I'll call you." He veered left to join a short line under the 'EU Citizens Only' sign, making an effort to look ahead and keep his eyes off Debra.

Jay's French passport-of-convenience and the European Union's bureaucratic ambiguities eased his passage through security. He stepped up to the line. The customs guard waved him to the inspection zone and asked him to open his briefcase. Again.

"Vintage photographs," Jay said. He showed the no-commercial-value notice stamped in New York. "I'm returning them to the Gilford Foundation." Jay used his smoothest accent, the one he'd picked up from his French aunt.

"You're a dual national?"

"Correct."

"Please show me your American passport."

Jay complied. The guard scrutinized the passport photos, comparing them to Jay's angular features: above-average height, dark hair, blue-brown eyes. He moved his lips as he read, pausing to glance at Jay's mismatched irises. They made the guard frown involuntarily.

At a newsstand Jay bought a copy of last night's *Le Monde*. By 9am he'd caught the RER commuter train heading into town. Clean, fast and quiet, the train reeked of disinfectants. They hinted at unclean secrets. A paramilitary SWAT team worked its way between the passengers. Rain painted the train's windows, masking the housing projects and spaghetti-bowl freeways beyond. Jay almost regretted not sharing a cab with Debra, the talkative, troublingly attractive woman from Kentucky. He guessed she was thirty, his junior by too many years. They'd just spent seven hours together, roaming the world's wonders, and talking about Paris. Jay hadn't wanted to seem overly eager to prolong their chance encounter. Debra. No memories attached, at least not spelled that way. Debra Wright. She'd said she was 'rapturous' about her newfound life in Paris. Jay shivered as he recalled her enthusiasm. Sleeping around had lost its appeal to him. But for the first time in a long time he felt conflicted. He was going to marry Amy. He loved Amy. They were engaged. Why had he met Debra? Why now?

At the Villepinte station Jay rearranged himself on the vinyl seat, making room for a thickset rider. He wore a knee-length sheepskin coat. The man's face looked the color of dead fish. It had been ravaged by acne in a now-distant adolescence. He stank of cheap aftershave.

In contrast to the orderly surroundings at Villepinte, the station platforms were scrawled with graffiti, much of it obscene. Jay puzzled at the fresh aerosol lettering of a phrase he hadn't seen before. *Abraham is Sacred* it screamed. The words were spelled in French and English and—he assumed they were the same words—in Arabic. He noticed the acne-scarred man reading the graffiti, his lips moving silently, like the customs guard's lips.

Rows of commuters leaned against the walls, waiting. *Métro, boulot, dodo* ran the Parisian blue-collar refrain. It translated to *Subway, slog, sleep . . . Subway, slog, sleep. . . .* The words repeated themselves in Jay's head, accompanied by snapshots of Amy and Debra. Day and night. Familiar and unknown. Comfortable and exciting. As the train pulled out again it occurred to him that he'd been commuting most of his life. First he'd shunted between his divorced parents in New York and Paris. Later he'd been a photographer, constantly on the move. Now he was a vintage photography consultant. Traveling had become joyless in the post-9/11 world. But he was an addict. He had wanderlust, and on a deep level it troubled him. He didn't often scrutinize himself. That was too painful. Still, he couldn't help noticing the dissimilarities between his native and adopted cities, and the way they affected his character and mindset. To'ing and fro'ing between Paris and New York and noting the variations was a way of keeping them in separate sub-files.

The first hours after arrival were the best for the kind of revelations he enjoyed sharing with Amy. She'd been marooned in Paris since the early 1980s. He paused. It was hard to credit. They'd actually met in a French *lycée.* They'd been high school sweethearts. And their relationship had gone sweet and sour ever since. Inside his designer suits Jay still felt like the curious, vulnerable teenager she'd loved. But middle age was staring them down, and now he had responsibilities, major responsibilities.

The train rocked. Jay studied the acne-scarred man pressed next to him on the seat, wondering which newspaper he read. Carefully opening his copy of *Le Monde* Jay glanced at the headlines. The fear of more riots and Islamic extremists was tangible. Turning the pages as the commuter train accelerated, his eye fell on the Culture section. He read a single-paragraph item twice, his grip on the newspaper tightening.

During an end-of-year auction to benefit a charitable foundation, a last-minute offering had startled bidders. It was something serious collectors would expect to find at Christies or Sotheby's. The item was a rare, 1843 French stereoscopic daguerreotype titled *La Liberté Grée en Goélette* by Quincy Alphonse Louis Thomas. The plate had garnered the exceptionally high price of 160,000 euros. That was over $300,000. Seller and buyer were anonymous.

La Liberté: Study of Schooner Shrouds Jay repeated to himself, sucking at the train compartment's stale air. He folded the newspaper. Why would Madeleine de Lafayette sell her favorite daguerreotype? She had millions in the bank. To give a gift to that pet charity of hers? More than once she'd told Jay she felt guilty for living past ninety. The charity needed her legacy, she'd said. But she couldn't bring herself to part with her photography collection or sell her house.

Jay was tempted to phone her. He flipped open his satellite cell and then remembered he'd not only failed to send Madeleine a Christmas card. He'd also forgotten to telephone on her birthday. He hadn't seen her and her housekeeper in months. They might've misinterpreted his absence. But he would straighten that out. He'd surprise them with a present for New Year's instead of Christmas, and another for Madeleine's birthday. Maybe he'd persuade them to come to the Gilford Foundation's offices on the Champs-Elysées. Every December 31st thousands of people poured onto the world's widest avenue and at the stroke of midnight hugged each other amid flying champagne corks. Even a cynic couldn't help enjoying the fireworks and floodlit Arc de Triomphe.

He scrolled through his address book, found 'MDL' and hit the call button as the train pulled into Gare du Nord. With the phone in one hand he de-trained. At the end of the platform stood two ranks of gendarmes armed with machine guns. They watched Jay cancel his call, fold his phone shut and put it in his pocket.

Paris and New York were still different places, Jay acknowledged. Yet many things had become virtually identical. They included the SWAT teams. Despite them, public places were increasingly seedy. On his last transatlantic trip less than a month earlier, his laptop had been stolen in a scam, when a handicapped woman had thrust a screaming baby at him.

Jay had been a fair running-back at Bensonhurst School, not great but good. He tucked his briefcase under one arm and trailed his rolling carry-on behind. Paris might appear benign, seductive, even. But Jay knew better. Orange alerts made people trigger-happy. Red and black alerts were worse.

"Welcome to Paris," Jay muttered to himself. He counted his paces as he walked east past the abutting Gare de l'Est train station. Counting was a habit he'd picked up, he wasn't sure when or why. He checked twice to make sure he wasn't being followed, pretending to tie his oxfords and glancing back through his legs. His lips felt rough and dry. For the first time that morning he realized the temperature must be near freezing.

A few hundred yards east of the station the scenery changed. Sunshine coaxed mist off the Canal Saint Martin, its arc of green-hued water bordered by leafless plane trees. Napoleon had traced the waterway across eastern Paris in the early 1800s. Commercial traffic had stopped long ago. Now houseboats and barges cruised it.

Jay climbed a humpback bridge, the ironwork frame and

wooden treads frosted. He paused midway to check his watch. It was too early to show up at Yves' camera shop.

Jay and Yves had an understanding: no one arrived before 10am unless authorized. Like most of the paparazzi Jay had known, Yves Rossi wasn't exactly an early riser.

As the canal water slid by, Jay's thoughts drifted back to Madeleine. He thought of the customs guard at the airport. Old photos and plates like Madeleine's daguerreotype threw inspectors. Few understood the value of vintage pictures. One key Impressionist was worth all the rare photographs in the world. But Jay had never been tempted by paintings. The field was too crowded. His passion since adolescence, since his father had given him his first Kodak Brownie Box camera, was photography.

Glancing back Jay was not pleased to see the acne-scarred man from the train. He and another man in an identical sheepskin coat were making their way toward the canal. The new man wore a headset. He pressed his ear bud and spoke. Steam gushed from his mouth.

Ever since his laptop had been stolen and his identity with it, Jay had felt embattled. He decided it was time to wake Yves. Hefting his carry-on, Jay counted to himself as he covered the 221 steps east. He stopped counting when he reached the storefront. Cupping his eyes he peered in. The clutter of camera bodies, lenses and accessories didn't suggest high turnover. But the cigarette smoke curling through the florescent-lit interior confirmed that Yves Rossi, Jay's main supplier of vintage European photography, was at work earlier than usual.

$$\bigwedge$$

Yves' pale, pocked cheeks reminded Jay of the scar-faced man on the train. They'd lost the bronzing of a decade's service in the French Foreign Legion. Jay suspected Yves of actively avoiding daylight. He was an unlikely Casanova. Despite his gangling frame and pitted face Yves somehow conquered young women, most of them from Paris' rough-edged suburbs. Jay watched as a twenty-something twig of a girl brushed past trailing the scent of pencil shavings and talc. Her dirty blonde hair had been tucked into a ski cap. "Bonjour," she murmured in reply to his greeting.

Inside the shop, chemical and feral smells mixed. It was as if a wet Labrador had walked through. A radio played hits from yesteryear. Jay recognized the guttural voice of 1930s singer Edith Piaf.

Without removing the cigarette from his lips Yves thrust out a large, sinewy hand. He jerked Jay's with a swift downward motion. It was not an American shake. Frenchmen did it differently. And they rarely hugged. Hugs were for friends you hadn't seen recently. Jay had left Paris less than a month earlier. He wasn't sure he considered Yves a friend. A fellow ex-paparazzo and business associate, sure. And a talented forger too.

"I saw the article," Yves said in a smoker's rasping baritone. His lips twisted into a smile. "About the auction." He re-lit his cigarette before stepping into a back room. "We've got a pedigree. Next time you'll see a catalogue with provenance and reproductions of those letters." Yves returned to the shop's front room. He handed Jay an envelope. "How did that first letter go? *Daguerre told me to stand on the Boulevard du Temple and have my boots polished while he exposed his sun picture...*" Yves chortled. "Congratulations."

Jay unfolded his copy of *Le Monde* but hesitated. "I read about the auction on the way in," he said. "I had no idea Madeleine was selling the plate. I'm on vacation." Jay knew Yves was right about the plate's pedigree. But he didn't appreciate the irony, or the way Yves had said *congratulations*.

Yves waited. "Sure," he said. "Tell me another one. In ten years you've never taken a vacation."

Jay let the jibe pass. "I'm taking Amy to Normandy," he said, weighing the envelope in his hands. "Either we get married or break up for good."

"For good? Again?" Yves batted smoke out of the way. "What about the plate? Can you believe the price?"

Jay laid the contents of the envelope on the shop counter. Each set of photographs came in an acid-free pack. Jay sorted them, eliminating a dozen from a bag marked *1860s Paris: Nudes.*

Yves scooped up the rejects. "You always were a moralist." He paused, waiting to catch Jay's eye. "Too bad the old lady died."

"What old lady?"

Yves studied him. He reached for Jay's copy of *Le Monde* and flattened it open to the obituaries page.

Madame Madeleine Adelaïde de Lafayette, aged ninety-three, celebrated Résistance and Free French hero, Legion of Honor recipient, woman of letters and art collector...

Her maid had discovered the body.

Jay opened his mouth but could think of nothing to say.

"I thought you knew," Yves muttered. "She had a good life. It says she was ninety-three." He busied himself filing the rejected photos under the shop counter. In silence he amended and initialed a stack of delivery notices.

"I'll look later," Jay said. His voice was unsteady. He stowed two packs of photos in his briefcase and cleared his throat. "What about my father's Minox?"

Yves retrieved a slender, palm-sized camera. "Get another one off Ebay and maybe I can scavenge it," he suggested, taking a drag from an unfiltered Gauloise. "It was full of dust. You're getting sloppy. That isn't good if you want to keep doing what we do."

"I'm no longer in that business." Jay's face was expressionless. He locked his briefcase. "Bruno and I went clean a long time ago. You know that."

"Sure."

"I'm getting a digital Leica," Jay remarked, "so I won't be troubling you with my Minox."

"Sure," Yves repeated.

Jay inspected the camera. It was a Minox LX Walter Zapp special, a sub-miniature designed in the 1950s for P.I.s and industrial spying. When William Grant had retired from the State Department he'd given it to Jay without specifying how or why he'd bought it.

"One more thing. What about Madeleine's other pictures and plates?"

"We'll have to see," Jay said. He peered through the viewfinder, framed and clicked, testing the add-on motor and flash. The back popped open and Jay dropped in a roll of 8 x 11mm high-sensitivity film. Digital was fine. But nothing could beat the Minox for documents or night photography. "Contrary to what you imagine," Jay said. "I don't know how Madeleine's daguerreotype got to auction. Suddenly it's worth a fortune and it's sold without being listed in a catalogue. And then she dies. I really did not know she was dead."

Yves leaned back on a worn swivel chair. He propped his cowboy boots on the counter. "The seller was anonymous." Yves coughed and lit up another cigarette. "The buyer was a number, not a name. You know what that means."

Jay pocketed the camera. "It means you'd better find out who stole it, because Madeleine would not have sold it or given it away."

"A job for Inspecteur Maigret," Yves said, smiling around blackened teeth. "The maid, the nurse or the gardener?"

"Maybe," Jay said. "But not if they're the ones I know. And it wasn't her housekeeper either. Not Arlette."

Yves shrugged. "If you say so. You'd be amazed."

"I think," Jay said softly, so that Yves had to drop his boots and lean forward, "I think it'll be worth it for you to find out.

If that plate can sell for $300,000 think of what *Daguerre's Window* must be worth. Think about how you can get those other pictures back before someone figures out they're forgeries."

Yves rubbed his pockmarked face. It had turned a paler shade of white. "What about *Curiosity Case*?"

"It's junk," Jay snapped. He hadn't meant to. He'd never enjoyed bargaining or bluffing. He was jetlagged now and surprised by the news of Madeleine's death. "Why do you ask?"

A sardonic smile crossed Yves' face. He stared into Jay's bloodshot, mismatched eyes. "I say we get to work again. A couple more and we could retire. Digital is going to put me out of business down the road. With a little help at the auctions from Claude-Gilles we could cash in. The market's there. For instance a guy came in the other day asking about daguerreotypes, saying he was interested in finding someone who still made them."

"And what did you tell him?"

Yves shrugged. "That I might know someone but that someone wasn't in town right now." Yves paused and pursed his lips. "Funny little old guy. Spoke good French like your dad, but I could tell he was foreign. American. He had a brush-over and funny teeth. Long and bleached. You know him?"

Jay shook his head. "I don't want to know him." He paused long enough to regain composure. "Find out who sold Madeleine's picture. Make a couple of calls and we'll talk. Or text me." He opened the shop door and hesitated. "Do me a favor? Step outside and tell me if you see a couple of guys in sheepskin coats by the canal."

Yves grunted. "Since when are the guys on the bridge interested? It must be your pretty smile."

"I'll bet they don't bother you."

Yves grunted again. "Sometimes you're better off being ugly." He blew smoke through his nicotine-stained teeth. "No one's out here. This is Paris, not the Wild West."

"You're the guy with the cowboy boots."

Yves' face changed from chalk to bruised purple. "One day you might pray someone's going to ride to your rescue," he said, "and he might be wearing cowboy boots. With all the shit that's going on in the world, it might be sooner than you think."

Ⱥ

Yves' words and the image of the man with bleached teeth followed Jay northeast like hungry strays. The neighborhood was not picturesque. It fit Jay's mood. The less scenic the setting the more Jay felt atuned to it. He realized he was walking fast, almost running, but paradoxically began to breathe easier. Once he reached the wide Boulevard de la Villette and its traffic jams he stopped glancing back and felt safe, though he was unsure why safety was an issue. This was Paris, not the Bronx. He was no longer a paparazzo and his father was dead and gone. So was Madeleine.

He'd walked this seedy avenue a thousand times. Somehow today it looked fresh to him. Squinting, he framed the cityscape and stopped to take a picture of a leprous building held up by wooden pilings. Its grimy, weathered shutters creaked. Behind them slatted patterns of dust decorated a wall. He walked on, hardly noticing the cold, periodically checking over his shoulder for the men in sheepskin. A tear welled up and crossed his cheek. The wind, he told himself. Madeleine was not a sentimental type. He had no right to weep for her.

The peeling storefronts he passed were stenciled with overlapping layers of faded advertising and graffiti, as inscrutable and many-faceted as Madeleine's face. The words they spelled rhymed. *Boucherie, boulangerie, quincaillerie, droguerie.* He sang them out, ignoring the aerosol ravings of religious fanatics and reactionary racists. He was already feeling better, feeling more human and less paranoid than he'd been moments before, despite Yves' apocalyptic words. The men in sheepskin were probably security guards, he told himself. The guy with bleached teeth was a tourist. And Yves was right about Madeleine. She'd had a good, long life. Yves would come through with a name and a telephone number. Jay would scramble for a few days. He'd find out what had become of Madeleine's collection and lean on Claude-Gilles d'Arnac until he found *Curiosity Case*. It would all work out. It might not be the vacation with Amy he'd imagined. But maybe he was destined to live in limbo with her. Life was like that. Tomorrow he'd wake up and start putting out feelers. Tomorrow things would be better. He checked his watch. Only twelve more hours to stay awake.

A streetsweeper dressed in green scooped up trash on Rue de Belleville. He used a green plastic broom made to look like a wooden broom from the 1800s. Jay side-stepped it and paused to say "two hundred."

Two hundred paces up from the boulevard corresponded in Jay's mind to Bonjour Siam, his favorite Thai restaurant, where he ate most of his meals. Rakan, the owner, was a friend. Jay's mouth watered as he thought of garlicky quail and crab in coconut milk. Seeing Jay on the sidewalk, Rakan stepped out and offered his hand.

"You coming in today? I got some fresh crab. You might want some spicy."

Jay paused before dipping his chin. "Save one for me. Why spicy?"

"Did you get my message yesterday?" Rakan asked. "Some friends of yours dropped by asking for you. They asked a lot of questions."

"I just flew in," Jay said, yawning. "Who were they?"

Rakan wrinkled his wide forehead. He looked around before leaning toward Jay and continuing. "Never seen them before."

"Tell me about them later," Jay said.

"But I think it might be extra spicy," Rakan insisted.

"Okay. I'll come in once I check the loft."

Strange, Jay told himself, feeling uneasy as he started walking uphill again. 'Spicy crab' was their code for 'trouble.' Jay didn't have many friends in Paris. Rakan was one. The others were colleagues, connections, acquaintances, but not friends. They were hard to come by when you spent your life on the road.

With ninety-nine paces to go before reaching his loft halfway up Rue de Belleville, Jay lifted his eyes to the familiar plaque that marked the spot where Edith Giovanna Gassion, better known as Edith Piaf, was abandoned on a doorstep in the year 1915. Jay knew the date and the plaque's words by heart. Whenever he walked by it he couldn't help humming her tunes. He caught his breath. It wasn't that he cared for Piaf's music or felt nostalgia for her world. She was the foundling songbird of a bygone Belleville, the trilling, guttural voice of Paris during the Occupation and postwar purges of the late 1940s. They'd been years not of wine and roses but of black-and-white, grainy misery, peopled by shaven-headed collaborationist women and clumsy spies, like his father William Grant.

Piaf wouldn't recognize her neighborhood, Jay told himself. He'd had the good fortune to lease his loft before the flood of Bohemian Bourgeois *Bobos*. They'd driven prices as high as the Eiffel Tower. And like the tower they might one day come crashing down

Traffic stood bumper-to-bumper. The siren of an ambulance in the downhill lane sang *da-di-da*, a sound leftover from the Nazi Occupation. As Jay neared home he spotted a pair of policemen in blue slickers dragging a motorcycle off the street onto the sidewalk. Funny, he said to himself. It was a BMW C1 Executive exactly like his own.

The loft's battered steel door led through a passageway into a single-story industrial space. Above the concrete floors were iron uprights and walls of brick topped by crossed studs and wooden planks, with a cathedral ceiling of tin and glass. His aunt Jacqueline called it 'hideous' and wondered how anyone could stand the chemical smells.

Jay set down his luggage and threaded his way between leather armchairs, past a black BMW motorcycle, a linotype machine and a wooden camera obscura that might have been a Howitzer. The heater's on-off switch was in the kitchen area. Near it, disguised as a pulse-dial telephone, was the silent motion alarm. He dialed in the disarm code and caught his breath. Forty-two seconds. An easy margin of eighteen.

Behind a wall of fireproof filing cabinets were the sleeping and office areas. He hadn't yet made the move to the apartment above his office at the Gilford Foundation on the Champs-Elysées, a neighborhood fine for business but not for living. Stepping carefully Jay avoided the fax scrolls littering the floor, as if they'd followed him from New York. He glanced longingly at the bed. Though he'd snoozed on the half-empty flight, once the snacks had arrived he'd broken his golden rule. He'd wound up spending five unexpectedly long hours in conversation with his neighbor, the five becoming seven as they'd waited for a landing slot then taxied for what seemed an eternity. She'd smiled and said her name was Debra.

Debra Wright. Young, with a quick, smart smile, Debra had distressingly symmetrical cupids-bow lips. She'd been eager to hear about Jay's esoteric research. He was organizing an exhibition at the Gilford Foundation featuring Samuel Morse and Louis Daguerre. He'd explained to her how the artist-inventors met in Paris in the spring of 1838 and perfected not only the Morse code but also the daguerreotype.

Jay had leaned over and written out the Morse code for Debra. He'd shown her how, in enciphering, each of the message's letters was replaced by another letter or figure, whereas to encode was different. It meant using complete sentences, words or syllables. Instead of being bored, as Amy would've, Debra had listened with eyes wide and lips parted. He'd shown her how to tap Morse's short dots and long dashes, the dashes exactly three times as long as the dots. Holding her manicured fingers in his, he'd felt a troubling rush, a throb in his temples. Even when he did manage to close his eyes as the plane flew over Iceland, he couldn't sleep. Debra's smile had dogged him, like the Mirage fighter on the plane's port side. The result was the deep tiredness and sense of guilt he now felt, compounded by accumulated fatigue from too many darkroom days in New York.

Chasing away Debra's image, Jay busied himself unpacking. His peripheral vision picked up a green light flashing on the 1920s linotype that served as the room's centerpiece. Jay pressed the "play" button on the answering machine and shut his eyes.

The first message was a series of clicks and a choked voice. It sounded familiar, like Jeff, a friend across the landing back in Manhattan. Jay waited. The second message was no surprise —Rakan from Bonjour Siam. Next came his aunt Jacqueline. She'd called to confirm dinner at her Trocadéro apartment. Jay wondered why she identified herself as "your aunt Jacqueline Dumont" in stilted English, as if he could possibly have two retired English-teacher French aunts named Jacqueline. "I'm afraid I have sad news," she added. "Arlette passed away several weeks ago and Madeleine has joined her."

Jay hung his head. That explained it. One longtime companion goes, he reflected. The second follows soon after.

The third voice on the digital chip belonged to Amy Smith. "Hi, your aunt phoned to invite me over for dinner but I'm not sure I can make it. I'll try your cell when I have a second. Glad you're back. Love you."

With his old stovetop machine Jay made himself a double espresso and settled into an armchair. Like the linotype machine it was a worn leftover from the days of the loft's former owner, a typographer. He'd sold Jay the lease before moving to the suburbs. Jay glanced at the junk-mail faxes on the floor. Talk about an anachronism. A faxed note from his immediate superior at the Gilford Foundation, a convinced technophobe, wished him a happy New Year and hoped for peace and prosperity in the world.

Jay nudged the faxes aside. The beauty of email and text messaging was they never cluttered your floor. If you used them judiciously insistent correspondents gave up.

He rose and slipped an extra battery for his GPS cellphone into a charger. After gathering up his mail from the hallway floor he threw most of it in the trash. Restless, he poked around his darkroom in the far corner of the workshop, preoccupied by thoughts of Madeleine. To keep his mind off her he sorted through the bottles of chemicals and the boxes of vintage photography paper he'd bought before leaving Paris, wishing he could snap his fingers and slow or even stop his monthly commute. Where would he settle, he wondered. Here or there?

The trouble was he'd become addicted to change. He routinely lost patience with the Parisians. In New York he felt homicidal. Business was good in New York and impossible in Paris. But Amy had a good job here. She refused to move to the West Side apartment his father had left him. Their relationship was difficult. But Jay had a plan for saving it. The truth was, despite flirts, he recognized in Amy the woman of his life. The idea sat uncomfortably. And he would never dream of using the shopworn phrase to her face. She was the only person he'd ever known who unquestioningly accepted his checkered past and put up with his passion for photography.

But he and Amy had grown into different people. He was no longer the photo assistant-become-paparazzo of the 1990s. Now he wore expensive suits, not that he cared for them. The vintage photography world recognized him as an authority. Amy had evolved from dog's body at an unknown European news service. The company had prospered. Now she ran the Paris office.

Jay willed himself to think of her. But two distinct images returned like pop-ups—first Madeleine, then the lively face of Debra Wright, a stranger on a plane.

Å

Squealing and chattering woke him from his reverie. A page with a long black streak curled out. He caught it before it reached the floor, promising himself he'd buy a plain-paper fax in the New Year.

Yves had already found the anonymous seller of Madeleine de Lafayette's daguerreotype. *Gonflay*, Jay read aloud, *Monsieur Serge Gonflay.*

"Never heard of him," Yves had noted below in a nervous hand. "Must be new to the business. Unlisted. Try d'Arnac. He gave me the info. Don't email me about this."

Jay drew breath. Paranoia and technophobia. Yves was a hopeless case.

According to *Le Monde*, Maitre-Commisseur Claude-Gilles d'Arnac was the auctioneer who'd hammered up the daguerreotype's price at the Drouot charity auction. D'Arnac was a familiar figure at Drouot. His official title of *Maitre-Commissaire-Priseur* meant he was an attorney and bonded auctioneer. Jay saw him clearly in his mind's eye. The delicate aristocrat usually wore a blue blazer and matching fleur-de-lys tie, hiding his corruptibility behind a coat of arms. Everyone knew d'Arnac had a problem with horses and was easy to influence. The fact that he'd handled the daguerreotype raised bright flags.

Press coverage of the auction was minimal. *Le Figaro, Le Monde* and *Le Parisien* mentioned it. Jay read a few two-line entries off screen. A Google search on Serge Gonflay turned up nothing, not even a White Pages entry. Jay flipped through his address book and then punched ten digits into his phone. In the business, it wasn't done to ask art dealers or auctioneers for information about their sources. That applied especially to the incestuous vintage photography world. But this was an exception.

As Jay expected, when promised advance notice of the next Gilford Foundation acquisition, d'Arnac offered little resistance, providing him with the seller's telephone number and address. But he wouldn't divulge the buyer's identity. "More than strictly confidential," d'Arnac lisped. "Perhaps Monsieur Gonflay will be able to assist you."

Jay closed his eyes. The workshop spun, gently at first and then faster. He opened his eyes, unsure how long he'd been asleep. Footsteps sounded. To reassure himself he jerked open the front door. The lock clicked. He tested it again. Glancing down at his feet he saw a large manila envelope. Had he missed it before? He picked it up, feeling something long and flat inside.

More junk mail, he thought. He was about to throw it in the garbage when he noticed his name and address handwritten in sepia-colored ink. The postmark was English, from London. He slid his forefinger under the flap and tore open the envelope. A catalogue spilled out. It was from a company called Bonham's, sellers of classic automobiles. Jay turned to a page marked with a yellow Post-it and felt his throat tighten.

The car on the double-page spread was a 1968 Jaguar, a Jag XKE, British racing green. The convertible top was down. Someone had scrawled the words *For old times' sake* across the bottom of the page in the same sepia ink.

A draft blew through the loft. Jay shivered. William Grant had driven a '68 Jag. An XKE. William wrote with an inkpen and favored sepia. It looked like his handwriting, but how could it be? He'd died almost precisely one year ago, at the wheel of a late-model Jaguar, a sedan, not a convertible, on the French Riviera.

Stretched across his bed, Jay stared up through the skylight. He wrestled with his memory, searching for a face, at his father's funeral in Marseille. A pair of unnaturally taut cheeks built around long, white teeth welled up. Bleached teeth. But he couldn't summon a full picture of the man's face. Was it a foggy day? Or had it been raining in Marseille? The cloud cover had been thick during the funeral, he was sure of that. And he hadn't minded. He'd always loved clouds. He'd always had multiple loves in life. While growing up they were cameras and clouds, in that order. And ciphers. The three were related. They were tangled.

Jay roused himself and tossed the Bonham's catalogue aside.

The printers had shown him how the linotype machine worked. When he'd moved into the loft they'd left it behind, a toxic waste site full of melted, hardened lead. Inside was a hotpot for smelting lead lines. Jay opened the access hatch and felt around. Behind a layer of melted metal his fingers touched a box. He backed up to an armchair and sat. Inside the wooden box his fingers dug under wine labels, rusted keys and sawdust. They'd been there several lifetimes, since before he'd bought the box at a flea market in Burgundy.

Jay lifted out the waxy paper sheets enveloping the daguerre-otypes. Three of them were covered with random numbers and letters in script. They were all that was left of the enciphered plates his father and Madeleine had exchanged in the 1940s and '50s. Jay had found the cache in a closet in New York one summer and had hidden them in his belongings. Without the codebook to decipher them, the numbers and letters meant nothing. He'd speculated for years about his father's coded messages, and the rolls of sub-minature negatives he'd found with them. Something to do with Cold War operations. Ancient history.

Jay put the plates to one side and unwrapped a fourth da-guerreotype. It was the twin of the one he'd sold Madeleine, the second of a stereoscopic set he'd discovered, forgotten by its owners at the bottom of the wooden box. He'd called the pair of plates *La Liberté: Study of Schooner Shrouds.* Jay flicked the plate in the light of the linotypist's composing lamp. The hologram images were imbedded in the metal probably one hundred and sixty years ago. The plate had the rainbow sheen of a CD. He could see the white schooner-rigged sailing ship at its moorings. His eyes swept across the surface, taking in the spiderweb of ratlines rising from the ship's gunwales to the tops of the masts.

Jay flicked the plate and glanced furtively around the loft, as if he were being observed. On the plate's back was the en-graved signature he'd placed there. *Quincy Alphonse Louis Thomas.* It was dated 1843.

If this is what they want, Jay said to himself, I'll be damned if they'll get it. He wasn't sure who "they" were. Had *they* sent him the Bonham's catalogue? It made no sense.

He nested the plates in the box inside the linotype ma-chine.

Like his father, Jay had always maintained multiple secret hiding places. He had empty spaces behind the books in his aunt's attic rooms, gaps in the walls of the family farmhouse in Normandy, and nooks in his father's apartment in New York.

He turned on a praying mantis-style reading lamp and stretched it out. The head reached over the fireproof filing cabinet. In the cabinet's false bottom were packets of foreign currency, press cards, U.S. drivers' licenses, French national ID cards, credit cards and business cards. They'd come in handy in the past, when Jay had been a paparazzo. His fingers flipped and sorted. *Deputy Inspector Jacques Langlais, Brigade Criminelle de Paris.* He rubbed the dust off. The photo showed him a decade younger. But he still had the same angular face and dark hair. It looked like the real thing because it was the real thing, provided by his father's friends. He slipped the card into a leather holder and slid the cabinet's hidden compartment closed.

Before leaving the loft, he paused in front of a glass cabinet filled with objects. That was typical of him, he reflected. He'd never dismantled the still life after shooting *Curiosity Case.* His aunt's dusty shells and vases were still there, where he'd arranged them over a decade ago. Jay lifted the lid off the display case. He reached inside and took out a signet ring. Eighteen-karat gold, he recalled. It was too small for him now. But it could be a big problem. He tossed the ring in the air and pocketed it.

Å

From top to bottom Rue de Belleville's two lanes were an accordion of traffic. Motorcycles darted between cars. Jay's BMW splashed through slush. Though he was hungry, and needed to talk to Rakan, he drove past Bonjour Siam without stopping. Lunch would have to wait.

Paris was jammed. After 2,000 years the locals still didn't know how to handle rain or snow. The city hadn't been designed for a million motor vehicles, and had become a night-mare for drivers. His friends couldn't understand why he rode a motorcycle in Paris winter weather. The truth was, after boarding school in Vermont, he rarely felt the cold, and he still enjoyed dicing with traffic. Illusory freedom, he reflected. Most freedoms were.

A moat ringed Paris' spiderweb of streets. He rode west on the Boulevard Péripherique, a beltway built in the 1970s to separate the City of Light from the *banlieue.* The suburbs. They were blightsville, a no-man's land scattered with housing projects for the working poor, many of them from Algeria, an ex-colony that had never fully emerged from decades of civil war. Jay hoped he'd stay inside the moat for the duration. He'd done a pretty good job burying his past. But maybe not good enough.

Serge Gonflay lived on the second floor of an early 1900s apartment house near the city's eastern parklands, the Bois de Vincennes. The park wasn't as fashionable as the Bois de Boulogne and the arrondissement where Jay's aunt lived, in west-ern Paris. But it harbored fewer prostitutes and perverts.

He chained the BMW to an iron-and-wood bench on the sidewalk, ran across the street and rang for the concierge, noticing Gonflay's name on the building directory.

"Monsieur is out," said the concierge, appearing from be-hind an ironwork carriage door. She couldn't have been more than five feet tall, including her pinned bun of silver hair.

Jay wrote a cell number on a business card. "Do you have an envelope?" The concierge adjusted her bun. A wire-haired terrier with cataracts snapped at Jay. The concierge kicked it and disappeared into a back room. Jay thought for a moment. He flipped open a pocket agenda. On a blank page at the end he noted the titles of three key images he'd bought for Madeleine over the years. One was by Gustave Le Gray, an-other by Félix Nadar. As if it were an after thought, Jay added

Curiosity Case by Quincy Alphonse Louis Thomas. He put an asterisk by it.

The concierge returned with a wrinkled envelope. Jay slipped in his card, the note and a ten-euro bill. Before handing it over he asked for Gonflay's cell number.

"What's that?"

Jay held up his satellite phone. Frowning, the concierge checked a sheet on a corkboard, wrote the number on a scrap of paper, pocketed the 10 euros and slammed the door.

In Manhattan it's the doormen, Jay told himself. In Paris it's the concierges. She was pretty unpleasant. But she couldn't compare with Madame Goncourt, his aunt's concierge.

Across the street from the building he punched in Gonflay's cell number. An onion-shaped clock atop an antique lamppost showed the time. The sky hovered between purple and black. Jay stared at the second floor where Gonflay lived. As if by sympathetic magic the lights flickered on.

At a table on the glassed-in terrace of La Coupole Daumesnil, a café kitty-corner to Gonflay's building, Jay ordered an espresso. He spread open the house copy of *Le Parisien*. A tabloid newspaper, it covered local news and sports. *French Right Split Wider than Ever*...read one title. *Extreme Right Gains Votes from Moderates...More Terror Cells Discovered in Banlieue..."Abrahamian Brotherhood" cited in latest communiqué...Orange alert still in effect as New Year's Eve approaches...*

As Jay watched and waited, he reviewed in his mind the concatenation of events that had led him to the café. How had this crazy mess with Madeleine de Lafayette begun? As a joke, about ten years ago. Madeleine wasn't just one of his parents' and aunt's old friends, with family money and no one to spend it on. Madeleine was the closest thing to a mother Jay had known. She'd also been his greatest benefactor and conspirator, a patron of the arts. When she found out in the 1990s that Jay had begun dealing in daguerreotypes and nineteenth-century photographs, she'd insisted on seeing them. She'd not only complimented him. She'd asked to buy them, starting with an experimental picture he'd called *Curiosity Case*, in homage to Nicéphore Niépce, inventor of one of photography's early forms.

He hadn't set out to make a forgery. There was a detail in the background that gave it away. Yves had never noticed. Jay only understood the significance of his joke when it was too late to do anything about it.

The ring.

He'd included his Bensonhurst School signet ring among the shells and vases and other authentic antiques in the display case. Why? That was like asking Alfred Hitchcock why he had appeared in cameos in his own movies. It'd started out as a game, a hidden signature. Had Madeleine known the picture was a fake? He was never sure. He'd never figured out how to read her enigmatic mind. For instance, she was the first person to tell him about Daguerre and Morse and the photographic cipher they invented. The cipher transposed early Morse code onto sensitized copper plates. Madeleine told him a lot of things—things about World War Two and the Nazi Occupation, about his father William and the enciphered daguerreotype plates they'd used in the Cold War. Not that Jay had paid much attention. Back then the mention of his father sent him into a rage.

As he sipped his second coffee, Jay could feel the signet ring in his pocket. It was a painful reminder of Bensonhurst School, and the abusive reactionary named William Grant. Worst of all, it reminded him of his own lack of professionalism as a photographer.

Å

Jay looked up from his table. The lights flickered off from
room to room in Gonflay's apartment. A minute later a heavyset
man stepped out of the building with a lap dog on a retract-
able leash.

Because of the checkered woolen coat, Jay couldn't be sure
of the dog's breed. Probably a miniature fox terrier, he speculated. Whatever it was its ribbons and coat didn't match the
frumpy man behind it. He had to be Serge Gonflay. Somehow
he looked the part, a burglar or a bouncer turned fence, a guy
who'd made enough money to move from the suburbs to the
twelfth arrondissement.

As the man and dog neared, Jay snapped a few shots of
them with his Minox. The terrier added his pile to what
Parisians call *pollution horizontale* before the man could pivot
and step into the café. He yanked the defecating dog behind,
practically over Jay's shoes and through the mounds of cigarette butts below the tin-topped bar.

"*Salut*, Serge." The barman reached over to shake hands.

Serge lit what Jay guessed was not his first cigarette of the afternoon. The dog yapped and kicked up butts. Serge reeled it in.
"Shut up or I'll punt you." He gave the spin-casting leash a jerk.

The barman slid Serge an espresso and a cognac. He sipped
the coffee and slugged down the cognac, ordering another.
With thick fingers he took a stale croissant from a basket on
the bar and tore off a nub. After teasing the terrier he tossed
the nub in the air. "Eat it," he grunted. "Ruin your liver."

The barman twisted his lean face and dropped another
chunk of croissant to the dog.

"Goddamn animal," Serge said to no one in particular.
"The wife always has a headache so I'm the one who's got to
take it out."

Serge was wearing a cell clipped to his belt. Jay pressed the memory button on his phone. He held up the newspaper to shield himself. A second later Serge's cellphone rang.

"Allo? Allo!" Serge Gonflay cursed, hung up and clipped the phone back onto his belt.

Twenty-nine minutes after identifying the man who'd sold Madeleine's daguerreotype, Jay waited on his BMW. He'd parked behind the trunk of a plane tree. Eventually a car rolled out of the garage underneath Gonflay's building. It was a black, four-door Mercedes. Jay spotted Gonflay at the wheel. The car surged into traffic. Jay bucked in behind, squeezing through a red light.

Gonflay gesticulated as he drove, one hand on the wheel, the other holding a cellphone. He wasn't the type to wear a headset, Jay remarked. Gonflay honked, swerving, enraged by the bumper-to-bumper puzzle.

Jay pressed the memory button on his phone. It repeat re-dialed. He nosed his motorcycle parallel to the car.

"I'm listening. Who is it?"

"*Bonjour*, Monsieur Gonflay. Mr. Grant speaking. Jay Grant. Maitre d'Arnac recommended I contact you."

Gonflay smirked. "I got your card and message."

The traffic light changed. Gonflay's Mercedes crossed into a bus-only lane and slalomed ahead. Jay had difficulty keeping up. Another red light stopped Gonflay at Place Felix-Eboué. The circular, nineteenth-century fountain in the traffic circle's center was encased in ice.

"I'd love to take you to dinner," Jay finished saying, his hand cupped over the phone's mike. "I'm in the market for some pictures which I understand you might have."

Gonflay's body started forward in the front seat. "Quincy

Alphonse Louis Thomas?" Gonflay grunted. "Maitre d'Arnac told you about him?"

"I'm familiar with his work. Exceptional, and rare."

Gonflay grunted again. "Did you know Thomas worked with Daguerre, and Daguerre invented the Morse code? We French invented photography—you do know that? The English tried to hijack it. But it's ours, and so are the movies and the Morse code." Gonflay accelerated, leaving behind a cloud of diesel exhaust. "Daguerre did it all," Gonflay added. "Nothing better's been done since with a camera. Daguerre and Niépce."

"Yes," Jay said, "I look forward to talking to you about that in person."

"Lunch and dinner are tough, what about a drink instead?" Gonflay asked. "Around 4pm?"

"What, this afternoon?"

"The sooner the better. I have a picture that might interest you. It's supposed to go to auction, but if you'd like to have a look…"

"Absolutely," Jay said.

"We could meet at La Coupole Daumesnil. Not the Coupole at Montparnasse—that's for tourists. This one has a discreet back room where we can view the work and talk in private. Avenue Daumesnil, a few blocks from Place Felix-Eboué and my buidling. Four o'clock."

Jay recognized the name of the café facing Gonflay's apartment. He folded his cellphone and slipped his hands into the gloves dangling from the handlebars. A minute later, Gonflay squeezed through the logjam. He sped down another bus lane toward Place de la Bastille. The Mercedes disappeared then reappeared in time for Jay to see it veer into the Marais.

Historic townhouses lined this fashionable Right Bank neighborhood. Many of them had been transformed into art galleries and antique shops. Jay had a fair idea of where Gonflay might be heading: Saint Paul, the "antiquarians quarter."

Λ

The Mercedes zigzagged down narrow one-way streets, jumped the sidewalk and parked under a no-parking sign. Gonflay piled out carrying a suitcase. For a big man he moved fast, hiking up his slacks and striding down an alley past hole-in-the-wall shops selling collector's items and iffy antiques.

Jay stowed his motorcycle outfit in the box on the back of his BMW and followed. After crossing two courtyards, he caught up with Gonflay outside a stairwell. By the entrance was a brass plaque. *Expertises et Ventes du Marais, Salle d'Exposition. Appraisals and Auctions, Viewing Room.* A cardboard sign dangling from a blue ribbon announced a private viewing for European Antique Tours. It sounded familiar. Yves Rossi had told him about this small-time auction house. A dozen privately run places like it had sprung up around town. French legislators had only taken two hundred years to change the internal monopoly law protecting bonded and licensed *commissaire priseur* auctioneers. The new Europe-wide rules were ambiguous. They had spawned money-spinners for disreputable dealers, some clearly in cahoots with fences and forgers. That's how Yves knew about them. Why the police didn't crack down was an open question.

Jay unfolded a plastic raincoat and slipped it over his suit. He kept his face out of view and climbed the stairs with a group of Americans wearing European Antique Tours badges. The auction house's upstairs rooms smelled of paint. Exposed ceiling beams and parquet enhanced the feeling of age. The buyers checked displays ranging from artists' sketchbooks to Art Nouveau glass or brass, silverware sets to porcelain. Of the so-called "Impressionists" a few were bona fide talents, their paintings behind glass with motion-sensors. The others were daubers.

Jay feigned interest in the paintings. He closed his left eye and then his right one, seeing color first then black and white. Instead of letting his congenital one-sided color blindness handicap him, Jay found it helped reveal structures and tonalities. He sometimes preferred the color-blind side, with its grays and grain and contrast. Learn to read it, he told himself, and you discover a stripped down universe. It seemed timeless and permanent. But it wasn't. The colors were there, waiting to be perceived by normal vision. That's why nineteenth-century photographers had hand-colored their images. Color made them less threatening, less like images of the grave.

From the marketing standpoint, the trouble with early photographs was precisely their lack of color. Most didn't possess the right brand of nostalgia. The Impressionists painted poppies, sunsets and plump Renoir women flouncing outdoors. Old photos were gray, dark, mottled, like age-marked hands. Like Madeleine's hands. Jay was thinking of her again, remembering the knotted veins and blotches.

Gonflay's contact had arrived. He was also hefty, a big Frenchman standing about six-foot-two. The newcomer was well dressed, with a camelhair overcoat. Easing his Minox from an inner pocket Jay used his rain shell as a shield, taking shots of the men talking and making an exchange. Gonflay handed over his suitcase. The man in the camelhair coat handed back a wrapped object. Jay guessed it was a sculpture.

A minute later another man joined them, shook hands and led Gonflay to a back office. The man in camelhair buttoned his overcoat, signaled to someone outside and trotted downstairs. A window at the top of the staircase looked over a courtyard. Jay pushed back the blinds and photographed the man in camelhair as he was joined by a short older man. The old man's face was hidden by the rim of a fedora. Jay stared and blinked at the hat. His mind grappled with a recollection. But he couldn't bring it into focus.

Jay zigzagged back through courtyards and alleys, wrestling with the image of the man in the fedora. He'd seen him before. Where? Gonflay reappeared unexpectedly and the two nearly collided. Jay stepped out of the way and watched Gonflay press his car key and pack the wrapped object into a padded compartment in the trunk.

The Mercedes rolled south toward the Left Bank. Jay noted that Gonflay drove like a taxi driver hurrying to the hospital. Maybe he'd worked as a cab driver. Or a policeman. A cop turned fence. In France that was a natural revolving-door.

Traffic came to a standstill on Rue de Rivoli. The broad, straight avenue bisected the Right Bank. On it a group of protestors marched behind a banner. Gonflay, dead ahead, leaned on his horn. Seconds later everyone was honking. The banner moved toward a streetlight. Jay could make out the arabesques of its script and the translation into French. *Abraham is Sacred. Abraham is loved by all People of the Book.* He heard the chant *Jihad islamique contre la République* repeated over and over.

It was just the thing to help the moderates in upcoming elections, Jay reflected. A jihad against the French Republic.

Gonflay swung into the bus lane where a policeman stopped him. Jay pulled up and saw Gonflay flash an ID card and shake the traffic cop's hand. He was allowed to turn left and break away. Jay counted to five before pushing his BMW across a traffic island around the marchers. He caught sight of Gonflay's car one block south.

Side-by-side they crossed the Seine on the many-arched Pont Marie. But traffic stalled again on Ile-Saint-Louis. It was a picturesque island. The Rothschilds lived on the upstream end, surrounded by twenty-foot walls and crumbling townhouses with billion-dollar views. Gonflay followed the island's perimeter road, drove one block, veered left the wrong way down a one-way, crossed from north to south, jerked left and right then crossed the other arm of the Seine. Jay counted six traffic violations in less than two minutes.

After more rally maneuvers Gonflay steered onto the sidewalk on a Left Bank street in the shadow of the Panthéon. Jay drove past, reconnoitering at the next traffic light. He turned to see Gonflay carrying something into a barbershop. Jay circled, slowing as he passed. The barber's blinds were shut. Jay sandwiched the BMW between parked cars.

Checking his watch, he decided he had enough time to call Amy. She would be in full swing, he imagined. On her third or fourth cup of coffee and probably smoking a cigarette, though she was supposed to have quit. He punched in her number. Their relationship had taken a combative turn. After a decade of free-floating, she wanted a commitment. He hadn't given it. Now that he was ready, she seemed distant, cold even.

Through her wire-service job Amy had made useful contacts in French officialdom. A couple of calls and she could find out what floral arrangement had been made for English royals staying at the Ritz. Her phone rang unanswered. Jay was about to disconnect when she picked up. He could hear her take a drag on her cigarette before saying hello.

"Thanks for your message," Jay said. "Let's have a drink after you get off work."

"It'll be too late. I'm beat already." The line went silent.

"Amy?"

"How about tomorrow?"

"That's a plan," he said. "Could you do something for me?" he added cautiously. "Check out this art dealer named Serge Gonflay? Call your friends at the prefecture of police and see what they know about him?" He read out Gonflay's cellphone and license plate numbers, and heard Amy scribbling.

"Odd name," she said. "*Gonflay*? What do you want to know that you can't get off the Web?"

"He might have something to sell the Foundation." Jay

hated lying. It reminded him of his father. "Run an ID check, do a profile." He mentioned the pickup at the Marais auction house and the drop at the barbershop. By Amy's sighs he could tell she disapproved.

"I'll call Richard and see if the prefecture has something," she said. "He's my Google and I guess I'm yours."

"You're more than that," he said. "We'll talk in Normandy."

"Normandy?"

"I'll explain later. I'm on my motorcycle and can't talk."

Someone shouted in the background. Amy groaned. "They're marching again," she said in a tired voice. "I'll call you later, after the demonstration."

Ａ

Jay restarted the BMW, his pulse picking up as he revved the throttle and felt like a paparazzo again. Gonflay had left the barbershop by the back door and walked around the block. It was a clumsy attempt to go unnoticed. Jay squeezed off a couple of photos as Gonflay approached. This time he wobbled under something bulky. It looked like a painting. The car alarm sounded, the lights flashed, Gonflay hitched up his pants and a minute later bumped the Mercedes into the stream of traffic flowing south on Rue Saint-Jacques. He turned left, heading for the Seine and Right Bank.

An ambulance slowed Gonflay's progress. *Da-di-da*, sang the siren. *Da-di-da*. The ambulance shot over the Pont de Bercy into the twelfth arrondissement pursued by half a dozen chasers.

With few great monuments, the twelfth didn't attract tourists. It had maintained a provincial feel, with the best and worst elements of French society. Gonflay worked his way across it. Jay lost sight of the Mercedes again. Gone. He checked the time. His appointment at La Coupole Daumesnil was in eleven minutes. He felt his cell vibrate, pulled over and read the screen. It was a cryptic text, from Amy.

B careful. X-special forces. Corsica. Marseille. Never done time. Friends. Algeria. Interior Ministry. xo A

Jay smiled inwardly. It made sense. The Ministry of the Interior. Gonflay knew the people who furnished public buildings—the chateaux, palaces and historic townhouses used by administrative departments. An inexhaustible reserve. An old special forces military policeman and Algerian War vet, from Corsica or Marseille, with protection. Jay folded his cell away.

As he pulled into the flow, a dark Renault sedan sped up, its driver refusing to yield. Jay swerved out of the way, barely avoiding an accident. Just like New York, he muttered to himself.

Fifteen minutes later he rounded Place Felix-Eboué for the second time that day. The ice had formed beards around the mouths of the lions in the middle of the traffic circle. It was only a few hundred yards to the café where Serge Gonflay would be waiting. He was four minutes late.

The sidewalks were dusted with snow. Someone had shoveled away a yard-wide strip of it, creating an obstacle course flecked with dog dirt. Jay parked and sprinted to the café but slowed when he heard panicked voices and the peal of an approaching siren. A dog yapped. It was Gonflay's terrier. It ran from the corner to La Coupole Daumesnil, dragging its leash. An ambulance pulled up. Its *da-di-da* siren echoed off the buildings. Jay leaned on the doors of the café and paused halfway through. The place was empty.

The bartender stood on the street corner. A bus was parked at an unusual angle. Its emergency flashers blinked and made a clacking sound. Jay pulled out his camera as he approached and focused on the bus. Something was out of place. Something seemed to be wrapped around the back wheel of the bus.

Then he spotted it. Him. Gonflay. Jay held his camera above his head and walked closer, shooting film, the motor whirring. He counted five then six frames and stopped shooting at ten.

"Slipped on the ice and fell right under it," panted the bartender to someone standing near him.

"Serge? He slipped on dog shit," said someone else with disgust.

Other voices joined in. A few shouted. The man had slipped, fallen, tripped, been pushed.

"Someone shoved him, I saw it," insisted a woman with bottle-bottom glasses.

Jay turned. Firemen were redirecting traffic. A dark-colored Renault cruised by. Jay instinctively recognized it as the one that had almost run into him—a luxury model Vel Satis. He pushed through the crowd and stepped into the street, steadying his camera. The car accelerated, avoided the firemen and police and sped around the traffic circle. Jay made out two digits and three letters. 75 A *something* X *something* D. He hoped he'd gotten a shot of it. As a backup, he noted the license plate letters and numbers on the palm of his hand.

As Jay walked past La Couple Daumesnil he saw Gonflay's terrier. It stood tangled in its leash, shivering. Jay opened the café doors, used his toe to push the dog inside, and turned to go. He stopped suddenly, glancing back. On the bar was a thin, small, rectangular package. He'd seen it before, in the padded trunk of Gonflay's car.

The bartender was still standing on the corner, staring at Gonflay's mangled body. Jay listened. He stepped quickly inside the café and heard the sound of dishes from the kitchen. Someone whistled. The whistle attracted Gonflay's dog. Jay lifted the package off the bar and walked out without looking back.

A frame lay underneath the plastic sheeting and bubble wrap. It felt like the wrong format for *Curiosity Case*, unless

Gonflay had reframed it. Jay slipped the package into his brief-case and slid the briefcase into the BMW's luggage compart-ment. As carefully as he could, he rode slowly back across the Seine to the Panthéon, trying to come up with a plan. He had to act fast. The barbershop had to be a drop. It might be where Madeleine's photography collection was being stored, and if he played his cards right, he might be able to get his hands on it before the police—or Gonflay's men—did.

$$\unicode{x1F1EB}$$

Atop the Montagne Sainte-Geneviève rose the Panthéon's stone dome. The barbershop seemed a leftover from the 1950s. Two yellow recliners stood on a broken-tile floor. Jay walked by, glancing in. Combs, brushes and straightedge razors stuck out of ceramic jars on a Formica counter. The mirrors were mottled. A vinyl-covered bench stood against one wall. Facing it was a low metal table. The Venetian blinds were pulled halfway. Through them Jay could see an aging, pot-bellied man in a white smock and red tie. He was slumped in one of the recliners, reading a copy of *France Soir*.

A buzzer rang when Jay pushed through the door. The shop smelled of hair grease and menthol. The barber didn't stir. "Come back in half an hour." It was a southern French voice. The barber's half-smoked cigar smoldered in an ashtray near a pair of worn scissors. "I'm closed," the barber grunted, louder. Jay ignored him.

Soccer was the shop's theme. Soccer, Saint Joan of Arc and Algeria. A yellowed poster showed the French World Cup team triumphant at Paris' Saint Denis stadium, a distant me-mory from the 1990s. A trophy in the shape of a soccer ball sat on a shelf. It was draped with a Paris Saint Germain club ban-ner anchored at one end to a plastic statue of Joan, the mad-woman patriot the English burned alive in Rouen. The shop's sun-bleached business license hung on the wall. Jay stepped close enough to read the name. François Lecoq.

"You deaf or a foreigner?" The barber spoke over his newspaper. "Speak French?"

Jay's eye picked out another newspaper on the table. *La France Française.* It was the party organ of a nationalist political faction. Algerian War souvenirs and a portrait of young Lecoq in uniform were the other giveaways. Lecoq was an old soldier, one of the thousands who'd never given up French Algeria despite a decade-long war in the 1950s and early '60s.

Lecoq folded his paper and stared, muttering. He checked his watch and then used *France Soir* as a pointer. Jay locked the door and flicked shut the Venetian blinds. "What do you think you're doing?" Lecoq blurted.

Jay sat down in the empty recliner and held out his arms so the barber could slip an apron over them. Lecoq glared at Jay's reflection in the mirror. "Serge had an accident," Jay said softly. He counted to three. "They've sent me to make the pick up."

The barber edged around the chair. "An accident?" He studied Jay's jacket and slacks. "What are you talking about?"

Jay stroked the barber's tie and then jerked it, tugging the man's head down until one large waxy ear was near Jay's lips. "Listen François, I said Serge had an accident and I wouldn't want that to happen to you. Where's the stuff?"

The barber reached for his windpipe. "He didn't leave anything..." he croaked.

Jay slackened his hold and then tugged the tie again, harder. "Wrong. The package was delivered a couple of hours ago, the boss is mad and if you don't want to wind up like Serge you'd better start talking."

"I...can't...breathe..."

Jay let go. He ran his fingers through his hair, measuring it out. "Not too short, François. Make sure to even up the sideburns."

The barber caught his breath. He pulled his tie back into place. Jay crossed the shop to a radio on a shelf. He turned up the volume and spun the dial to 105.5—*France Info*. The 24/7 news station's unmistakable theme music came on. A sports report rolled by. Two skiers had been killed in the Alps. "Listen," Jay said.

A fatal accident in the twelfth arrondissement has cost the life of a man positively identified as Serge Gonflay, 62 years old. Eyewitness accounts confirm the man fell into Avenue Daumesnil as a bus was passing . . . traffic will continue to be rerouted as police authorities . . .

Jay turned down the volume. "Where have you been stashing the stuff?"

Lecoq flinched. "I'm just a drop."

Jay made a snipping motion. "Get to it, François. I don't have all day."

The barber picked up his scissors, ran a comb through Jay's hair and started to cut. His hands shook. "Careful François, you've screwed up already by double-dealing." It was an educated guess. "The boss doesn't like that." The barber trembled but said nothing. Jay pulled out his cell. "Keep cutting. I'm counting to ten. Then I'm calling the boss and you can kiss your ass goodbye. As soon as you've finished my haircut they can do what they want."

Lecoq staggered back. "I didn't know Gonflay was double-dealing Leyzanges." His accent had become more marked. He sounded like a character from a 1940s movie. "I'd never do that to Henri's crowd, I swear."

Jay waved at the straightedge razors in the jar. "The boss likes his friends very clean-cut, François."

The barber straightened his tie again. His tongue licked his bloodless lips. With a peg-leg limp he crossed to a storage cabinet. "Look." He held it open. "I don't have anything. That bronze was the last thing Serge brought over. The Degas.

Check the closet if you want." He threw the door open wide and jerked a dangling string.

Jay could see the room was empty except for a broom and mop.

"I swear, I don't have anything."

Jay flipped open his phone and started to punch in a number. "I'm listening François."

"All right, wait." With fumbling fingers François Lecoq rooted out a pair of reading glasses. He opened a drawer in the mirrored cabinet and flipped through the pages of an address book until he reached the letter "O." His finger zigzagged down a list of names. "This is all I have. Serge said to call someone at Lamartine named Jean-Paul in case of an emergency."

"Jean-Paul?" Jay raised the blinds part way.

The barber nodded. Through the half-drawn blinds he looked out the window. But no one walked by. "I don't have his last name."

Jay read the telephone number aloud to himself, punching the digits into his phone's memory. "How do you know I'm not Jean-Paul?" He motioned for the barber to step back, then pulled open the drawer of the cabinet. Underneath the address book was a package the size of a deck of cards, sealed in black plastic. "What's this, François?" The barber stared. He said something incomprehensible. "You'd better lie low, understand? Close the shop after I leave and take a vacation. Not a word."

"But. Where will I go?"

"What the hell do I care? If you're holding back, someone's going to give you the closest shave of your life."

Jay slipped the package into his briefcase. He made the snipping motion again and François Lecoq reluctantly finished the haircut.

"Keep the change," Jay said, stuffing a twenty-euro note in the barber's breast pocket. He brushed the hair off his jacket and raised the Venetian blinds a few inches. Sleet was still falling. Umbrellas jogged by. Across the street about a hundred feet from the shop, a dark four-door subcompact waited in a tow-away zone. "You know those guys?" Jay motioned with his chin. The barber shook his head.

Two men sat in the car. The wipers swept the windshield, paused then swept it again. "You better hope they're not from the *Renseignements Généraux* or *Police judiciaire,*" Jay said. "Where's the toilet?"

"In the courtyard."

"The courtyard connects to the back building, on the other street, right? Serge went out that way earlier."

The barber nodded. "If it's them, what do I say?"

"Nothing. You didn't see me. Gonflay was a customer like anyone else. Show them the empty closet." Jay paused. He picked up the address book and tore out the page marked "O."

The courtyard led to the service stairs of an apartment building. Its main entrance faced south, away from the Panthéon. The street ran parallel to the one where the unmarked *R.G.* car awaited. Jay walked through the courtyard and back building and then jogged around the block to his BMW, pausing to tie his shoelaces. He slipped his briefcase into the luggage compartment and straddled the motorcycle. There was no time to put on his raingear. Before pulling out, he glanced into the side mirrors to see if he'd been tailed. He did a double take. It couldn't be. Not her.

Crossing the street behind him was someone familiar. Jay watched Debra Wright lower her umbrella and quickly turn the corner, trotting out of view. He held his breath and then counted slowly to five.

Accelerating north, Jay wondered what Debra was doing near the Panthéon. Cold sweat prickled his back. A fluke. It had to be. Concentrate, he told himself. Think. He thought about the black package in his briefcase, and the names.

Leyzanges, Jean-Paul, Henri and *Lamartine.* The barber had slipped up and given away four clues, he told himself. *Leyzanges* was someone or something. *Jean-Paul* was a common first name. Was *Henri* a first or last name? *Monsieur Henri* or *Henri* something? It could be either. *Lamartine* had to be a last name or a company name.

He pulled over a few blocks beyond the Panthéon, glanced around and when he'd decided there was no one following him, dismounted and put on his rain gear. Then he got back on the motorcycle and flipped open his cell phone, still unsure of his next move. What were the chances Jean-Paul's telephone number would work? Close to nil, Jay told himself. He waited for the ring tone and examined the torn page of the barber's address book. Underneath, in parenthesis, was the name "M. Henri." An answering machine with a synthesized voice responded. *Laissez un message s'il vous plait...* Leave a message.

Jay knew what the telephone company would say. He called anyway to ask for the name and address to match the number. Unlisted, *liste rouge*, said the operator. Predictable. Whoever Jean-Paul was he wouldn't be that sloppy. It was a job for Amy and her friend at the prefecture of police. Jay folded the torn piece of paper and put it into his pocket, wondering yet intuitively knowing what the small black package contained. A daguerreotype? Why? And why wrap it in a vacuum pouch? He glanced at his watch. In his darkroom he could open the package and take a look. But first he'd have to see Yves and get his Minox film developed.

He hit *memory* and *auto dial* and listened as Amy's voice-mail kicked in. "Amy? A whole bunch of stuff is going on. Gonflay's dead. I'm damned if I know why and I need your help." He read out the numbers and letters of the Renault's license plate. "It's all I could make out. Call Richard at the prefecture and find out who owns the car, okay? Find out who Gonflay's people are?" Jay paused. He read out the names the barber had mentioned. "And see what Richard can find out about an American woman named Debra Wright, with no 'O' or 'H' in Debra and a 'W' in Wright. She works at a place called Anchor and Compass Consultants. Thanks, Amy. I'll call you later."

Å

Jay felt his hands tremble as he drove through deepening darkness toward Yves' shop on the Canal Saint-Martin. He clicked back through the pages of his life, trying to make sense of what was happening. Gonflay was dead. Someone was playing hardball. The daguerreotype plates were the key. They had to be. But which plates—Madeleine's or his father's?

He rewound ten years to when he'd made *Curiosity Case* for Madeleine as an innocent joke. She'd been mesmerized by the Calotypes and daguerreotypes. He couldn't have imagined she was playing a game, or what it would lead to.

Jay backed up even further. He hadn't gone straight to college. His years at the Paris *Lycée* where he'd met Amy had turned him off higher education. So he'd taken courses at an adult-education program called ADAC funded by the city of Paris. They were great for learning photography, engraving and printing techniques. They also introduced him to a world of misfits trying to recycle themselves. That was where Jay had met Bruno, an ex-assistant to a notorious paparazzo. Through Bruno Jay had landed a job as an apprentice to a photo-engraver in Belleville, the one whose lease he'd wound up buying.

Over the years, starting with his Brownie Box camera, Jay had read everything he could about daguerreotypes, Calotypes, tintypes, silver prints, mezzotints and the other obsolete but magical vintage techniques for impressing images on paper, glass or metal. After his training and apprenticeship he had the know-how not only to restore but also to make seemingly authentic vintage works himself. At first that had proved awkward and slow. Later his mastery had increased. It turned out he had a natural talent born of a passion for the past. Jay hadn't known or cared where his love of the craft had come from. He was thankful to have a vocation and enough skill to transform his visions into reality.

Then came the bread-and-butter years as a photo assistant. From gofer he rose to stand-in for the famous Fabrice de la Montagne. Fabrice had been too drunk and disorderly to work some days, like the day they'd rented a camel from the Paris zoo and a studio with miniature sand dunes. They'd spent $100,000 shooting half-naked starveling teenage models riding leather trunks and baggage. When Fabrice had passed out Jay had taken over and had never looked into his rear view mirror again.

He realized he was getting ahead of himself and clicked back again to another page, dragging the pop-up window of his life sideways and then searching inside it for clues. He'd turned his knowledge of nineteenth-century photography into a money-spinning venture by a fluke. He'd begun printing "vintage" pictures for a friend, a guy who sold antiques at the Porte de Clignancourt flea market, an ex-Legionnaire and paparazzo named Yves Rossi.

Yves sold Jay's first forgeries. They were clumsy, especially the daguerreotypes. The plates were never perfect. The chemical solutions and the timing for exposure and mercury vaporization never seemed to work. Once Jay had almost poisoned himself with carbolic acid. But then the quality had improved. The daguerreotypes and tintypes, even the paper-negative Calotypes that seemed fished up from an ink well, began to look authentic. One day an expert decided they were.

Early 1990s fashion ragamuffins posed on expensive leather luggage led Jay by a crooked path to photo-reportage for magazines like *Géo* and *National Geographic.* Measured in monetary terms it was the wrong way around to success. But Jay hated the lies in advertising and fashion. Then somewhere in a smoky café in the twentieth arrondissement on the edge of Paris he'd found out that Yves Rossi and Bruno Puy knew each other. Both had been paparazzi. Maybe if they worked together with Jay they could set up an agency combining fashion and advertising and celebrities. If they worked overtime and cashed in on other people's fantasies they could spend the rest of their time indulging a shared passion for independent lifestyles and unprofitable photographic anachronisms.

The paparazzo fashion business had turned from adventure to farce. Bruno and Yves hadn't lasted long, winding up in hospitals or jails a few too many times. Jay could have continued on his own. But he was alarmed to learn that he actually enjoyed tracking people. He had a talent for what he came to think of as the flipside of spying. He savored the ugliness, the tarnish. It was in his blood, the blood of William Grant. He'd enjoyed being a paparazzo until that morning. He'd woken up on the French Riviera, scarred by stings from wasps in a fig tree where he'd sat all night, waiting for a starlet and her adulterous lover to show. And he'd realized he was becoming what he hated most—a supplier to the gutter press. He wasn't exposing anyone with his photos stolen through ten-inch lenses. He'd begun to play their game, transposing Eurotrash from observed reality to published fiction sold by the million.

So he'd given up the six-figure earnings and gone back to college, adding a B.A. in history to his resumé. On the side, he'd learned digital Scitexing, PhotoShop and electronic photomontage. That was when he'd caught Amy on the rebound from a depressive philosophy professor. Jay, Yves and Bruno had settled down by then and become legitimate dealers of vintage photography. Yves made fakes on the side for fun. If people enjoyed them and believed they were real then why disabuse them? What difference was there between that kind of deception and the soft-porn deceptions of advertising? *Caveat emptor*, Yves liked to say. Let the buyer beware.

Two-dozen semi-key forged images from the 1840s onward: that had been the core production of his partnership with Yves. It had been stimulated and financed by the enthusiasm of Madeleine de Lafayette. Once they'd gone down the road far enough, private collectors had become interested. Some were in France and America, others in London. He'd also sold or traded through complacent auctioneers like Claude-Gilles d'Arnac. Each image took weeks or months to research, execute and place on the market. There were the "lost" 1840-1843 *Menagerie* daguerreotypes commissioned by Lerebours, the great photographer-entrepreneur of the French *Commission Photographique.* Jay had also forged the gold-paper Calotypes of Fox Talbot that had supposedly self-destructed a hundred years ago. He'd made seascapes and landscapes by Gustave Le Gray and Quincy Alphonse Louis Thomas. All were artworks that had disappeared like thousands of other masterpieces. Jay was not some nickel-and-dime fraudster. He considered himself a skilled artisan who brought back to life artworks that had deteriorated beyond reclaim. Sometimes he created them from scratch. Quincy Alphonse Louis Thomas was his invention.

He and Yves had found the name, an obscure amateur photographer of the 1830s and '40s, and reinvented him to give the forged pictures a pedigree. They'd hired a calligrapher in Tunis to copy forged letters in period French script, on nineteenth-century Neapolitan paper. They'd spent a full month planting the letters in the National Library. This was before the days of Wikipedia and the Internet. It took time and skill to create a pedigree. Originally he and Yves were going to reveal the project as a hoax. But things got out of control. And somehow, somewhere along the way his father had reappeared, asking for help. Help with a set of undeveloped daguerreotypes. *For old times' sake.*

As he bounced across town on his BMW, Jay thought of the bubble-wrapped package in the luggage compartment, and tried to guess what was in it. If it contained *Curiosity Case* his troubles might be over. He would be free of the past. At least one part of it.

He hit Boulevard Beaumarchais and picked up speed, trying to imagine what would happen to him if his past were revealed because of the signet ring in *Curiosity Case*, and what any of it might have to do with a 1968 Jaguar XKE or a spook with bleached teeth asking to buy daguerreotypes from Yves. One thing was clear. Jay was in trouble. He might go to jail or be declared persona non grata and lose his American passport. A spy and son of a spy, mixed up with forgers and murderers. Rogues breed rogues, he told himself, recalling his father's words. He could easily lose everything, his future with Amy, his job at the Gilford Foundation.

Jay's cell vibrated as he reached the northeast side of the Place de la République. He pulled over before answering.

"Jay? You there?" It was Jeff, his neighbor across the landing in Manhattan. "Are you all right?"

"Yeah, I'm all right. Why wouldn't I be?"

"I sent you a text and left you a message," Jeff said. "Didn't you hear it? Then I tried calling and the phone was always busy. So I thought I'd better call your mobile."

"What's up?"

"Whoever it was beat up José pretty bad."

"Jeff what are you talking about?"

"A big guy with nine fingers," Jeff said. Jay could imagine Jeff's plump features, the features of a caricature, with flared nostrils and balding head. "The police got here about half an hour late," Jeff continued. "When the alarm went off I called you but there was a shoot-out on 132nd in the projects. The guy didn't break through your front door. But he got away after punching José a couple of times. In the ambulance José kept saying *finger, finger, the man had no finger, big hands, sausage fingers . . .*"

Blood pounded in Jay's ears. He tried to organize his thoughts. A burglar had seen him leave his New York apartment last night and had tried to break in. José the building superintendent had intervened and been slightly injured. No panic.

Jay memorized the hospital's telephone number, thanked Jeff and folded his cell. After loosening up his neck muscles he called. The nasal-voiced automatic operator said the number didn't exist. He tried again and got the same error message.

The important thing was José would be okay. The burglar hadn't gotten into his apartment or stolen anything belonging to the Gilford Foundation. Best of all, he was safe on the far side of the Atlantic.

Safe.

The word should have surprised him. It didn't. Everyone seemed to live in fear. He went over the events of the last day, starting with Debra and the acne-pocked passenger in a sheepskin coat. His mind cut between thoughts and images, mixing metaphors and verb tenses. Madeleine's plate, Madeleine dead and his 'friends' who smelled of spicy crab, looking for him at Bonjour Siam. The man with long bleached teeth asking Yves about daguerreotypes. The wreaked BMW on the sidewalk across from his loft and the Bonham's catalogue with his father's handwriting on it. Gonflay dead. And now this. It had to be a series of flukes.

Jay heard his father's voice in his head. *There is no such thing as coincidence, only a lack of information.* That was probably William Grant's favorite saying, especially when he'd been drinking.

Rattled, unable to drive any further until he'd thought things through, Jay dismounted his BMW but left the engine running. He stared up at a stone plaque on the wall of the gendarmes' barracks on the corner of the Place de la République. Jay knew why he'd stopped there, and what was engraved on the plaque. The photography studio of Louis Jacques Mandé Daguerre had once stood here. It was a place of pilgrimage to people like Jay. From the windows of his studio Daguerre, flanked by Morse, had taken his shots of Boulevard du Temple. They were the earliest and most beautiful daguerreotypes known.

Standing on the edge of the square Jay aligned himself with the plaque and looked across the Place de la République past the leafless plane trees and the towering statue that symbolized the French Republic. Headlights and taillights left tracks like tracer bullets. In Daguerre's day, Boulevard du Temple had run straight up to where he stood. Parisians called it *le Boulevard du Crime* because of the racy performances in the theaters and music halls that had lined the boulevard in the early 1800s. Daguerre's studio had doubled as a magic lantern theater. It was the precursor to the movie theater.

Why had Gonflay mentioned Daguerre and Morse together? Hardly anyone knew of their friendship or the Daguerre-Morse daguerreotype code. Unless he'd heard about the photography show Jay was organizing. But how could he have heard about it?

Jay felt giddy with exhaustion and confusion. He wanted to forget Gonflay and Madeleine and the nine-fingered burglar in Manhattan. He desperately wanted to close his eyes, reopen them and be standing in the Boulevard du Crime, looking up at a third or fourth floor window, at the mustachioed Daguerre with the giant camera obscura. He wanted to stop time. Daguerre's camera had had the magical power to freeze time and capture space on a metal plate, transforming four dimensions into three. Because the plate was not two-dimensional. It had thickness and weight, and was acid-etched with a sun-traced map of pits. They formed a picture of reality.

Reality? Taking a cautious step forward, Jay felt the side-view mirror of a car brush past. He swiveled. A Renault. A big, dark Renault. Another six inches, it occurred to him, and he would've been as dead as Daguerre or Serge Gonflay. Shaken, Jay watched the Renault disappear, heading north on Boulevard de Magenta. He got back on the BMW and drove in the opposite direction, circling the square on his way to the loft in Belleville. At the traffic lights near the statue of the giant warrior woman the traffic light turned red. He pulled to the curb. Someone had sprayed graffiti in red and black paint. Islamic Jihad to to bring down the French republic? At least they hadn't cited Abraham this time. He waited for the light to change, his eyes on the gendarmes by the barracks. Then he noticed a car one row back. A Renault. The same big Renault Vel Satis. How could it have circled back already?

Before he could think, Jay jerked the BMW through the red light and into passing traffic. He swerved to avoid a clapped-out Fiat, hit a pothole and felt his motorcycle skate over the slush. As Jay flew sideways the Renault accelerated. Jay watched from the clouds, from a body not his own. He saw tracer bullets, heard horns and felt cold wet air. A cartoon bubble held the shout and the exclamation points that trailed from his mouth. Sparks showered from the edges of the BMW's chassis. It spun 360 degrees. In a disembodied state he felt the contact. His flying body landed backwards on something metallic. It crumpled. As he rolled to the mud and ice on the sidewalk he saw he'd hit the hood of an old Citroën Deux Chevaux.

Seconds later he was standing. The Renault was gone. The BMW lay on its side. Someone in a long leather coat helped him lift the motorcycle and push it onto the sidewalk. Before Jay could thank him, the man was gone.

In the muddy gutter Jay found his satellite phone and

camera. He opened the luggage compartment on the back of the BMW and retrieved his briefcase. The gendarmes near Daguerre's plaque did not drive over to investigate. Maybe they hadn't noticed, Jay thought. Probably they didn't care. He was just another motorcycle rider who'd slipped on the ice.

When he saw that the BMW's chassis was bent, Jay gave up trying to straighten the front fender. A pretzel. *Totaled.* The word came to him. *Totaled,* like his father's car, a Jaguar sedan William Grant had tried to fly without wings.

$$\unicode{x00C5}$$

The métro, Jay told himself, trying to stave off panic as he realized someone was trying to kill him. Get into the subway before the car circles again. Ride one stop to Jacques-Bonsergeant station and cross the canal on foot to Yves' shop.

He limped down two flights into the station, struggled through the barriers and climbed the northbound platform on line five, checking behind him. Something like paranoia had dogged him for much of his adult life. It usually wore his father's face, a genetic bequest. Now it wore his own face, and he felt increasingly like his father, a man persued. He wondered if the passenger at the far end of the subway platform was tailing him. If so, how? Why? Jay watched the train roll in. Its brakes squealed. Riders pushed out, others pushed in. Jay hesitated, waiting to be the last on board. The man down the platform also waited. Jay got on. The man got on. The warning horn blew. The doors began to slide shut. Jay jammed them open and squeezed back onto the platform, pulling his briefcase behind. Two cars down, a man struggled to pry open the sliding doors. They held shut. The train lurched. Jay ran toward the exit. The train raced alongside. He looked into the cars as they clattered by. Hundreds of faces were pushed together behind the glass. Hundreds. He recognized one of them.

As the train rattled out of the station, the face swam into focus. Debra. Debra Wright. Again.

Jay had no time to think. He sprinted toward the far end of the platform. A fresh crowd of passengers came down the stairs. At the top of the staircase two men stood looking down the corridor between northbound and southbound tunnels. One of them wore a camelhair overcoat. The other wore sheepskin. Jay stopped short. He focused for a split second and then turned and sprinted back, following the signs to line 3, *direction* Gambetta.

Jay ran, suddenly aware of the sweat stinging his eyes. An eastbound train approached. Its wheels shimmied. He looked over his shoulder. The men were pushing through the crowd. The train rumbled closer. He had two, maybe three seconds to decide. Shoving past a woman at the edge of the platform, he jumped onto the tracks, took three steps across the rails and vaulted onto the eastbound platform. The incoming train blared its horn. It lurched, halted then rolled into the station. As he ran, Jay ducked and bobbed through the crowd. Once the train had pulled alongside the platform, Jay forced his way onto a car halfway down. Riders muttered but no one challenged him. He turned his back to the windows and felt the train rattle out, praying the men tailing him hadn't had time to climb on board.

Body-to-body packing had transformed the passengers into sweaty shrink-wrap bundles scented by sour breath and wet wool. Everyone wore an overcoat, either woolen or sheepskin or camelhair. In Jay's agitated state, the scene looked to him like a contemporary art installation or a scene from a modern-day *Inferno*.

Using his briefcase to push his way out at Père-Lachaise, the first transfer station, Jay ran upstairs through the ranks of marching overcoats. Tunnel after tunnel appeared. Two subway lines converged on Père-Lachaise. He rushed through the swinging arms and legs, up and down concrete staircases, counting his steps.

Ride back to République and change to the number eleven line to Belleville, Jay told himself. The subway map in his head was a tangle of colored threads.

But there would be nowhere to hide if he got off at Belleville. And he needed to get to Yves. What about Père-Lachaise? It's the best place in Paris to lose a tail. I can lose anyone in the cemetery.

He allowed himself to be lifted bodily and swept by the crowd through the station. It was impossible to run. His knees bumped against the men and women in front of him as he climbed the steps. He wrestled his arm upwards to check his watch. His mind grappled with calculations. He had three, no two and a half minutes to get out of the subway, cross the boulevard and breach the southwest gate before closing time. From there he'd need twenty, maybe twenty-five minutes to get to Yves' shop. And from the shop, where? The airport?

Wind blew down the staircase. Jay pushed his way outside and then weaved between the bumper-to-bumper cars on Boulevard de Ménilmontant.

A cemetery guard was bent double in his blue cloak, preparing to swing shut the big green doors to this, the city's great ghoulish tourist attraction. The guard tilted his kepi back and chipped at ice. Jay darted past and took the stairs two-by-two, pulling himself up with the handrail. *Heat, warmth, electricity*, he chanted, denying the pain in his back. A whistle blew. The guard shouted, forced the door closed and ran up the staircase in pursuit. Jay sprinted into the grid of tombs. They sheltered under skeletal trees whose forlorn branches had set their leaves adrift. He ran, stumbling on tree roots, broken masonry and overturned urns. His lungs burned. The eyes of melting stone Virgins stared down from towering cenotaphs. Grim reapers swung their scythes in the air. Freshly dug graves yawned.

Behind and below, the guard's shouts faded. Whistles blew. But they were far from the hill Jay had climbed. Other shouts replied from the crest near the crematorium. With difficulty Jay made out the silhouette of a chimney against the darkening sky. He slowed, trying to find his bearings among the mossy columns and lichen-frosted crosses that merged now in the thickening twilight.

It was the living Jay feared in this city of the dead, an acropolis filled with bone and ash. Père-Lachaise spread over one hundred acres on the hills of eastern Paris. Jay had always loved the graveyard. But now it seemed to have turned against him, as if it had resented his earlier visits when he'd been a tourist, like 2 million others who each year tramped between the funerary monuments of the famous dead. The tables had turned. Now Jay was one of them, the dead. He was trapped inside the tall stone perimeter walls topped with razor wire and steel spikes.

Breathless, his back in pain, Jay ran in what he hoped was a northeasterly direction, ducking at shadows and sounds. Branches scraped on sandstone. Plastic flowers rustled in the wind. Feral cats chased rats.

If only he could make it to the northeast exit, he told himself, the one the tourists never use, no one could get him. No one.

He paused long enough to think again and felt a spreading paralysis. *If they know who I am, how can I go back to the loft?*

Jay slumped in the lee of a tomb. He felt feverish yet cold, freezing cold. On the tombs around him he read the same soot-blackened words over and over: *concéssion à perpétuité.* Jay realized he was wet, the rain and sleet running down his neck and back. A whistle blew nearby. He broke into a run and fell, tearing his motorcycle rain gear on a rusted railing. The sleet slashed down. His mind repeated the line. *Concéssion à perpétuité.* Groping, Jay searched for a tomb big enough to crawl into. He recognized the curving path that led to the grave of Jim Morrison, a hallowed spot scattered with keepsakes and trash left behind by rock 'n roll pilgrims.

By a bizarre twist of fate James Douglas Morrison had been fished out of a bathtub in Rue Beautrellis on July 3, 1971 and been buried here, in Père-Lachaise, the repository of France's great and good. Morrison had become the object of cults. People crawled around his tomb day and night wailing *Jim, come back to us.*

Jay got down on his hands and knees and wriggled his way through a rusted door into the chapel of a family tomb. He kicked an empty bourbon bottle out of the way and wrestled his cellphone out of an inside pocket. The battery had come loose. He set down his briefcase and shook the phone, tapping it against the graffiti-scrawled walls. The auto-dialler wouldn't work. He entered the digits manually. Somewhere out there Amy's mobile began to ring. One, two, three rings. Jay counted, peering through the chapel's broken glass.

"Amy?" he crouched among the rotting leaves and fast food wrappers, whispering. "Amy?"

"Boy have I got some news for you," Amy began.

"Later. Listen."

"Where are you? Jay? I can barely hear you. I'm stuck in traffic near Place de la République, I was heading for Belleville..."

"No. Don't. Not Belleville. Go to the east exit of Père-Lachaise, the back way out, the door on the staircase on that dead-end street." He spoke in a hoarse, hushed voice. "Hurry. They're following me."

Jay folded the phone closed and held his breath. His hands were cut and bleeding. The gravel crunched behind the chapel. A flashlight raked past. The eyes of a stray cat lit up, disappearing as leaves rustled under approaching feet.

Jay had done a lot of crazy things in his life. Dangerous things. But he'd never hidden in a graveyard after closing time.

He sank behind the marble altar at the back of the chapel and pulled a decaying linen cloth over his legs. The light beam danced around and away.

"I don't see anyone." The guard's adenoidal voice bellowed into a walkie-talkie.

"Keep looking," came a squelched answer. "Repeat, keep looking."

How long would it take Amy to get here? He began counting, imagining her route. She'd have to drive up Avenue de la République and around the back of the cemetery. That made thirteen cross-streets in the eleventh arrondissement and how many stoplights? He calculated the distance from where he was hiding to the cemetery's back door. Four hundred yards give or take.

The flashlight faded to a blur at the bottom of the main east-west access road. Jay crawled out of the chapel clutching his briefcase and picked his way on unmarked dirt paths between the tombs. His teeth began to chatter. Leaves and mud made the footing unsure. He recognized the tomb of Auguste Comte, headed north-by-northeast to Saint-Simon, paused by Richard Wallace and crept across the wide, curving Avenue des Acacias toward Félix Tournachon, better known as Nadar. Nadar was the greatest of the early photographers, a portraitist and inventor, the first man to take a camera into a hot-air balloon. Jay leaned on the cold gravestone, trying to keep his balance. He wondered in a delirious half-second what it must have been like to photograph Paris from a balloon back in 1858.

Through the whistling sleet he heard heels clicking on the cobblestones. The back exit was another one hundred and fifty, maybe two hundred yards away. If the heels belonged to a cemetery security guard, Jay reasoned, he could step out, tell the guard he'd lost his way and ask to be let out of the northeast gate. It was an honest mistake, officer, I assure you I had no intention of remaining inside.

The flashlight glanced over the glistening cobbles. Jay was about to step forward when he saw the silhouette of someone else beside the guard. A tall heavy-set man bulged from his overcoat. Was it camelhair or sheepskin? Jay held his breath. He pressed his back to the gravestone. The flashlight swept closer. The heels were no more than ten feet away. The men's voices battled against the wind. Their words were shredded by it, like sailcloth, like the shrouds in Madeleine's daguerreotype. "Dangerous" Jay heard one man say. "Get the dogs. . . . Dead or alive . . ." The guard's cape fluttered. The other man tipped his umbrella against the wind. The wind lifted his overcoat. A camelhair overcoat. Jay closed his eyes and held his breath. Branches rubbed against the tomb. Their scraping sound covered the noise of the walkie-talkie and heels.

Twenty minutes had passed since Jay had phoned Amy. She might be outside the cemetery already, waiting. Or she might still be stuck in traffic. Either way he had to get out. Now. He would have to jump, climb the wall and jump. He'd always heard it was easier to get out than to get into Père-Lachaise. Jim Morrison fans did it. They hid out after closing time and climbed over the walls before dawn.

The stone perimeter wall was as mossy and wet as the tombs. It dipped to four or five feet near the back entrance. Jay scrambled onto it. He bit the handle of his briefcase and clung to the cyclone fencing on top of the wall. But his back convulsed in muscular spasms.

It'd been easy to get onto the wall. Getting down was another story. On the city side a fifteen-foot drop ended on slippery cobbles. Jay teetered. He clutched at the wire fence. A lamp glowed over the dead-end street and the cemetery's back staircase. He was about to jump when he noticed a rectangle of light spilling up the stairs into the cemetery, where it struck the gilded lettering of a star of David. How could there be light on the stairs? The door had to be open.

Jay clamped the briefcase between his legs. He raised his wrist and used his teeth to drag back his sleeve. It was exactly six o'clock. Impossible. The gates of Père-Lachaise always closed at five-thirty in winter. Oversight? Or a trap? Jay teetered on the wall, looking down again at the glistening cobbles. *Concéssion à perpétuité*, he heard himself thinking. He shook the sleet out of his eyes. He would break his leg or sprain an ankle if he jumped. He took a deep breath and bit the briefcase handle again. Convulsed by pain, he flipped back to front and slid down the wall back into the cemetery.

Jay always counted steps and seconds wherever he went. He wasn't sure why. But now his mind was exploding with a new set of calculations. *Concéssion à perpétuité, à perpétuité* his mind screamed. He was unable to quantify or count perpetuity, forever, infinity. All he wanted was out.

His last thought as he stepped through the door was of the graven, gilded star of David, a memorial to wartime deportees.

Beyond the gate, the dead-end street stood empty. He ran down it without looking back, sprinting until dizziness and pain transformed speed into slow motion. He was running in a dream, a bad dream. He saw a bathtub with Jim Morrison floating in it and heard his father William chanting *à perpétuité, à perpétuité*. A man in a beige raincoat standing on the deck of a freighter floated into the dream, holding a subminiature camera and a pair of round eyeglasses. *To Buenos Aires*, he said, *à perpétuité*.

At the bottom of the cobbled street, traffic flowed on busy Rue de Bagnolet. Jay stumbled on the sidewalk. A car jerked over, blinding him with its headlights. He staggered back, barely able to see or hear the voice shouting at him. "Taxi? You called a taxi?"

The cabbie reached back and threw open the passenger door. Jay scrambled in. His muscles forced the air out of his lungs. "Thanks, yes, thank you," he lied. A second later he blurted Yves' address and leaned back, closing his eyes.

"Slippery," the driver said with a strong foreign accent. "Dangerous tonight."

Jay wheezed agreement, reaching into his pockets for a quick damage-control assessment. The camera had been in his breast pocket when he'd crashed the BMW. Jay tested the shutter, zoom and flash. Despite the shock, the Minox seemed undamaged. The bubble wrap and leather briefcase had saved Gonflay's picture. The battery had detached itself again from the body of his banged-up satellite phone, but he worked it back on and wiped the mud off the keypad. Jay pressed the buttons and shook the phone until he winced from the electric shocks in his ribs.

"Amy? Change of plan. I'll be at Yves' place in half an hour. Don't ask. I'll explain later." He folded the phone and closed his eyes again.

No broken bones? The blood on his scuffed hands and cut knee had already begun to crust over. His motorcycle suit was torn and muddy, and his slacks were split, but he'd be all right as long as he could get into some dry clothes.

They rode in silence, the traffic thick and noisy, the radio playing a chat show about dog salons in Burgundy.

$$\unicode{x1F5FC}$$

Relieved to be alive and safe in the taxi, Jay wished the ride would last forever, so he could sleep and clear his mind. The vision of the last thing he'd seen before exiting Père-Lachaise —the memorial to wartime deportees—burned in his head, behind his temples. For a long time, for years, he hadn't understood why his father had hidden the sub-miniature film strips in his Manhattan apartment, in a waterproof fishing tackle box under the bathroom heater. When the heater had sprung a leak, the plumber had lifted it out. Jay had been standing nearby.

Inside the tackle box were the negatives and contact sheet, dated June 17, 1950. "Roll Two" was marked on the bottom of the sheet. There was no other information.

With a loupe, Jay had studied the contact sheet, making out a wharf, a ship, a gangway, smoke funnels and a deck. He had no idea who the man in the pictures was, a tall, thin man leaning on the freighter's railing with one newspaper rolled inside another, held like a riding crop in his right hand. Jay wondered why his father had taken so many photographs of the ship and the man, and another man in clerical robes, a monsignor or bishop. He'd speculated about the seaside location, and had decided that, because of the mountains and cityscape, the date and the lettering on the newspapers, it was Nice or, more likely, Genoa. The name of the ship was not in the frame. The raincoat the man wore was beige, like the one his father always wore. The ship's flag might have been red, white and blue. Jay wasn't sure. But there were no stars and stripes. Who was the man with round glasses? Could he still be alive?

"Monsieur?" It was the taxi driver. "Is this the address?"

On the canalside road near Yves' shop Jay paid the cabby, giving him a generous tip. Glancing up as the taxi pulled away, he saw its roof lights were off. The light on the license plate was off, too. He smiled inwardly. Only a guardian angel would've picked him up like that, by mistake, on a night like tonight. An angel wearing cowboy boots. Or a beige, standard-issue Company raincoat.

The voice of Edith Piaf crooned from a radio somewhere in the camera shop. Jay guessed *Radio Nostalgie*. White noise for blue-rinse ladies and, apparently, ex-Legionnaires. Yves covered the telephone mouthpiece. "Sit down."

But Jay couldn't sit. His body ached. He was cut and filthy and freezing cold. With shaking hands he opened the briefcase and propped the picture against a whisky bottle. While Yves signed off, Jay grabbed the radio and tuned into *France Info*. The item ran by, repeated almost verbatim, spooling on its 7-minute cycle.

A fatal traffic accident in the twelfth arrondissement on Avenue Daumesnil near Place Felix-Eboué has cost the life of Serge Gonflay, a local resident. Eyewitness reports...

"Gonflay," Jay repeated, turning down the volume. He pushed two rolls of exposed film across the counter and gave Yves a telegraphic summary of events, from Gonflay's wrecked body to the barbershop, the accident on the BMW and his escape across Père-Lachaise.

Yves lit a cigarette from one he'd smoked halfway down. The mask of a Foreign Legionnaire in some god-forsaken Algerian desert slid over his face. "What's in the bubble wrap?" He didn't wait for an answer. "Where did you get it?" He let his cigarette fall and ground it out with his boot. "I always thought *Fall Woods with Brook* was one of Quincy Thomas' better pictures."

Jay cursed silently, shivering, and waited for Yves to stop coughing. "It's not the picture I need," Jay said. "It's not the one *we* need."

"I don't understand."

Jay set the signet ring on the counter. "Seen this before?"

"I don't remember."

Jay felt his blood drain out. "Okay," he said. "*Curiosity Case.*"

"The first one you made. The one you said was junk."

"What was in the case? Shells and vases. And this." He pressed the ring into Yves' hand. "Get your loupe. Bensonhurst is on the bezel with my name. Bensonhurst was founded in 1925." Jay watched the penny drop.

"Why didn't you get the picture back if you knew about the ring?"

"I forgot." With bloodied, trembling fingers, Jay wiped condensation from the shop's window. He looked out through camera bodies and lenses. "I screwed up. How would I know Madeleine would buy our pictures? How would I know her stuff would wind up being stolen and fenced?"

"So Claude-Gilles knew it was a fake?"

"He must've. So did Gonflay."

"Shit." With bony fingers Yves picked up the exposed rolls and shook them like a pair of dice. "You want to lie down? You're all ripped up and wet." Yves lifted the whisky bottle. Jay shook his head.

"I'll be back in fifteen minutes. Amy's on her way. Maybe I'll have figured out what to do."

He stepped into the sleet. His eyes watered. Taillights flashed along the highway of his life, a one-laner with a horizon-line halfway up the frame, and goons on either side. No more job and no more Amy, a voice said in his head. Back to frame one.

He felt intense cold. Rubbing the moss and filth off his hands, he walked down the canalside esplanade to a café. Images chased their tales in his head. He saw the humpback bridge. No one was on it.

Inside the café Jay contemplated his cellphone. He gulped his café-crème and fiddled with the signet ring. This couldn't just be about Madeleine's photos, he told himself. Something else was going on. Shit was happening, and it was spelled William Grant.

La Liberté: Study of Schooner Shrouds. Shrouds were what you wrapped the dead in. Madeleine, for instance, and William Grant.

Shrouds rhymed with clouds, billowing, shroud-like

clouds. Clutching the coffee cup for warmth, Jay drifted back to his troubled childhood. He'd learned to love clouds by watching them through the skylight in the ceiling of his room at his aunt Jacqueline's apartment. He'd spent his adolescence counting and classifying not trains or planes as some kids do but clouds. The skylight was his viewfinder, a giant Brownie Box camera, like the one William Grant had given him when he'd turned ten years old, the year his mother had died.

He'd told his father about the skylight in Paris, in a letter he'd sent care of the commercial section of the Teheran embassy. That had been William's posting at the time. Within a month Jay had received a copy of *Knowing Clouds* by return mail, in a diplomatic pouch. Inside the pouch was the cryptic note "One for each." Thick and illustrated, *Knowing Clouds* had been published in London in 1935 by T. L. Murray & Co. It was a rare first edition. A registered letter arrived a few days after the pouch, containing William's first cloud cipher.

The sky always seems bluer on the far side of the sea.

Jay had known what to do. He'd written out his alphanumeric correspondence table and come up with a numeric series. With it, following their protocol, Jay had deciphered the phrase. Decades later he still remembered some of the numbers. After flipping through the pages of *Knowing Clouds* and finding the lines and letters, he'd written out the enciphered message.

B-G-U-D-L-U-V-J-A-G-Z

Be good, love Jags.

Tucked between the pages of *Knowing Clouds* he'd found a photo of his father leaning against his Jaguar XKE. With his magnifying loupe, Jay had read the car's vanity license plate: LUVJAGZ. He'd torn the message into flushable pieces and headed for the attic room's bathroom, tears welling. Only Jay knew his father's nickname for him was JAG. Jason Anthony Grant. Fitting. William the spook would choose an acronym for his son.

For old times' sake. The phrase from the Bonham's vintage car catalogue came back to him now. What did it mean? The cloud book was hidden at his aunt's apartment, upstairs. It was the only possible explanation.

The camera shop was double locked when Jay got back. He stepped in quickly, behind Yves. Strips of wet film hung in rows, dripping over the darkroom sink. One contact sheet was ready. Yves fished the other out and hung it up. He switched on a hot air blower. "You change your mind about the whisky?"

Jay shook his head. "What do the negatives look like?"

"Good. Good contrast." Yves poured himself a shot. He handed Jay a magnifying loupe.

A light-table filled one corner of the lab. Jay scanned the contact sheet and negatives, hop-scotching from frame to frame. The images showed Yves' face, his outstretched hand then Gonflay and his dog. In the second row came Gonflay and his car. The auction house in the Marais. The guy in the camelhair coat. More Gonflay with packages, coming and going from the barbershop.

Yves took the loupe and glanced at the frames Jay indicated. He laid out the second contact sheet and negatives. They showed Gonflay crushed by the bus and the Renault getting closer. And closer. The driver was out of focus. But he looked to Jay like the man in the camelhair coat. It had to be. It was the same car. Jay noted the full license plate number. He compared the series of images again.

"Take a look at the guy driving here and the one with the camelhair coat here," he said.

Yves lowered his head and jumped from image to image. "There are a thousand guys with coats like that," Yves muttered. "And a thousand guys with big Renaults like that one.

Besides, he looks like Gonflay's best friend. See how they're shaking hands and smiling?"

Jay re-scanned both sheets. "Why would the driver be wearing a heavy overcoat at the wheel?" Jay crossed his arms, noticing his torn sleeve. "You take your coat off when you drive, right? We're not in Moscow. So why does this guy have his coat on, unless he jumped into the car. Like he'd just pushed Gonflay under the bus."

Yves shrugged. "Maybe he's cold-blooded. Give me the loupe." He pored over the tiny images. Jay could hear him breathing, exhaling sour mash and nicotine. "Someone's in the back." Yves' voice was guttural. "Behind and to the left of the driver."

Jay peered into the lens. He tried his right eye—color blind but strong on tonalities. And he saw it, a latent image. A man. A man wearing an overcoat and a hat. He was raising his hands to cover his face. The image was too small and too dark to read clearly. "These are the same guys who ran me down."

"I'll make some blowups," Yves said, "and work on the guy in the back seat. Maybe you'll be able to recognize him." Yves blew a plume from his cigarette. "Tell me this. How come these guys look like old pals here, and, if you're right about what happened, the guy just pushed Gonflay under the bus, here, in this one? And why are they after you? What changed in a day?"

Jay waited. Yves said nothing. "Some crucial information must've come in."

"Yeah." Yves nodded. "What I'm asking is, what changed in the basic equation? Who arrived in town and started asking questions and throwing money around?"

Jay blanched. "Can you think of anyone who'd like to see me dead?"

"Other than Amy?" Yves sucked on his cigarette. "Some strange shit's going on." He reached behind the light-table and fished out a newspaper. "The afternoon edition." Running across the top of the front page was a headline in bold, *Far Right Splits Again.* The subtitle explained, *Not Since the 1940s Has the Extreme Right Been So Divided.* Yves folded the pages back. "Read this. I was going to call but figured you'd seen it."

Jay's eyes swept back and forth over the double-column interview with Claude-Gilles d'Arnac. The slug-line read, *Who Was Quincy Alphonse Louis Thomas?* The subtitle gave Jay a start. *Could Q. A. L. Thomas have been the mysterious link between Niépce, Daguerre and Morse, the fathers of Heliography, the Daguerreotype and the Morse Code?*

Pedigree, provenance, Jay thought. He reread the story. Quincy Alphonse Louis Thomas' forged letters had been found at the National Library and *Le Figaro*, France's largest circulation daily, had sought out Maitre d'Arnac for a professional assessment. The auctioneer had used terms like *cautious optimism, fascinating potential, astonishing quality, rare stereo image* and *the mysterious messenger.* It was a command performance.

"First Madeleine dies," said Yves. "Then the schooner daguerreotype sells for big bucks, then Gonflay gets bumped off and someone is after you." He drained the whisky from his plastic cup and stared at Jay. "I typed a couple of things into the search engines and guess what? There's a French Wikipedia entry on him. Quincy Alphonse Louis Thomas. It wasn't there yesterday. I know. I checked."

"You checked?" Jay dropped the newspaper on the lighttable, shaken by a sudden chill. "I've got to see my aunt. She knew Madeleine. She knew my parents. And I think she knows the maid who cleaned Madeleine's house. Find her and we might find the pictures before we wind up in jail."

"Or dead."

Λ

A pair of headlights flashed their high-beams as Jay stepped outside. He felt cold again. Through the sleet he recognized the car.

"That goddamn phone of yours!" Amy floored it. The Peugeot rocketed over a pedestrian crossing. Umbrellas dueled in the headlights. "I'd been trying to get you for an hour." Amy's voice betrayed exasperation. She ran her eyes over him. They were big, pale blue eyes. "Jay?"

His head had started to spin. "Turn up the heat," he said. His teeth seemed to belong to someone else. He couldn't stop them chattering. In the half-light he saw Amy's long pale body, its sinews tense as she stretched back and grabbed a picnic blanket off the package tray. She draped it over him, her long chestnut-brown ponytail swinging like a pendulum.

Christmas decorations winked in the sleet. They were strung from pole to pole along Rue de Bagnolet. Pedestrians cowered, jumping clear whenever cars sprayed mud from the gutters.

"Where's your motorcycle?"

"Gone." A pain in his back caught the word. Amy stared at him. "I had an accident on the way over." He told her. The stoplight changed. The Peugeot bucked northeast. "Turn right," Jay said. The pain in his back was getting worse. "Drive by my place. I'll explain. Just drive by without stopping so I can see if it's being staked out."

Amy avoided a fender-bender and headed west on the tree-lined Boulevard de Ménilmontant. "Why can't we stop and get you under a hot shower?"

Jay recovered his voice. "Either I'm losing my mind," he said, "or I'm in worse trouble than I thought." He didn't know where to begin, and decided to start with Gonflay and tell her about the barber and being chased across town and through the cemetery. In mid-sentence he pulled the blanket over his head. "Look right."

By the main entrance to Père-Lachaise a group of burly men in rain slickers were talking to cemetery guards. "See them?"

Amy dipped her chin. Then she realized Jay couldn't see her. "What's it about?"

"Me."

Back streets led them into Belleville. Jay finished telling Amy about the chase. What really worried him, he realized, was the professionalism of the teams tailing him. He'd shaken them. But they'd picked him up again, they'd seemed to know where he was going.

Near Jay's workshop they spotted an unmarked car. They always stood out. That was the irony. Jay crouched again. The one-way street left no options.

"I'm scared." Amy white-knuckled the wheel.

Jay knew the cops weren't cops but the French equivalent of the FBI and CIA. They had to be secret service. *Direction de la surveillance du territoire.* DST. Or maybe the RG or PJ, the police of the police. He clamped his jaws and concentrated on the pain. But his mind ran ahead. Why did they know who he was and where he lived? The short answer was, they'd listened to Gonflay's phone calls. Or maybe they'd found his Gilford Foundation business card on Gonflay's body. That hadn't been wise. He should've had the presence of mind to use fake ID. But he couldn't have imagined what he was stumbling into.

Amy slowed. Jay sensed the Peugeot's side mirror about to graze the double-parked secret service car. She stopped and rolled down the window. Jay started to lift the blanket when he heard Amy folding her mirror back out. She veered downhill, a whimper of relief trailing from her lips. He counted to ten before rearranging the blanket. Electric pain played up his spine. "At least I'm not paranoid," he said. "They were following me. They know where I live."

Amy fumbled. She found a pack of cigarettes and ran her

fingers around inside it. The Peugeot rolled through a yellow light into a blocked intersection. Amy hit the brakes. The pack fell. She groped for it. Horns blared. Drivers nudged to within inches of the Peugeot. A deliveryman stalked toward them. Jay's radar picked up traffic cops. One zigzagged through the jam, carrying a walkie-talkie. The cars ahead of them moved, the accordion wheezing. Amy glided downhill. "The DST is looking for you?" She lashed her hair out of the way.

Jay spoke calmly. "I left you a voice message." He waited. Amy nodded. "Did you find anything on Jean-Paul, Henri, Lamartine or Leyzange?"

She shook the cigarette pack. It was empty. "We've got to see a lawyer," she said, braking at the bottom of Rue de Belleville. "I did find 'Lamartine.' We'll have to look through the stuff together." She tossed the pack behind. "Where do we go? Not your place. Mine?"

Jay counted to five. "My aunt's," he said, checking his watch. "It's early but I've got to talk to her. She's expecting us for dinner."

"Dinner?" Amy stared. "You want to eat dinner with your aunt? The DST are after you, you saw one guy get killed and you don't even know what I found out today from Richard." She paused long enough to draw breath. "I vote we call a lawyer." She crawled across the next intersection. Her horn bleated. She hit it harder. "There's Vondelmeyer. He's always handling Americans' problems," she said. "I have his number at home."

Jay pointed right. "Head to Opéra and my aunt's," he said. "Please." He took Amy's arm. "I'm freezing and bleeding, and I've got some clean old clothes at my aunt's place. I need to talk to her, and check some things in the attic. Besides, my aunt knows Madeleine's maid and nurse."

"So what? What does any of that have to do with a lawyer?"

"Okay," Jay said, massaging his temples. "Gonflay sold a

daguerreotype I once owned. He sold it for a lot of money, way too much. It was reported in *Le Monde* today. The plate belonged to Madeleine de Lafayette. You remember Madeleine."

"Remember?" Amy asked. "She's practically your surrogate mother."

"I think Gonflay had the picture stolen, probably by the nurse or gardener or the housekeeper."

"The housekeeper? Arlette wouldn't do that. She's worked for Madeleine forever."

"Arlette is dead," Jay said. "She died a couple of weeks ago."

Amy's pony tail fell forward over the steering wheel. She pulled it out of the way. "Why am I only hearing this now?" She paused long enough to sit up straight. "Who's the new housekeeper?"

"I don't know, someone Madeleine hired a couple of weeks before she died."

"Before who died?" Amy shook her head. "Let me get this straight," she said. "You think Gonflay had the new maid steal this picture and you're trying to get proof of this for some reason?" Jay nodded. "Then why don't you just tell Madeleine?"

"Because Madeleine's dead. She died two days ago."

Amy pulled to the side and cradled her forehead. "I'm sorry, I . . . Madeleine was a lovely woman." She paused. "This is starting to sound too weird to be true. Please go to a lawyer tonight, okay?"

Jay looked out the window. "It's complicated."

"Why don't you let the lawyer un-complicate it?" Amy stuck her jaw out. "Wait. I'll get Vondelmeyer's number off my cell."

"No. Listen. By French law I'm French and your lawyer will make things worse. I'm a dual-national and the son of a dead spook. I can just see it. I've got an American passport and an American lawyer and I'm trying to pull some kind of super-power thing on them." He paused to search his pockets. His movements became frenzied.

"Now what?"

"No ID," he blurted. He checked his wallet and found only the fake police identity card, a New York driver's license and two credit cards. "I left my passports at the loft."

"Smart."

"It's not like I was expecting this to happen," he said, pain stabbing him in the back. "I'll get another one at the consulate."

"You want to go there now?"

"It's too late." He pulled the blanket around him. "There's also this forgery thing. It's a felony here. I've got to get that picture back."

"Which picture?" Jay sighed. He ran through the tale of *Curiosity Case* and watched as Amy reluctantly changed course, turning right on Boulevard Saint Martin. They passed Paris' former city gates, encrusted with stone armor lit by flaring spots. *La Gloire de la France*, Jay thought. The stone-dead glory of dead kings.

"Wait," Amy said. "What if you didn't sell those photos as originals?" She paused. "You could've sold Madeleine those pictures as fakes, like the ones you used to sell at the flea market. You just play dumb. The DST guys aren't after you. They're after Gonflay's people. You're just a dummy who got caught up in this by mistake. You don't know about the rest of it. You're so dumb you don't even know Gonflay is dead, right? You just happen to go to the same barber as he does. Jay, ignorance can save you. You sure don't know what I know."

"For instance?"

"The car you took pictures of when Gonflay was killed? It's leased to a Champs-Elysées law firm called Lamartine. I've got the name in there." She waved at a pile of papers on the floor.

"What else do I not know?"

"Lamartine represents a defendant in that government corruption trial that's been going on for years. You didn't know that, did you? And you don't know the defendant was Serge Gonflay's partner in Marseille." Amy stared ahead at the cat's cradle of speeding cars. Conflicting emotions etched deep lines into her face. She tapped her left ring finger nervously on the steering wheel.

"Go on," Jay said, noticing how beautiful she was when worried, and how long and perfectly formed her fingers were.

Amy seemed to notice for the first time that he was bloodied and filthy. "Hold up your hands," she ordered, pulling a box of alcohol-soaked wipes from the glove compartment.

"What business were they running?"

"Real estate. On the Riviera, in Provence, around Marseille."

Jay's lips had split from the cold. He couldn't whistle. "So, Serge Gonflay gets caught ripping off the government, leaves the special forces and goes into real estate and antiques with his friends from the Ministry of the Interior."

"Right." Amy accelerated. "It gets worse." Traffic flowed past the opera house. Wide avenues and money made it flow. Jay turned in his seat, trying to determine if they were being followed. But it was too dark and too wet to see. "It's sleazier than usual," Amy continued, "Richard said there are some seriously bad-news people from Marseilles and New York involved. He couldn't tell me everything."

"New York?" Jay smelled the alcohol on his hands as he massaged his temples. He stared at his fingers and counted them silently. The pieces were beginning to fall into place. Too many things still didn't make sense. How did Gonflay know about Madeleine's photo collection in the first place, let alone the pictures by Quincy Thomas? From d'Arnac? Why would d'Arnac risk discovery by giving that interview to *Le Figaro* if he knew Gonflay was dirty or had doubts about the authenticity of Quincy Thomas? Jay fought back the tendrils of suspicion reaching toward the only person who could join all the dots. Yves. And what would any of this have to do with William Grant?

"I say we check into a hotel. Maybe they know about me, too," Amy said. Before Jay could comment she took a hand off the wheel and used her fingertips to illustrate several points. "Maybe they know about your aunt. They might know you're related and look there. We've got to call a lawyer, a good French lawyer. Ask your aunt. Call her now and tell her you've hurt your back, which is true, and you need a lawyer. Use my phone. It works."

Jay took the phone. It was the path of least resistance. He pressed the keypad and watched it light up. "Maybe," he said. "You're right. I'll ask my aunt in person about the lawyer. No one's going to know she's my aunt. Dumont is a different name from mine. The DST have no idea who I am. I'm just a guy who was supposed to meet Gonflay and then ditched my tail in the subway. It's like you said. Besides, I need to ask my aunt a couple of things. You're right, though, that's the thing to do."

Jay watched Amy. He wasn't sure he'd convinced her. She stared at the cars ahead. He turned on the radio. *France Info* wouldn't announce whether the DST had an all-points bulletin on him. This wasn't America. Not yet.

The news spooled by. They passed SWAT teams near the Arc de Triomphe. Fifty or more riot police trucks awaited the New Year's Eve festivities. The SWAT teams had become a fixture, around ever since the anti-terror laws of the 1980s. It may have taken 9/11 to awaken the sleeping American giant, Jay reflected. The French had been dealing with bombs and hijackings before that. On December 31st, a sharpshooter would be posted on the roof of the Gilford Foundation offices. Others would position themselves on balconies or roofs up and down the avenue and atop the Arc de Triomphe. Each year they did it. Just in case. In case of what? What better target than Europe's most famous avenue filled with a million partiers? Only blowing up the Eiffel Tower would make for an even more spectacular atrocity. But the ironwork would be hard to knock down. Post-9/11 simulations had shown it wouldn't burn or implode like the Twin Towers. An Algerian GIA terror squad had hijacked a plane and tried to topple the tower in 1994, but they'd been grounded and killed in Marseille. The details were still a state secret. Even the all-knowing Google could only provide links to conspiracy theorists.

"Jay? Are you asleep?" Amy drummed the steering wheel with her ring finger. "Just remember, nothing you've done so far is strictly illegal," she said. "Not even those fake letters. That could have been a joke or a hoax, whatever. I've been thinking about it. You tell the lawyer it was a hoax to debunk the experts. That you were doing it as a kind of provocation and had planned to write the editor of *Le Monde*, from the point of view of the world expert on daguerreotypes at the Gilford Foundation."

He watched Amy clicking her ring finger against the steering wheel again, unconsciously tapping out Morse code. Click. Click-click. Click. The thought of Morse and Daguerre led to Debra Wright. "Did Richard find anything on that Wright woman?"

Amy stiffened. "Debra you mean?" She paused. "No. Nothing. She's not registered with the French. She has no residence or work permit. And the company... Did you look at their website?"

"She might be trying to stay under the radar. I'll bet she gets paid in America. You did that once."

"So did your father." Amy pursed her lips. "You want to tell me about Debra, with no 'O' or 'H'?"

Jay counted to five before answering. "There's nothing to tell. She sat next to me on the airplane. We talked. She's from Kentucky." He waited. "There's something I can't figure out about her."

"I'm sure."

Jay shook his head. "Would I be telling you about her? Okay, she's attractive and eager to get to know me for some reason, but there's nothing going on." A light flashed in his head. It was the closest thing he'd had to an epiphany. "Wait a second," he said, sitting up. "Wait just one second. If I can get a hold of that picture with the signet ring in it," he sat up straighter and reached into his pocket. "I can use the flaw in the photo as a defense."

"Are you changing the subject?"

"No, honestly. I say to them, look, this is obviously a hoax, as you suggested, because of the ring. I have the ring right here." He held it up. "This ring is in the curiosity case in the picture. I put it there on purpose. It was a joke, Amy. The whole thing was a stupid joke. So I tell them, it's not my fault if a bunch of con men have got this all wrong. Look at the ring. It's my signet ring. It's got my name engraved inside it." Jay smiled. "I can't believe it. Why hadn't I thought of that before? All I need to do is find the damned picture."

"I'm lost," Amy said. "Why did you put your ring in the glass case?"

"It was a joke." He paused. "We have to get out of here, to New York maybe, and let the lawyers deal with it. Like you said. We get married in New York. We go to Niagara Falls."

"Married?" The car swerved.

"Absolutely. I was planning to ask you in Normandy. Then all this stuff started happening."

Amy flushed. "What if I said 'no?'"

"I guess I'd have to ask again until you broke down and agreed." He took her left hand and slipped the signet ring on the third finger. "A temporary fix," he said. "Sorry it's so clunky."

A tear rolled down Amy's cheek. "You jerk." She wiped it away. "So where's this picture?" Her voice cracked. "I can't believe you're asking me to marry you in the middle of all this."

"The picture?" Jay braced himself. Amy pulled over and

used the touch-technique to shoehorn her way into a parking place near Trocadéro. "I have no idea."

The maternal side of Jay's family had lived for the last hundred years facing the Passy cemetery, Trocadéro esplanade and Eiffel Tower. The building's sculpted faux turrets and wrap-around balconies gave it what Jacqueline Dumont's society friends called *le grand standing*. In other words, it was a good address. Jay had always hated it. He'd never really had the privilege of living there, except during summer vacations back in the 1970s. They were the bad old days, when Jay's divorcée mother Marie-Anne Dumont had fallen from the apartment into the graveyard below. The word "suicide" was never mentioned. A Dumont wouldn't contemplate self-murder.

Jay followed Amy at a distance, watching her ponytail swing across the shoulders of a fake leopard overcoat. His back ached and he couldn't keep up. His eyes raked the street for unmarked cars. Limping, he touched the cemetery wall, wondering if he should have stopped and bought flowers for his aunt, and for his mother's tomb. The one crowned by the melting sandstone Madonna he now saw hovering ahead, high above the perimeter wall. With relief he remembered the gates closed at sundown. He'd had enough cemeteries for the day, enough for a lifetime.

"If anyone were after you they wouldn't face much of a challenge," Amy said.

Jay keyed in the entry code and pushed the heavy door to the courtyard. Like an automaton, Madame Goncourt pulled back the lace curtains of her concierge's lodgings. She stepped out, wearing pink rubber gloves. They made her hands look like lobster claws. "Bonsoir Monsieur Jay," she said. "Bonsoir Mademoiselle."

Goncourt's greeting sounded friendly enough but Jay sensed its subtle poison. The concierge had always refused to call Amy *madame* even though she was patently no longer a *mademoiselle*, a term reserved for virgin girls or old maids.

"Bonsoir Madame Goncourt," Amy said. Jay didn't have the energy to deal with Goncourt and merely nodded. Her sullen face had changed its default expression over the decades from Jack O'Lantern to baked apple. "Whose side was she was on during the war?" Amy asked. Goncourt retreated and raised the intercom. Jay heard her reporting, telling his aunt *Monsieur* Jay had arrived with his *Mademoiselle*. She followed them with her eyes until they reached the elevator.

"When my aunt starts the professorial stuff," Jay said, "just think back to those happy days in high school and let it slide. She'll never change."

The elevator stopped at the top floor. Hilary, Jacqueline Dumont's housekeeper, pulled the door open. She blinked through a pair of flour-dusted eyeglasses, her square jaw and prominent mole signaling perplexity. "Oh dear. You're early. Your aunt hasn't finished her massage session." Hilary didn't speak. She peeped in an unmistakably English accent.

She took Amy's overcoat and Jay's briefcase and averted her eyes from his dripping clothes. They were spotted green from moss and torn around the knees. "Is everything all right?"

"Splendid," Jay said, limping to the kitchen. He called back to Amy over his shoulder. "Go to the living room, get *Le Figaro* and read about Claude-Gilles d'Arnac," he said. There was always a copy of *Le Figaro* in the living room. The climate might change, the world would become globalized, but he could depend on his aunt not to miss a day of *Le Figaro*.

The parquet in the hall creaked louder than it used to. Jay could hear Hilary's breathy soprano as she queried Amy. Why early? And what happened to Jay's clothes?

The spasms in Jay's back doubled him over and took his

breath away. He stopped at the end of the hall in front of a wooden pegboard hung with sets of keys. Struggling to reach up for the bunch marked *attic rooms*, his mind played the old Velvet Underground earworm. *If only if only if only*. If only he could get under a hot shower he would be all right.

Jay heard heels approaching. Jacqueline's husky voice rose. "I feel ten years younger, Rosalie. You *are* a miracle worker..." The flow stopped.

Jay stood straight in time to face his aunt. She was five-foot two, with eyes of blue, and wore a matching blue silk dressing gown and a frown. Her unnaturally black hair had been coiffed, her lips rouged. Tennis, sun lamps and regular facelifts since she'd retired kept Jacqueline Dumont looking the same indefinable age as her younger partner Hilary. You'd never guess her to be eighty.

"Why on earth are you here so early?" Jacqueline gathered her gown around her. "Jay, this is Rosalie."

He reached out to shake Rosalie's hand. "Delighted to meet you," he said. "I'm the American nephew."

Rosalie bowed her head. She seemed an unlikely masseuse. Too young and fashionable. Rosalie had a bright Hermès scarf wound around her neck, and an expensive black woolen coat over a tight-fitting dress. She also wore a black felt hat cocked at an angle.

"What's happened to you?" His aunt addressed him in English. She recoiled when her hands touched the moss stuck to his motorcycle outfit.

"I had a little accident on my motorcycle," he said. "I'm afraid I need to get upstairs to my room and take a shower."

"An accident?"

Hilary approached. She whispered to Jay's aunt that Amy was in the living room.

Rosalie apparently understood English. "A motorcycle accident?" She took off her coat and put her right hand behind

Jay's back. "Breathe slowly. I'm a nurse." She felt just below his ribs while lifting gently with her other hand. "Follow me," she said. "You should probably be in the hospital."

"We're so very sorry to trouble you, Rosalie," Jacqueline exclaimed, trying to keep her gown closed. "How inconvenient. I hope this won't spoil our dinner, Hilary."

At some point in recent decades Jacqueline Dumont had given up the pretence that she and Hilary lived separately. She'd quietly converted what had been Jay's mother's childhood bedroom into an exercise room. It was equipped with a treadmill and massage table. Rosalie unhooked a white smock from a coat rack and slipped it on. Jay couldn't help staring. He wondered if she'd been a gymnast.

"Please take off everything except your boxer shorts." She spoke with clinical authority, pocketing a diamond solitaire. Rosalie washed her hands and rubbed them with mentholated ointment. Mud from the cemetery clung to Jay's motorcycle suit and clothes.

"I should shower first," he said.

"Your aunt did tell me you're American and I have heard that Americans are obsessed with personal hygiene." She paused. "Shower after I've had a look at you."

Rosalie helped him onto the massage table. She had a provincial accent, Jay noticed. From the Dordogne, he guessed. She pronounced consonants you never heard in Paris and used an *ng* sound as a kind of universal suffix.

Rosalie pummeled, stroked and gouged at his spine. He couldn't help gasping at the strength of her fingers. When he opened his eyes they focused on Rosalie's long, muscular legs in black nylons. Not even the white hospital smock could hide her athletic build.

"Your aunt says you're a photographer," Rosalie commented. She pulled down the elastic band of his boxer shorts and felt his coccyx.

"I used to be," he said, one word at a time. Her fingers jabbed higher, steel prongs separating each vertebra, pinching, pulling and realigning.

"Turn over please." She faced away. When Rosalie turned back she draped a white cloth over his midsection. She moved to the head of the table to work on his shoulders and neck. "You're nothing but bone and muscle," she remarked. "Have you taken up sports since leaving photography?"

"No," he groaned. "I played football, did some boxing."

"Like all good Americans, *non*? It seems you used to be many things, Monsieur Jay. What are you now?"

He hesitated. "Just a boring white-collar employee."

Rosalie nodded. She told him to breathe deeply, let the air out and allow her to manipulate his neck. "Don't resist," she said. "I'll lift and pull now."

Jay felt as if his head were being wrenched off his spine. Terror gripped him. "Relax," he heard Rosalie say. She pulled again and he felt something pop. "There, that's better." She loomed over him. "Lie still, Monsieur Jay. Don't move. Close your eyes."

He could hear her unwrapping a package and pulling gloves on. She rubbed her hands again. It sounded like she was preparing a lotion. This one had a chemical smell. Her plastic-gloved fingers spread the cream over his shoulders, neck and back, kneading. He squeezed his thighs tight and gritted his teeth. She took off the gloves and dropped them into a garbage can. Water ran in the corner sink. "The muscle relaxant will be absorbed in a few minutes. How did you hurt your back, Monsieur Jay?"

Rosalie's lilt had a mesmerizing effect. Jay was unsure if he was expected to answer. He felt himself floating. "I slid on ice." He tried to explain what had happened, stopping to lick his lips. They were dry and puffy. The ointment burned his skin. He wanted to tell Rosalie about the cemetery, about crawling through the tombs and sliding down the walls, and his vision of his father in a beige raincoat. But he thought better of it. So he stuck to the story of the BMW and suddenly wondered if it had been hauled away or scavenged.

"Oh, I don't like motorcycles," Rosalie said, as if he'd been talking to her. "You could have been killed. And then your aunt Jacqueline would be all alone, except for Mademoiselle Hilary of course." Rosalie stood behind Jay. His eyes were still closed. He could hear her searching through the medicine cabinet. "Sit up now and take these. They're homeopathic muscle relaxants. You had a knot in your back and an alignment problem. It's not a slipped disk, though you might want to get it X-rayed tomorrow. Dress warmly, take it easy and I'm sure you'll be fine."

Rosalie handed him the pills and a glass of water. "They'll relax your muscles, that's all, and tomorrow you'll feel like new." Jay hesitated before swallowing. "Good. You can take your shower now. I must be off. Don't forget to have your fiancée apply more cream later."

Jay stretched cautiously. The pain had gone. He could hardly believe it. He twisted, trying to provoke a spasm.

"Go easy," Rosalie chided. Her eyes appraised his torso.

"You are a miracle-worker," Jay said. "My aunt is right."

While he dressed, Jay heard Rosalie cross the parquet and say goodbye to his aunt. The front door shut.

Jay returned to the pegboard. The heavy old keys to his attic room felt familiar. He weighed them in his hand and counted the steps as he climbed.

A cast-iron radiator pinged along one empty wall. Across from it on brass tacks hung a vanity license plate from his father's Jaguar, and a yellowing Jim Morrison poster. Jay stared at them. The ceiling curved down to form a mansard roof around a small gabled window. Above the bed was a rectangular skylight. A taller man could have spread his arms and touched both walls. Jay glanced out at the Eiffel Tower. It sparkled and shimmered. The New Years' countdown read "3 days, 4 hours, 15 minutes, 38 seconds." He wondered how many lonely maids and au pairs had lived in this *chambre de bonne* before his aunt had converted it into an attic apartment in the 1970s. Hilary had lived downstairs with Jacqueline for as long as he could remember. Hilary had been the teenage au pair of 1966 who'd stayed on. Everyone knew it. So his aunt had finally relented and decided that she herself had had the idea of sending Jay upstairs during summer vacations and Christmas holidays. The other attic rooms were for the cook and governess, neither of which had survived as institutions into the twenty-first century.

He sniffed the mothballs in sachets scattered around the room. Hilary kept the apartment clean. Thanks to her nothing had changed, not even the Jim Morrison poster on the wall. Jay wondered why. He hadn't slept there more than twice in 30 years. Why were some people stuck in the past?

Jay let the rust run out of the hot water. The soap flaked. When the hot water finally arrived it filled the bathroom with steam. His back spasms had stopped but he felt mauled. He recognized the shampoo, something he'd bought at the U.S. commissary. Brut, he speculated. The label had peeled off. He coaxed out enough to work up a head of foam, washing out the snippets of his unexpected haircut. The suds stank. They conjured images of the smoky discos of his teens. Had he really known Amy that long? His mind clicked back to high school, to *Come on Baby Light My Fire*, to sex, drugs and Jim Morrison dead in a bathtub, a seminal moment in his adolescence and his troubled relationship with William Grant. It was another world.

Jay toweled off and surveyed the room. Most of his friends had grown taller and thicker as they moved toward midlife. But he'd topped out at six feet when 18 years old, and was as slim as he'd ever been. He rummaged through closets and drawers still packed with teenage castoffs, laughing inwardly. The bell-bottoms and platform shoes were back in style. He ferreted out a pair of worn jeans and a thick gray sweater. It was emblazoned with cracked iron-on letters that spelled out *Bensonhurst School.* The clothes still fit. He wasn't sure it was a good sign.

At the bottom of a closet, he found the battered 1960s Pan Am carry-on bag he'd last used in high school. He filled it with underpants, socks and T-shirts, and then found a stained pigskin aviator's jacket. Memory lane. He draped it between the bag's long handles. The clothes would keep him going long enough to get out of the country. He'd get a new passport from the American consulate tomorrow, some cash from an ATM and be home free once he'd seen a lawyer.

Jay picked up the French rotary phone on the nightstand by his bed. It was the kind with an *écouteur*, an earpiece dangling from a wire. In the France of his youth, husbands routinely listened to their wives' conversations. There was no dial tone. He traced the phone line to a three-pronged jack under the bed and plugged it in. The dial buzzed lazily as he spun it. The tones shot off in a musical stream.

"Bonjour Siam!" Pots and plates clanged and voices shouted in Thai. Jay could almost smell the garlic and ginger down the phone line. A hand fumbled with the receiver on the other end. "Allo? Allo!" Rakan shouted. "Bonjour Siam!"

"It's me."

"Ah, you coming tonight?"

"I wish. Any news?"

"News?"

"Did my friends come back? The curious, spicy guys?"

Rakan barked something in Thai. "No, not those friends. Another friend. A good one. Fresh crab tomorrow? I'll make it with coconut milk. Okay?"

Jay said thanks and cradled the receiver. He stretched out

on the bed and stared up through the skylight at the gray sky. Not a single puffy cloud was in sight, and no moon, not even a sliver. The scent of his perfumed hair and the position of the bed under the skylight conjured another image, this one of Amy at seventeen, her body pale and firm in the square of light cast over the bed by a waxing moon. Madame Goncourt had called Amy a slut that first night he'd brought her home, up the service stairs, to listen to music, to The Doors, to the dead Jim Morrison guy his father the spook had fished out of a bathtub in Rue Beautrellis. *Dirty little whore*, Madame Goncourt had spat as he and Amy had crept by her loge. *I was still a virgin at your age.*

Jay considered dialing New York. He checked his watch and figured Jeff would be on Wall Street by now. José must be all right or he'd have heard otherwise.

From the gabled window he scanned the streets surrounding the cemetery, looking for unmarked police cars. Later, he told himself, feeling faint from hunger. Check the codebook and photos after dinner. He lifted the carry-on bag by its long handles and headed downstairs.

In the kitchen Hilary rattled something on the stove. Jay slipped by. The scent of roasting meat wafted down the hallway. Hilary returned the pan to the oven, turning to see who was there just as Jay edged out of the front door. He tucked the bulging Pan Am bag behind the elevator's wrought iron cage. "Pan American Airlines," he said to himself, pausing to read the tall white letters. He was old enough to have grown up flying Pan Am and BOAC in those pre-Lockerby days, when bombs and suicide madmen were something no one had heard of. Jay turned and was about to step back into the apartment when he heard the elevator. It stopped, and the heavy wrought iron door swung open. Jay squatted out of sight. Through the cage he saw a short, heavyset figure step out. A pair of pink rubber gloves swung into view.

"*Mon Dieu!*" cried Madame Goncourt. "What are you doing Monsieur Jay? Trying to kill me with a heart attack?" She thrust a tattered manila envelope at him and wagged a finger. "This came with the evening post."

Jay couldn't help smiling. "The evening post," he repeated. Did such a thing still exist in Paris? Another charming anachronism. He looked at the envelope and only half-listened to Goncourt.

"I don't understand," she said, waving her rubber-gloved hands. "The envelope says *insouffisance de affranchisement* but I guarantee you it couldn't have been returned to sender for insufficient postage because the mailman would have simply marked it *taxé* and your aunt would've paid the fine. It's not my fault it took so long to get here. Understood?"

Jay watched her with a kind of horrified fascination. "I'm sure I understand," he said.

"I'm telling you it's not my fault the letter was sent back. Look at the postmarks. It's a year old!"

Jay raised an eyebrow. "It doesn't matter Madame Goncourt. Thank you."

He stepped into the entrance hall, studying the torn, tattered envelope. It was covered with stamps. Some had been cancelled, others not. Black letters spelled out in English the words "additional postage required." The handwriting and sepia ink were familiar. Jay carried the envelope with him into the dining room and poured a glass of white wine from a bottle in an ice bucket.

Amy and Jacqueline were in the sitting room. Jay heard a few snatches of conversation. "*Suitable address,*" "*regular working hours,*" "*not too late for family*" ... The words drifted in with the smell of dinner. He stared at the envelope and was about to open it when he heard his name being called. "Coming," he said, slipping the envelope into his briefcase. He walked back through the entrance hall. "Coming," he called again, wondering how he was going to get through the next two hours.

Å

It looked as if Hilary had spent the day making creamy celery root salad, and Alsatian noodles swimming in butter to go with the Norman-style rabbit in cream-and-mustard sauce. Dessert was a chestnut pudding cake soaked in liqueur. *Nouvelle cuisine* had never fazed the self-taught English maiden. If not in language or manners then at least in cooking style she had become more French than the French, circa 1900.

Somewhere between the salad and rabbit Jay tried to pick his aunt's brain. But he gave up. First they would have to submit to Jacqueline's blow-by-blow account of recent events, linked seamlessly to a homily on his future. Amy had told her about Jay's marriage proposal. He could tell by the way Jacqueline fixed her bright blue eyes on the signet ring and raised her brow in disapproval. She wasn't the kind to improvise an engagement.

"We're going away on a little trip," Jay said as the salad bowl disappeared.

"Oh," his aunt remarked, "and where will you go?"

"To Normandy. Before that I'd like to pay my respects to Madeleine."

Jacqueline frowned. "Has something come over you—the motorcycle accident, perhaps? Perhaps it touched a buried nerve? A proposal of marriage and paying respects to the dead in the space of a day?"

"It's never too late," Jay said. "Look at you. You're developing a sense of humor."

"Don't provoke your aunt," Amy said.

Jacqueline struck a pose. "I'm used to it. He's always behaved this way. His father was jocular, too. It was a peculiar thing in a man with such serious responsibilities. Did you know Jay's father, I can't recall?"

"Amy saw him a couple of times," Jay said.

"Mr. Grant wasn't well."

"That's a nice way of putting it," Jay remarked. "He was drunk and kept asking her if she was a Commie." He took a helping of rabbit. Amy's cheeks were crimson. "Where is Madeleine buried?"

"I'll write that down for you later," Jacqueline said. "All in good time." She allowed Hilary to serve her.

"What did she die of?"

"It's not really dinnertime conversation."

"Do you happen to know, while we're not on the subject of Madeleine, anything about her nurse and maid or the gardener?"

"Of course I do, what a thing to ask. I saw Madeleine once a week for years."

"He probably has a minor concussion," Amy said. "He's been having headaches and rubbing his temples all the time." She nudged Jay under the table.

"Headaches? How odd, so have I. And Madeleine was having headaches, too. Do you think it's something in the water?"

"Air pollution," Amy said. "You should see the statistics."

"What about the maid and the nurse?"

"Dear me, Jay. Is this in relation to a friend who's seeking domestic help? Why else would you want to know?"

"How did you guess? My friend needs a maid and a nurse so I thought I'd ask you."

Amy drained another glass of wine. With her fork in hand, she chased a sauce-covered rabbit leg around her plate.

"Very well," said Jacqueline, "seeing that you won't relent." She told Jay what little she knew about Manuela Santiago, the maid. She was from Manila, was wonderful with ironing, but had an irksome penchant to dress in shades of pink or purple.

She spoke fair English but little French and seemed as honest as the day was long, at least by the standards of "that volatile country she comes from."

"And how might I be able to speak to her?"

Jacqueline rolled her eyes. "You might try going back upstairs to the attic and knocking on the room next to yours. Manuela also works for me. She has now, for the last year, not that you would know, since you rarely deign to visit anymore. The agency sent her and I'm very pleased."

Jay took a deep breath. "What about the nurse?"

Jacqueline rattled her gold earrings. "But that's Rosalie, dear, and you've just met Mademoiselle Trichet now. She's not only a masseuse she's also a registered nurse. Her specialty is gerontology. She's Charles' niece. Do you think I'd have just any masseuse come in?"

Jay stood up. "Why didn't you tell me Rosalie was Madeleine's nurse, and you have the same maid?"

"Why on earth would I think to tell you that?"

He circled the dining room. "Someone was stealing things from Madeleine. Someone stole a very valuable daguerreotype and sold it recently. The authorities have asked me to assist them. Naturally I thought of the maid. If it wasn't the maid, the logical next suspect is the nurse."

Jacqueline's jaw subsided into the stretched flesh of her neck. "That is absurd," she said. "Absurd. I don't know what you're talking about young man but I'm telling you once and for all, Rosalie and Manuela wouldn't steal anything from anyone. What makes the police think anyone was stealing from Madeleine?" She cast a worried glance at Amy. Over her shoulder Jay could see a folded copy of *Le Figaro* on the sofa where the two had been sitting.

"We've both read the interview with the auctioneer," Amy confirmed.

"I'm sure Madeleine gave your photograph away or let

Maitre d'Arnac auction it for charity," Jacqueline added. "She was very active with charities. You know she was generous. Generous to a fault." Jacqueline paused. "For such an intelligent woman she was also surprisingly capable of doing unwarranted things." Jacqueline sat upright and signaled to Hilary. "According to the article, your Quincy Alphonse Louis Thomas seems to have been quite an important photographic pioneer."

Jay stopped pacing. It did seem crazy to think someone like Rosalie would steal antiques from Madeleine or have anything to do with Serge Gonflay, and if the maid was trustworthy too it meant Gonflay had used someone else. "I see your point," he conceded.

"*Ah, finalement!*" Jacqueline recomposed herself. The mustard sauce had congealed on her plate. "Now may we speak of other things?"

Jay shook his head. "I've got to ask you a few pointed questions because I'm straightening out a complicated business deal and for Amy's sake I need your cooperation."

Jacqueline seemed taken aback. She touched her pearl necklace and avoided Jay's gaze. "Hilary," she called. "Please, let's move on to the pudding." Jacqueline knit her fingers. "What do you wish to know, Jay? I envisaged this evening as a holiday celebration, since you were not available for Christmas and goodness knows where you will be on New Year's Eve."

"Do you remember anyone named Gonflay having anything to do with Madeleine? Serge Gonflay?"

Jacqueline snorted. "Gonflay? What an absurd name. It sounds like *gonflé*, as if he's all puffed up, full of himself, a ridiculous buffoon. I'd have remembered that name."

"What about Jean-Paul or Henri?"

Jacqueline said she knew half a dozen *Jean-Pauls* and *Henris* and heaven knew if Madeleine had known them too. There was Jean-Paul the greengrocer in Rue de la Pompe, Jean-Paul the plumber in the Normandy village near the family farm-house, and there was the Pope of course. Though he was dead.

"What about Henri?"

"Do you mean *Henri* as a Christian or a surname?" she asked. "A first or a last name?"

Jay said he wasn't sure. All he'd heard was "Henri." Provincial Frenchmen seemed to stick *monsieur* in front of first names a lot of the time. "Madame Goncourt does that," he said. "Rosalie did it just now. She called me *Monsieur Jay*. So, I don't know. It might be Monsieur Henri, Henri Deyzange, a name like that."

"Deyzange?" Jacqueline repeated. "Surely you mean *des anges*?"

"Yes, something like that. It could be important."

His aunt became pensive. Hilary cleared the dishes and brushed the crumbs off the tablecloth. Jay and Amy tried to help but Hilary shook her jowls, signaling them to stay put.

"I know *Maitre* Henri," his aunt said when Hilary went back to the kitchen. "But *monsieur* and *maitre* are different titles." She adopted her professorial tone. "*Maitre* means lawyer, or bonded auctioneer, and then of course in that case *Henri* would be a surname. A last name. Maitre Henri," she began again. "Of course I know *Maitre* Georges Henri. Everyone knows him, even you, Jay. He's a wonderful man and was a great friend to Madeleine and your parents."

Jay watched as red flags and fireworks shot into the sky. "Was he at my father's funeral?"

"No dear," Jacqueline paused. "He attended your mother's funeral, but that was a very long time ago."

Amy blanched. "He's a society lawyer, isn't he?" she asked.

Jacqueline nodded. "Maitre Henri is the senior partner at a very successful law firm." Her head bobbed with pride. "He is a model of altruism. I know for a fact that he spends his waking hours selflessly raising money for good causes. He sits on the boards of half a dozen charities. Now that I think of it, one of them is called *Les Anges de la Charité*. 'The Angels of Charity'. Madeleine willed her estate equally to them and *Opus Angeli*. So there's your solution. *Les Anges* means the angels, not *Leyzange*. It's not a man's name at all." Jacqueline paused to draw breath. She seemed pleased. "Don't tell me you've forgotten Maitre Georges Henri?" Jacqueline Dumont the retired English teacher looked at Jay and Amy in turn as if they were D- students. "The only flaw in Georges' character is that he's what you Americans call a *workaholic*. He simply cannot delegate. He was here a fortnight ago personally overseeing several legal matters we're in the process of resolving. Imagine, a man his age of his caliber taking the time to help simply because he's an old family friend."

Jay's hands flew up to his face. How stupid could he have been? He saw the one that got away, a fish swimming toward him from the depths of memory, a fish wearing a gray fedora hat in the courtyard of the Marais auction house, and in the back seat of a big, dark Renault. Jay grabbed his aunt's forearm. "Remind me what the name of Maitre Henri's law firm is."

She flinched, looking at her nephew's hands. "The law firm? Why, it's the firm we've always used dear, the firm I would fully expect you to continue to rely upon once I'm gone."

"What's the name?"

"The name? How can you be so forgetful? It's Lamartine Associés."

Jay glanced at Amy. She nodded back.

"You remember Maitre Henri? You met him when you were a boy, Jay, when your parents divorced, and afterwards, when your mother passed away." Jacqueline looked pleadingly from Jay to Amy and back to Jay. He tightened his grip. "Your father knew him," Jacqueline said. There was worry in her voice. "They worked together, long ago, after the war. Maitre Henri was with the Free French like Madeleine. Your mother knew him too. They were close friends. He was a photo cipher specialist and gave you your first camera, in Normandy."

Jay let go of his aunt's arm. "My father gave me that camera." He realized he'd shouted. "Jacqueline, are you telling me Maitre Henri was a spy and worked with Madeleine, and my parents, both of them?" Jacqueline looked away. "Well I'll be damned," Jay said. He walked to the French windows and threw them open. The balcony railing shook. His eyes swept the cemetery and street below. A wave of nausea hit him. Cold air blew past, fluttering the curtains. He could hear Jacqueline whispering to Amy. He felt their eyes on his back.

⅄

Names played in Jay's mind, a scratched CD. *Maitre Henri, Maitre Georges Henri. A friend of your parents. Your mother. After the war.*

There were pictures of them together, Jay knew. Photos. Lots of photos. Upstairs. And the codebook.

It took him twenty-five seconds to cross the apartment, retrieve his briefcase from the entrance hall and unhook the attic room keys from the pegboard. In another forty seconds he'd climbed the staircase and opened the door to a storage room at the end of the attic hall.

The steamer trunk with the photo albums looked as if its lid had been freshly dusted. A brass plaque gleamed, inscribed with the name *Ambrose van Eecks*, a paternal great grandfather. While he dragged the chest down the hall into his room, Jay recalled family stories of Ambrose. A sea captain, he was the family's own Flying Dutchman, a pickled-herring eater.

Possibly because this ancestor and Jay's own father liked eating pickled herrings for breakfast, Jay had always loathed them. He lifted the trunk's top and threw aside a dust-cloth. The family photo albums had been stacked there for as long as

Jay could remember. They were labeled on their leather spines, catalogued by date and theme. Jay lifted one and flipped the pages. A plastic binder marked "Brownie Box" in his own handwriting caught his eye. He opened it and pulled out the thin, dog-eared owner's manual. He and his father had used the manual as their first codebook. The photos Jay had taken with the Brownie Box thirty years ago had faded. The mossy greens of Normandy were grassy now. The reds had gone scarlet. The sheep around the farmhouse looked even dirtier than he remembered.

In a section marked "1971" Jay found the photos he'd taken on July 4th at what he later thought of as the Jim Morrison Memorial Barbecue. The photos showed the farmhouse caretaker at his grill with tongs and a glass of wine, the clotted cream of his complexion darkened now by chemical discoloration. A yellowed *International Herald Tribune* newspaper clipping showed a series of photos taken in a Paris street. The newspaper's headline was three inches high. *Rock Idol Dies in Paris Bathtub.* A group of clean-shaven men in summer suits stood behind the gendarmes. Though partly covered by the eternal beige raincoat, one suit was familiar. Someone a long time ago had circled William Grant with an orange crayon. Jay wondered what kind of expression his father wore as he peered into the bathtub and cursed Jim Morrison, the drugged-out subversive idol. Morrison's greatest crime turned out to be his inconvenient date of death. July 3rd. How many all-American family barbecues had he ruined?

Jay slipped the Brownie Box owner's manual into his briefcase and closed the binder. That was one mystery he would never solve without resurrecting William Grant.

Jay looked through the albums again. The one marked *1947-51—Paris* was thicker than most, the spine worn from flexing. Apparently someone still enjoyed looking at it. He debated whether to take the album or remove the photos. He flipped through quickly. Forgotten words and images swam to mind. There might be more material than he remembered, more photos of them taken together, he said to himself.

He opened his briefcase and his fingers touched the small black package from the barbershop, and the tattered manila envelope the concierge had given him. Delivered a year late, he remembered. Why deliver it now?

Sitting cross-legged on the floor Jay poked a finger through a tear in the envelope's edge and worked it open. A two-line note fell out. Jay recognized his father's handwriting.

For old times' sake. Now you have the plates as you always wanted. Dad

Jay's face flushed. He reread the lines.

Inside was another envelope. He tore it open and shook out a vanity license plate, the twin of the one hanging from brass tacks on the wall behind him.

LUVJAGZ

Jay shut his eyes, struggling to find a distant memory—the coded message, that first cloud-cipher they'd used.

The sky always seems bluer on the far side of the sea = LUVJAGZ

Jay held the license plate up to its twin. He lifted the envelopes and compared them. The inner envelope had been postmarked in Marseille just over a year ago, a few days before William Grant had driven off a cliff into the Mediterranean. Drunk driving, the police report had said.

The envelope's other postmark was illegible. But the larger outside manila envelope bore a hand-inked inscription, *insuffisance d'affranchisement.* Insufficient postage. It had been returned to sender. By then the sender was dead. A new set of stamps had been applied. But they hadn't been cancelled.

Jay shook his head in disbelief. Why now, he asked himself again. He looked up through the skylight and knew. The cloud-cipher. The codebook. The Paris ratline to Genoa.

From the shelf above his bed he pulled out a boxed set of illustrated history books and set them on the floor. He reached through the gap between the books and found what he hoped was still there, a copy of *Knowing Clouds*.

On a sheet of typing paper he found in a desk drawer, Jay hastily drew up an alphanumeric substitution table.

A B C D E F G H I J K L M N O P Q R S T U V W X Y Z
1 2 3 4 5 6 7 8 9 10 11 12 13 14 15 16 17 18 19 20 21 22 23 24 25 26

For old times' sake. Now you have the plates as you always wanted. Dad

F = 6. O = 15. R = 18. His fingers raced back and forth across the pages and lines of the book. 6-15-18. He wrote out a total of fifty-four letters. They would decipher as eighteen triple sets of numbers corresponding either to page, line and letter, or page, line and word. He assumed his father had used the old protocol where Z = 26, and so began to write out the message.

He checked *Knowing Clouds.* Page 6, line 15, letter 18. That was "M". The next one, 15-12-4, was "D". 20-9-13 was "L".

M-D-L.

Madeleine de Lafayette. He worked out five more sets. They spelled B-H-I-N-D.

Behind. Behind what?

"Jay?" Amy stood by the door. "Your aunt wanted to send Hilary up to get you but I said I'd come instead. Dessert is on the table. Everyone's upset."

Jay closed the cloud book with the note between the pages. "A voice from the past," he said, standing. "Probably just one of my father's little jokes."

"Is that the envelope the concierge gave you?"

Jay nodded. "You have eyes on the back of your head." He slipped the license plate back into the tattered envelope and dropped it into his briefcase. "My father and I played this game when I was a kid, with coded messages. Morse code then ciphers. I guess he always hoped I'd follow in his footsteps."

"I'm glad you didn't."

"Me too." He paused. "We sent each other ciphers so my father's minders and the Bensonhurst censors wouldn't be able to understand."

"Censors?"

"It's a long story."

Amy stood next to him and stroked his neck. "How's your back?"

"Fine." He paused. "Amy?"

"Yes?"

"I want you to look at something."

"Okay," she said. "What about your aunt?"

"She can wait. Sit down." Jay opened the photo album and turned the pages. "This is France in the late 1940s."

Amy took the album. Her blue eyes blinked. "Your mother was a beautiful woman, much prettier than your aunt, much taller and more feminine."

Jay reached over and flipped forward until he came to the section where his father entered the Dumont family, in 1947. William Grant hadn't always been overweight. Here was proof. He was of above average height, sandy haired with a winning smile, and he wore his three-button worsted suit with confidence. His gray felt hat sat at a rakish angle. His wife, or perhaps his fiancée at the time, Marie-Anne Dumont, stood stiffly to his right. To his left was another young man, shorter, with an intelligent but hard face. The man's scarf hung low, falling to his waist, and on his head sat a fedora, also light gray, but not cocked.

"Maitre Henri?" Amy asked. The tip of one long finger tapped the image. "He's famous."

Jay studied the photo's tonalities with his color-blind eye. "That's him."

The black-and-white print was in excellent condition. Jay removed it from its cardboard corner-mounts. On the back he read aloud *Georges, Marie-Anne, William, 1-1-1948*. The handwriting was a woman's, his mother's maybe, or his aunt's. Maybe it was Madeleine's. She'd been deputy Paris station chief at the time, so she might have been behind the camera. Jay wondered about the order of the names, and the expressions on the trio's faces. Georges, Marie-Anne, William. A glance from Amy told him she wondered too. He'd actually seen the picture before, years before, but had barely glanced at it then. Now it had a story to tell. It whispered from the grave.

A group-shot two pages later had aged less well. The colors had altered. An American friend of his parents' had probably taken it, Jay figured, because few Frenchmen would have had access to color film or a color lab back then, in 1948. The Marshall Plan had just kicked in. Rationing was the watchword. That was one reason why Robert Doisneau and Henri Cartier-Bresson had used black-and-white film to cover the postwar-Paris scene. It was the visual correlative of Edith Piaf's songs about a proud, impoverished, humiliated country broken by the debacle, the Occupation and the drawn-out Allied presence, a country terrified by Communism, unsure of its future in the age of the atom bomb and Anglo-American military primacy.

The men and women in the group photo didn't look like the kind to stand in line for bread and milk while the post-Occupation Nazi Collaboration trials moved forward. Actually they didn't move forward. The Nazis and Vichy-sponsored Milices, the French Fascists, somehow kept slipping out of the country. Later, decades later, it was quietly reported that the Vatican and Allied secret services had helped smuggle them via Marseille and Genoa to South America. But hardly anyone knew the operation's codename. The ratlines started a year after William Grant's employer had changed its acronym from OSS to CIA, incorporating half a dozen specialized intelligence groups including CIC—Counter Intelligence Corps.

Lost in the past, Jay stared at the family photos. He compared the same three faces again in the two pictures. In the color snapshot they were grouped towards the center of the frame. His mother's face, her lips red with lipstick, her long legs showing under a fuchsia-blossom dress, was symmetrical and petite. His father's head mushroomed slightly and was large and pink. And what about Georges Henri? He had a hatchet face, Jay decided. Georges' scarf was blue, an unusual blue that might have been navy or royal blue once but had faded now. A third man stood at the edge of the frame, a small, dark man with thick eyebrows. Jay had no idea who he might be.

On the back of the color picture what looked like another woman's hand had written *Marie-Anne avec William, Georges, Charles, Free Europe Committee, 1949.* Jay repeated the words to himself.

"Free Europe Committee?" Amy's eyes glistened.

"Cover. A research unit, maybe, part of CIC. Probably planting articles in the newspapers, reserving cabins on freighters to Buenos Aires for Gestapo sweethearts. Maybe we should ask Georges Henri or my aunt." He paused. "Madeleine was the deputy chief of station, I knew that much. She showed me lots of old photographs my dad took, and the daguerreotype plates they used for transmitting ciphers. It was boring stuff, mysterious men on the deck of freighters, transportation orders and bank account information, that kind of thing."

Amy's eyes widened. "You mean they really sent coded messages on plates?"

Jay couldn't help smiling. "You think that only happens in the movies? Caesar used a cipher. They've been around since

Phoenician times." He lifted out the black package from the briefcase. "What you want is to somehow hide or disguise the cipher and there are lots of ways of doing that. What Daguerre did was make a photographic plate of an image of Morse encoding, with dots and dashes. He wrapped the plate in black paper without developing it and shipped it to Morse in New York. Morse developed it and read the code. That's how it started, it was like a game for them, like sending a scrambled email." He paused. "I'm writing a lecture about it for an upcoming show we're sponsoring. I must've told you."

"Morse was into daguerreotypes?"

"He was the first American to use them. I'm sure I've told you. Morse was in Paris with Daguerre when the process was perfected. In 1838. A couple of decades after Daguerre died, the imperial forces under Napoleon III used a similar photocipher to send secret messages with carrier pigeons, during the Franco-Prussian war."

"In 1870?"

Jay nodded. "In 1870-'71. The Germans used something like it during the First World War, but they introduced a codebook because Morse code was too well known by then and too easy to crack. Then the Nazis got rid of the photographic element, modifying Morse code and broadcasting the messages by radio. The only way to decipher them was to have a codebook. That's what the Enigma code was all about. You know, at Bletchley Park."

"You're losing me," Amy said. "I've got this image of a pigeon carrying a daguerreotype plate from Bletchley Park over enemy lines." Jay started to explain about the invention of wet collodion, celluloid film and microscope cameras—the precursors to microdot technology—but Amy stopped him. "I'm too tired and your aunt must be furious by now." Jay nodded but didn't move. "Should we open it?" She fingered the edge of the black package.

"Not unless you want to expose the plate so no one can read it."

"You mean that's one of their coded plates? You think it's still good?"

Jay shrugged. "It can't be from the 1940s because it's in a plastic vacuum pouch, but I won't know for sure what's on the plate until I get to my darkroom."

Amy shook her head. "You can't go back to Belleville. They're watching."

Jay was about to tell her Yves had a setup he might be able to use, but he decided to change tack. He needed Amy's help. "You know, cracking the Enigma code got a lot of people killed in World War Two. It won the war and wound up giving us the first real computer. Then after all that trouble people like my father helped the bastards get away to South America."

Amy tugged Jay's hands. "Your father must've thought whatever he was doing was right," she said. "He was following orders."

"Remember Nuremberg?" Jay asked. "You don't just follow orders or you get death camps and torturers."

"We're too far removed. We can't know what was really going on in the '40s and '50s. You've got to forgive him for whatever he did to make you hate him so much."

"I never hated him." Jay flipped a page and read his mother's handwriting off the back of several other pictures. "I pitied him."

Amy turned the album's pages. The pictures showed summery scenes in a weirdly green countryside, with ruined castles and stone farmhouses as backdrops. *Free Europe Corporation* was written across the back of one of them.

From "committee" to "corporation", Jay thought. That was progress.

How innocent the venture must've seemed at first to the young William Grant, Jay reflected. He'd been too young to fight in the war, but old enough to clean up the mess afterward. How heroic, beating the Commies by whatever means necessary, even if that meant helping torturers to escape, helping the rats climb the ratlines. How young they'd all looked. Yet how old they'd been.

"William Ambrose Grant," Jay mused in a tired voice, culling pictures from the album. He was troubled by the carousel of bleak images from a dead world spinning in his head. "Instead of being a hero he wound up a drunk. I wondered for years what it was that broke him." Jay slipped the cloud codebook and the Brownie Box camera manual into his briefcase. He nested the old photos and black package between them. "Let's go downstairs."

"Jay?" Amy wrapped her arms around him. As she started to speak, his satellite phone shrilled.

$$\unicode{x2567}$$

They both jumped. Jay instinctively stepped toward the gabled window. "Allo?"

"It's me."

Yves. A long pause followed. "I'm looking at the Eiffel Tower," Jay said. "In three days, three hours, twenty-two minutes and six seconds it'll be New Years. Are you there?"

"You think they're listening?"

"Maybe."

There was another pause. Jay strained his ears, trying to detect an echo or a hum. As usual the satellite connection sounded scratchy and hollow.

"We've got to meet," Yves said. "I'm heading out of town. You know where I go? I'll be there in twenty minutes. Ask the bald bartender for my table."

"Give me an hour," Jay said.

"Don't come if you're followed."

Jay flipped the phone shut. He stared at the dancing lights of the Eiffel Tower. Amy stepped in front of him and with both hands turned his face toward her. "Yves wants me to meet him at Terminus Nord," Jay said. "I've got to go." He watched Amy's expression. Before she could object he wrapped his arms around her. "I'll take you home. Or to a hotel. That would be safer. I'll drop you somewhere on the way to Terminus Nord."

She shook her head. "What if it's Yves? How do all these people know so much about you and your stupid photos and plates? What if it's Yves, for god's sake?" She fought back anger. "What do you know about him? You're clueless. Maybe he's a fanatic or a terrorist or something. You think he's happy to see you bailing out of the business, like Bruno did? You're the guy's only friends as far as I can figure out and you've both gone legit."

Jay bit his lower lip. "It's not Yves." He tried to sound reassuring. "Because he was a Legionnaire? Is that why you suspect him? They're not touchy-feely types you know."

"*Semper fidelis*," Amy said.

"Semper fi is the Marines, not the Legion."

"Same difference. They both storm beaches and kill people and torture people because they're following orders." Amy leaned on the wall. "I'm going with you." Before he could object she snapped the briefcase shut and walked down the hall with it.

"Go ahead," he said. "I'll be there in a second. Tell my aunt I got a call from New York and we have to leave right after dessert."

Amy hesitated. She set down the briefcase. The parquet creaked under her long strides. Jay waited until she was out of view. Then he knocked on the maid's room next door.

Λ

"Hello," Jay said, "I'm sorry to bother you but I'm looking for Manuela Santiago and my aunt said this is her room. Are you Manuela?"

The woman opened the door and smiled. "You are Madame's American nephew?" Manuela stepped back and showed him in. Her pink maid's outfit hung from a hook. Her slender figure was cloaked by a puffy, bright purple overcoat that reached to her calves. The sleeves were rolled back, revealing two thin, brown wrists. She was short and had the impish features of a teenager. But Jay guessed she was closer to fifty. "I was about to go out," she remarked.

"I'm sorry to trouble you, but you might be able to help me. Madeleine de Lafayette was a friend of mine," he said. "Some things seem to have disappeared from her house, and I'm helping the police investigate. Keep this to yourself, if you would. Don't mention anything to my aunt. It's a fraud investigation."

Manuela stared with black, widely spaced eyes. "I don't understand," she said. "I told the French policemen and ladies everything already."

Jay nodded. "Some new evidence has been found. This is a sensitive, internal enquiry. Do you understand?" Manuela glanced through the gabled window at the Eiffel Tower. Jay reassured her. She had nothing to fear.

In halting English Manuela repeated what she knew. The old lady had died of old age. That's what they'd told her. The old lady had been sick. She'd had headaches and nightmares, imagining things. She, Manuela, would never risk losing her job or her residence permit by stealing anything. "I have working papers," she said, opening a black plastic purse and digging them out. "I work for an agency. You can check. Your aunt knows. Please don't get me in trouble sir."

"There's nothing to worry about," he said. "I was just wondering when you last saw Monsieur Serge Gonflay?" The maid shook her head. "A tall heavy man with a red face?" The maid shook her head again. She'd never met any Frenchman like that at Madeleine's house, she swore. She'd never heard the old woman mention him.

Jay wrote the name out in capital letters. G-O-N-F-L-A-Y. The maid looked at it. "I'm not illiterate sir. I went to a convent school."

"Did anyone remove art objects or photographs from the house while you were there, or ask you to do so?" The maid swung her head. Her eyes tracked Jay's. "Perhaps someone you trusted and are now afraid to denounce?"

"Madame never trusted me," the maid said at last, pulling the purple sleeves of her overcoat back from her wrists. "Because I'm dark-skinned and I don't speak French." She peered at Jay. "Maybe someone else was taking things," she continued. "I don't know. There were many things around, just like your aunt's apartment downstairs. Pictures with carved frames and metal artworks and pieces of furnishing. Many French people came over to see Madame Madeleine, especially in the end."

"In the end?"

"Before she died."

"She died suddenly?" The maid nodded. "And you found her the following day? Did you have the impression she was sick?"

The maid nodded again. "There were so many things in the house sir," she said, tripping over her words. "Things moved from one room to another."

"How do you mean?"

Manuela twisted around. "Madame said everything got up and moved. I think the house was haunted. I never liked it." Manuela crossed herself. "Maybe Madame was not right in the head. I think she moved things herself sir. She often carried an old picture with her and talked to herself like she was talking to God."

"A picture or a photo?"

"I'm not sure. It was a funny-looking thing. Made of metal, sir."

Jay nodded. The maid told him haltingly about her experiences at Madeleine's house. How independent the rich old lady had been, how gentle and kind to everyone, even though she was a racist, like all the rich French people the maid had worked for in Paris, except, of course, Madame Jacqueline. Only at the very end had Madeleine begun to seem ill, behave strangely and complain of bad dreams.

"I don't know what she dreamed because Madame didn't like to talk English to me and I didn't know what she was saying sometimes. She took some pills and had special drinks. But I just cleaned the house sir and bought food and cooked once or twice a week when your aunt visited. Madame didn't like my cooking." Manuela glanced at her wrist watch and drew a sharp breath. "I'll be late for the movie," she said. Her fingers clutched at her rolled up sleeves as she and Jay walked along the hallway. "What do the nurse and gardener say sir? They know I don't know anything. They work for the same agency I do."

"I'll need to speak to them." He noted the name and address of Geronto Services, the agency, and the names of the nurse and gardener. Mademoiselle Trichet and Monsieur Gonzalez. Manuela didn't know their first names. "Rosalie," Jay said. "She's the nurse. I'm not sure about the gardener."

"The agency has plenty of work for me," Manuela added. "They know I am an honest woman and so does your aunt. I went to a convent school." She crossed herself. "There are many old women like Madame Madeleine alone in this city. The men die first. In my country too."

"This is confidential," he told Manuela again as they reached the stairwell. Her dark eyes refused to look at him. "Telephone me at this number day or night if you think of anything. It's my private number. Do not give it to anyone, not even another policeman or my aunt. I might want to show you some photographs and ask you to identify the people in them." Manuela dipped her head. He wrote his satellite telephone number on a page of his notebook and tore it out. "Strictly confidential, Manuela."

She crossed herself, said *goodbye sir* and scurried down the service stairs.

In the downstairs hall, Jay hooked the attic room keys back in place and stopped short. He stared at the pegboard. He could hear Amy talking to Jacqueline in the dining room, spinning tales. Glancing around for Hilary, he reached up to the pegboard again and lifted off a set of keys. They were labeled *Madeleine de Lafayette*. The keys jingled in his pocket. He sat uncomfortably at the dining room table.

Jacqueline waved away Jay's apology. She dipped her spoon into the chestnut pudding and pointed to the champagne Hilary had brought out. They raised their glasses in silence. Jay's temples were pounding. He felt the urgent need to leave.

Haldemann, Erlichman, Mitchell and Dean, put them together, what does it mean...Haldemann, Erlichman, Mitchell and...

The anti-Nixon chant tormented Jay for years. He'd heard it time and again in the early 1970s, during the Watergate investigation, when he thought he'd never again be able to bridge what people called the Generation Gap and talk to his father. William had called him a Commie and Jay had called him a Fascist, an agent of repression.

The political chant had become a riff in a jazz standard Jay hummed in his senior year at Bensonhurst. *Compared to What?* It was an act of unconscious subversion. He'd heard the song that spring day in 1974 when an impeachment march had passed under his father's windows in Manhattan. The marchers waved banners showing Tricky Dick Nixon, his nose erect. They shouted *Haldemann, Erlichman, Mitchell and Dean, put them together, what does it mean?*

What did it mean? He remembered now that William Grant was drunker than usual that day and shouted down from the ninth floor at the anti-Vietnam, anti-Nixon protesters. *You don't know what the hell you're talking about*, William had roared. *You can't even dream what the real world would be like if we hadn't gone in.*

He'd leaned out of the window and thrown a beer bottle and gone on a rampage through the apartment while Jay, his visiting teenage son, sat motionless in a corner. William had shouted names, names from the past, his dead wife's name, and others Jay struggled now to remember. They were German names, Arabic-sounding names and French names. *Georges, she loved Georges, not me . . . for all I know you're not even my son.*

Not even your son?

The police had come around. The embarrassed officers had advised William Grant the CIA operative that it was illegal to throw beer bottles from a ninth-floor window. "Sir," one of the policemen had said, "you might hurt someone."

"You don't get it sonny boy. I *want* to hurt someone. You know what they're calling you? Pigs. Pigs!"

When the officers had seen the distinguished service awards from Langley, Virginia, scattered and splintered on the living room floor they'd let William off with a reprimand, ruffling Jay's long hair in a pathetic gesture of what? Solidarity?

Jay sat silent now in the Peugeot's bucket seat. Amy drove slowly, methodically across town toward Terminus Nord. But he didn't hear her conversation or the sound of traffic. The chant resonated in his head, reformulated with a contemporary French lilt. *Gonflay, Georges, Yves and me, put it together what can it mean . . . What can it mean?*

The other names ruined the rhythm, Jay decided. He'd never been strong on scansion or meter. The other names were Madeleine, d'Arnac, Lamartine, Les Anges, Opus Angeli, Jean-Paul, Manuela Santiago, Charles, Marie-Anne, Debra... Put the names together, he spurred himself. Put them together because if you don't very soon someone else will. Someone who's out to get you.

But his mind rebelled. The irrational drumming of the Nixon-era chant returned. "I don't know what it means," he shouted. "I don't know!"

Amy's right hand felt its way through the passenger compartment to Jay's face. "It's no coincidence is it?" she asked. "I mean, that someone just sent you that license plate."

"Coincidence? No such thing. *Dixit* William Grant."

Earlier, as they'd done their best to sneak unseen to her car, Amy had given up any talk of going to the police. And there was no way to contact a lawyer at 10pm between Christmas and New Year's Eve, not in Paris.

She accelerated north across the Champs-Elysées, rolling down the boulevards without encountering a single traffic jam. Minutes later she double-parked alongside other cars in front of Terminus Nord.

The landmark café-restaurant faced the Gare du Nord train station. Wind and rain swept by. How many freight wagons had rattled out of the station to the death camps, Jay wondered? How many black-booted SS officers had swilled beers at Terminus Nord and shaken hands with zealous French bureaucrats, men with names like Maurice, François or Georges Henri?

Not, at least, with William Grant, the latecomer. The spy. Jay wondered how his father could stomach sending Nazis and Fascists to freedom in Argentina, Uruguay, Paraguay, Bolivia or Brazil once the war was over. *Anything to stop the reds. Anything. To keep Europe free.*

Jay heard his father's voice in his head again. *There is no such thing as coincidence, only a lack of information.* It was William's pet saying when drunk. The roadmap of burst capillaries on his cheeks traced the itineraries of a lost life.

The words flitted through Jay's mind as he and Amy made a dash for the restaurant's revolving door. *Only a lack of information.* They shook themselves in the lobby like wet retrievers. Despite the hour Terminus Nord was filled with travelers and after-theater diners. Platters of oysters and shrimp were propped on stands. The Maitre d' asked Jay to wait by the podium.

Wait? No problem. Waiting had been Jay's nursery theme. Waiting had marked his adolescence and grown-up years. He knew Terminus Nord from business trips to Belgium, Amsterdam and Cologne, and from the history books, and his father's slanted recollections of the war's aftermath. The restaurant's beery, brassy interior hadn't changed much since the Occupation. It was a place full of people waiting for a train and a revelation, surrounded by ghosts.

Jay caught the bald barman's eye and followed his chin as it dipped toward a booth.

They slipped past waiting couples and slid in. Yves lowered his copy of *France Soir* and glanced into the mirrors around him. He shook Jay's hand, moaning almost imperceptibly.

"Your face, " Amy said.

"I tripped. Come to think of it, maybe it was those two guys who wanted to tie my shoes."

"Burglars?"

"Maybe they'd mistaken the back of the shop for the front. An honest mistake. A key can look like a crowbar."

Jay had seen Yves deal with crowd-control police. It wasn't a pretty sight. You learned tricks in the Foreign Legion.

"What did you do to them?" Amy asked.

Yves grinned. He took a drag on a corn-paper Gauloise. "One of them went swimming in the canal," he said. "The other is in a dumpster. A big green one." He pulled back his duffel coat sleeve. "The kind the garbage trucks pick up at night. Right about now."

The waiter took their orders. Amy sat silent. Yves lifted his mug and gulped. He offered her a cigarette. She stared at the pack but didn't move. Yves raised an eyebrow. "New look?" he asked Jay. "I'm not sure I've ever seen you in a bomber jacket and bellbottoms."

"Deep disguise," Jay said. The waiter left Jay's double-espresso and Amy's mini-bottle of Perrier. "What did they look like?"

Yves' Adam's apple bobbed. "One was your size," he said. The foam caught on bristles around his lips. "Black hair, strong foreign accent. Unremarkable except for a little moustache."

"The taxi driver," Jay said. "The one who picked me up after the cemetery."

"The other guy was a weightlifter type," Yves said. "Stocky. Looked like an animal."

"DST?"

Yves showed his blackened teeth again. "Last month the DST was folded into the DCRI," he said. "Direction Centrale du Renseignement Intérieure. Our new Homeland Security. These guys are private contractors. That's what the cards say." He dropped a wallet on the table and poked out a plastified ID card. *Les Gardiens Parisiens.* A passport-size color photo showed the man's face. *Fabrice Gouge.* Jay wondered if the dumpster-collectors had made their rounds. He pushed the wallet back.

"He was in the subway, following me," Jay said. "We seem to have something they want."

Amy clutched her glass. "You recognize them?" She paused. Her eyes raked from Jay to Yves. "Do you guys always talk like this? *Guy talk*? Is this how tough guys talk when they've been beaten up and chased around, or maybe just killed some other hormonal *guys*?" She looked at the water she'd spilled and rolled her head to loosen up her neck muscles. "Okay," she said. "I'll stop being emotional. I'll shut up. It's really none of my business, except this hormonal guy here is supposed to marry me and it looks like he's going to wind up in that cemetery over at his aunt's place instead, like his mother, who turns out to have been a spook like her husband. But you probably knew that, right Yves?"

Yves' expression gave nothing away. He reached under the table and pulled out a dirty manila envelope, handling it with his tobacco-stained fingernails. "I've got a train in twenty-five minutes," he said. "If I were you I'd save the family arguments for later, package this with gloves on, send it to a reporter and blow town."

"Good advice," Amy said.

Jay used his coffee spoon to ease out the prints and blowups.

"Friends of Gonflay's?"

"Former friends. Some former DST renegades moonlighting or recycling themselves, probably. Or Ministry of the Interior agents. There's some kind of connection with an African-American woman. It doesn't figure."

"Unless she's a spook." Yves blew the smoke over his shoulder, signaling for another beer and the check. "I'd forget the police."

"You don't know the half of it," Amy remarked. She rearranged the prints and blowups with her long, red fingernails. Yves had done a good job. A gallery of faces stared up.

"He's the guy who was driving when Gonflay was killed," Jay said. He tapped the man in the camelhair coat. Amy and Yves bent close and peered at the grainy enlargements.

"Here's your man in the back seat," Yves said, pushing the oversize image to the center of the table. "Funny thing to be wearing a hat and a scarf inside a car, don't you think? Like you said before, it doesn't seem normal."

Jay contemplated the images. He set three of the vintage snapshots from his aunt's album on the table.

"Nice paper," Yves grunted. "Fiber, probably from the 'Fifties?"

"Not bad. Try 1948 and '49."

"Who's the woman? This guy's wife?" Yves tapped on the faces of Marie-Anne Dumont and Georges Henri.

"Other way around," Jay said. "She goes with him. My father."

Yves shook his head. "Doesn't look that way." He coughed. "I get it. This is the guy from the car," Yves added. "The guy in the back seat with the hat. He's got the same hatchet face almost 60 years later. Looks like a mean bastard. Amazing. He's wearing the same kind of hat and scarf sixty years later?" Yves shook his head. "Cheap son of a bitch."

"Georges Henri," Jay said. "Otherwise known as Maitre Georges Henri."

Yves took another beer from the waiter. He gulped and shook his head. "Never heard of him."

"Ever hear of Maréchal Pétain, Adolf Eichmann, Hans Globke, Charles de Gaulle, François Mitterrand, Père Labé?"

"Or Opus Angeli?" Amy added.

"Opus Dei."

"Not the same."

Yves drank. But his mug trembled. "They're all dead, right? And Père Labé went gaga, everyone knows that." Yves wiped his cheeks. "Gonflay was ripping off the ministry and these guys?"

"Looks that way."

"What about the third one, in the color picture?"

Jay shook his head. "On the back it says *Charles*."

"Probably dead."

"Probably."

Yves coughed. "And d'Arnac? Where does he fit?"

"That's what I was going to ask you."

Yves flinched. "Bruno was right," he said, turning to look at the door. "When I told him what'd been going on, Bruno said, 'Better get out, fast. Go to the moon.' If I were you I'd put together everything you can and disappear tonight. I don't know how you did it, Jay, but you sure got us up shit creek. Père Labé is untouchable. These French secret service guys are not to be messed with. And now you're starting to suspect me."

Jay paid the check. They left through the service door. The alley faced the station. Rain fell. "Stations and airports are the first places they'll look," Jay said.

"Just remember Norbert in Calais," Yves said. "If I need to see you I'll get Rakan to call. If Rakan says 'spicy crab' it means I'm trying to reach you." He paused long enough to dangle a set of keys. "These are to Bruno's office. Call him. He'll help. He said he would. You know his door code?" Jay shook his head. "Think of the French Revolution. 1789."

"The year Daguerre was born," Jay said.

Yves stooped to peck Amy's cheeks. "I'm sorry," she whispered.

"For what? If I were you I'd be suspicious. I'd still be suspicious."

$$\mathbf{\unicode{x1F5FC}}$$

Computer and TV screens flickered, photocopiers flashed, radios babbled, modems squealed, fax machines throbbed and printers spat out page after page of paper. Electronic gnomes inhabited the headquarters of the wire service. Pasty-faced technicians and journalists drifted among the IT stations checking, sifting, tearing and feeding the machinery with fresh paper or cartridges.

No one from the second shift was around to ask Amy why she'd come in again and brought her boyfriend with her. Her humanoid co-workers signaled their recognition by a nod or a raised paper cup. *Too tired to talk*, their expressions telegraphed in facial Morse code. *December in Paris. Stop. Rather be in the Bahamas.*

It felt to Jay as if, for the last few hours, Amy had been on the edge of a breakdown. But now that she was on familiar ground she'd become a demon of efficiency. The photocopies, wire service reports and print outs from the Web provided more information than they could handle. Jay felt fatigue and panic. With a coffee mug in hand he scanned documents, highlighting paragraphs, pushing his brain.

Maitre Georges Henri Knighted by President Mitterrand... Opus Angeli Cited as Model Charity... Opus Angeli Inaugurates International Gerontology Foundation...

An in-depth report in *Famille Chrétienne* magazine provided a concise history of the ever-expanding evangelical charity, starting with its founding by militant priest Père Labé just after the Second World War. From its beginnings in abandoned Nazi armaments warehouses near Paris, by the 1960s it had developed a network of institutional donors worldwide. In the 1980s, several multi-million dollar estates had been auctioned on its behalf. As it grew, other financing came from spin-off activities, everything from used clothing and furniture shops to real estate agencies, a domestic help and nursing agency, several clinics and a hospital. By the early 1990s these lucrative, tax-free charitable foundations had transformed Opus Angeli into the country's leading nonprofit. By then Père Labé had become a cult figure, a nonconformist spiritual guide in this most secular, anticlerical of European republics. His bright blue eyes burning with zeal behind thick lenses were a common sight on French TV. That raucous voice always seemed to be on the airwaves. Labé's square jaw and Kirk

Douglas dimple had softened with the drooping of advanced age, but his pugnacity had remained undiminished. Then senility had sapped him. Père Labé's spokesperson was forced to admit that the man many considered a saint was suffering from a degenerative mental disorder. He was ninety-five by then.

As far as Jay could deduce, only one uncontained spill had ever sullied the charity's operations during their fifty-plus years of service to the handicapped and the elderly. There had been unsubstantiated allegations of Opus Angeli funding an extremist group of former Algerian War paratroopers based in Marseilles, a group called *La France Profonde*, and a radical Christian sect in Brittany, *Les Enfants de Sainte Jeanne d'Arc*. The groups had been disbanded, Opus Angeli's mid-level management reshuffled, and the affair squelched. Since then ten years had gone by without incident. By now no one remembered the scandals.

Over the years Maitre Georges Henri was always shown with his trademark scarf and fedora. He'd remained above suspicion, the proverbial man-behind-the-scenes. Adoring crowds focused their attention on the charismatic Père Labé. Henri was a minor Résistance and Free French figure. His wartime record was as ambiguous as that of former French president François Mitterrand. Mitterrand had made Henri a Knight of the Republic in the mid-1980s. Only a few commentators drew attention to the similarities in the men's careers. The Socialist president came from an aristocratic clan while Henri's background was humble. His father had been a colonial administrator in Algeria, when the country belonged to France. After being knighted Henri was hailed across the political spectrum as the "self-effacing financial miracle-worker" who'd turned Père Labé's stumbling volunteers into a "crack force of French patriots nicknamed the Angels of the Aged." After Labé had gone senile, the charity empire had shifted into

Henri's hands. Still in the shadows, Georges Henri was sometimes cited by government insiders as "the model apolitical altruist." He'd been a friend over the years to both the center-right and the Socialists, including past and present ministers and presidents.

Amy read the highlighted sections of the pages Jay handed her. An alarming scenario played itself out in Jay's mind. He waited for Amy to finish reading. The florescent lights painted her cheeks green. He scratched at his stubble.

"I tried earlier with Google and it didn't work. But if you had a subscription and went to *Le Figaro*'s website and looked in the obituaries columns over the last few years," he asked, "could you see what came up?"

Amy drained her coffee. "I'd have to see what kind of search options they have and when they put the paper into electronic format. Everyone was ten years behind here." She turned the flatscreen so he could read it. "What's the keyword?"

"Lafayette," Jay said. "Or de Lafayette."

Amy accessed the archives, typed in a string of commands and keyed in the name. The files went back three years, according to the pop-up message.

"That ought to be enough," Jay said. Amy hit *enter* and a second later the name *Nicolas de Lafayette* appeared. "Madeleine de Lafayette is what we're after," he said. Amy gave him an impatient look. She lashed the mouse and *Madeleine de Lafayette* popped up. There were three references. The first was two paragraphs and didn't tell them anything they didn't already know—Madeleine's age, the reasons she was worthy of being mentioned in *Le Figaro*, where she'd died, when and how. Amy clicked to the second and third entries. *Madame Madeleine de Lafayette, renowned art collector and heiress to the Verlain shipping fortune, died in her sleep yesterday following a fatal brain hemorrhage...Heirless, her possessions were willed to the charitable trust Opus Angeli...The funeral will be held*

Thursday at 11 o'clock at the church of Notre Dame de l'Assomption, with inhumation to follow at the Cimetière de Passy...

Without waiting, Amy changed the keywords within the obituary section to *d'Arnac Opus Angeli* and entered. There were three hits in France within the last year involving three elderly women, Madame Louise Vialat-Prélenfrey, Madame Georgette Dupont-Lartigues and Madame Hélène Furstenstag. Each had willed her estate to Opus Angeli. The auctions had been run by Maitre Claude-Gilles d'Arnac at the Hôtel Drouot in Paris.

Amy pulled each entry up and read it aloud. "Died in her sleep...brain hemorrhage...Died at Saint-Xavier de Collonges Clinic, stroke...Died after falling down a flight of stairs at home...No heirs. No heirs. No heirs."

Amy glanced at Jay.

"None of them was super-rich," he said, "or we would've heard about them. None of those names is familiar."

Amy stared at the screen. "Not *super*-rich," she echoed. "But I'll bet they were all *filthy* rich. Secret rich. The old-money type of rich. Like Madeleine."

Jay swallowed. When he'd been a paparazzo he'd encountered the rich and famous. They were always surrounded by household staff and professional vultures. The 'secret rich' were an easier target. Retiring, thrifty, sometimes pious they often had no more than a loyal housekeeper or cook to help them. Sometimes they lived alone. And sometimes they were heirless.

Jay rubbed his eyes. He sat on the carpeted floor at Amy's feet. "I'll bet there were no autopsies," he said slowly, "and that Georges Henri and Claude-Gilles d'Arnac wept at every funeral."

Amy shifted in her chair. "I wonder who the nurse and gardener were. If they were the same team each time."

They stared in silence across the florescent-lit room.

Another penny dropped into Jay's slot. "Can we go back to that other obit? The one for Nicolas de Lafayette? He was Madeleine's son."

Amy turned back to the keyboard and mouse. The item reappeared. *Nicolas de Lafayette, 57 years old, only son of Verlain shipping heiress Madeleine de Lafayette, died Friday in an automobile accident on the Boulevard Péripherique in Paris when his vehicle, a late-model Renault, went out of control. Monsieur de Lafayette was unmarried and had no children . . .*

The blood seemed to drain from Amy's face. "And then there was Madeleine's housekeeper Arlette," Amy said. She clicked and typed in another search. "Hit and run. Just over two weeks ago."

Jay stood. He pulled Amy to her feet. "When did my aunt say she'd last seen Maitre Henri to talk about her will?"

Amy's expression told Jay she had come to the same conclusion.

"You've got to get some sleep." Amy's voice sounded disembodied. She pulled the curtains and fell into bed.

Jay felt uneasy. Her apartment faced the south side of the Musée d'Orsay on the Left Bank. What if they knew about Amy? With a rush of adrenaline, he dragged the loveseat from the book-lined living room and wedged it between the front door and kitchen wall. Anyone out there would have to break down the reinforced door and move the couch to get in. Jay sat on the edge of the bed and asked himself who would be trying to get in. Yves had taken out two of the men who'd followed him. One was floating in the Canal Saint Martin. The other had either been compacted by a garbage truck or was in traction. Maitre Henri was unlikely to break down the door. He was over eighty years old. True, the French secret services had found his Gilford Foundation business card and were tracking him, because he'd met Serge Gonflay. But how would they connect him to Amy? The DST and PJ were notoriously unsubtle. They would've interrogated her and arrested him by now. If there were rogue former DST agents involved they might be worrying after what Yves had done to them. They'd probably be on the run, afraid of being identified. Still, there was the nine-fingered man in New York and the guys in sheepskin. And Debra.

Jay stretched on the bed beside Amy and shut his eyes. But his jetlagged, exhausted mind wouldn't stop working. She'd already fallen asleep. Her head was hidden by a mass of hair. He wrestled a blanket over him and draped his aviator's jacket on top.

In the twenty years he'd known Amy, he'd rarely slept at her apartment. It was cramped and stuffed full of books, most of them on philosophy. That's what she'd majored in. He kept a few clothes there in case of an emergency. But he'd never done anything like settle in. One of the reasons she hadn't moved to a bigger place was she was waiting to see which way things would break. Now they were breaking. Into pieces.

Jay turned over. The mattress was too soft, the sodium streetlights and traffic on the riverside expressway too jarring. He was too tired and too wired to sleep. At every noise, his eyes popped open. He forced them shut, only to feel the bed spin Wizard of Oz-style. Images of Madeleine and his father and mother danced in a whirlwind with Georges Henri and the barber. Jay saw Madeleine's son, the tall, dark-haired, pale Nicolas de Lafayette. His spidery arms and legs and gloomy character had always made Jay think of a daddy longlegs. Nicolas had worked as a librarian and was considerably older, so he and Jay hadn't really known one another well. There'd been that one embarrassing encounter in a Latin Quarter nightclub years ago. Nicolas never came out of the closet. It was surprising to see him in S & M drag, on the masochistic end of the leash. A year later, Jay and Nicolas had driven across town together after a visit with Madeleine. Jay remembered how fearful Nicolas was at the wheel, no typical Parisian male. Maybe that was how he'd lost control of his car. Maybe Nicolas de Lafayette had been too agitated or distracted to get out of a road warrior's way on the beltway. Maybe. But Jay doubted it.

Tomorrow Amy would have to check on Louise Vialat-Prélenfrey, Georgette Dupont-Lartigues and the other woman. Jay groped for her name. Hélène Furstenstag. Something like that. Amy would have to check if they had lost sons, daughters, husbands or trusted housekeepers in banal traffic accidents, leaving them heirless. Heirless dowagers with wills made out by Maitre Henri.

Amy would have to help put together a watertight, damning dossier, he told himself, a report with all the arrows drawn in. Because no one in France was going to want to believe that Maitre Georges Henri, Résistance hero and selfless second to Père-Labé, seemed somehow involved with the underworld, murderers of the elderly, or what looked like an extremist reactionary group. There would be massive denial. It would be like the Terror of 1792. Heads would roll. Jay would have to put together enough pictorial evidence to cast doubt on the accidental death of Serge Gonflay. The photos would show Henri in the killer's car. An investigation into the charities' activities might turn up answers. One way or the other, Jay was bailing out, leaving town, climbing up the ratlines and diving into the ocean from the rigging.

If only he'd been at the scene of Gonflay's murder a few minutes earlier, Jay told himself, flipping onto his other side. *If only if only if only...* The tune started up again in his head. No matter how he tossed and turned he could find no comfort in Amy's bed. He was sure Gonflay had been murdered. Someone had pushed him. If Jay had arrived a minute earlier he could've taken photos of events as they unfolded, as he knew they must have unfolded. Now he would have to reinvent reality. He'd have to drive to Bruno's office, scan the prints and rework them with PhotoShop. He was impatient to check the black package from the barber shop, but that would have to wait until later.

The fridge shuddered, shaking the floor. Jay shot upright and searched the darkness. Amy slept fitfully, her breathing uneven, seemingly tearing at the stale air. Jay pulled his jacket back over him and settled down again. He caught sight of his briefcase across the room. He was conscious of the set of keys in his pocket.

Sometimes you have to lie to preserve the truth, steal to uphold the law, imprison to keep others free... make war to preserve the peace... think of the greater good... freedom, freedom, freedom.

William Grant had always despised philosophy. Yet he'd had plenty of pat sayings to share when he'd been drinking. Freedom was the harp he played. Freedom to do whatever you wanted, as long as you were strong enough. Freedom to impose freedom. Freedom of action. Freedom from this, freedom from that. Freedom was worth any price, William had often said. Any price. Then his wife had betrayed him and jumped off a balcony, and he'd drowned himself in a bottled ocean of lies stretching from Old Europe to Pinochet's Chile and the Shah's Iran. Such were the professional hazards of an operative in the lie business. The revelation that Jay's mother, too, had worked for the Company, segueing from the Free Europe Committee, made him sick. He'd always suspected it, had always lived in denial.

Here was the troubling thing, Jay told himself, fully awake with no hope of falling asleep. Georges, Maitre Georges Henri had felt no qualms. He'd thrived. Jay wanted to know why. He had to try to understand how, despite the freight cars full of Jews and Résistance fighters, despite the clicked heels of SS and Milice, despite the reams of false documents generated by the secret services of the world to keep the ratlines secret, despite the decades of posturing and deception at the head of a charity, how had Georges Henri lived with himself? What messianic fire disguised as altruism burned under Henri's gray fedora? What was the key that opened the lock, the key to the why of it all?

Jay rolled over again. He felt the keys to Madeleine's house jab his thigh. He knew what he had to do.

Paris, December 29, 2007

Jay left the bedroom carrying his shoes. His greatest fear was that Amy would wake up when he slid the loveseat away from the front door. But she didn't. He padded down the stairs in stocking feet and slipped on his oxfords in the entrance hall.

It was 2:45am on the illuminated dial of Jay's wristwatch, 2:44am on the giant clock on the Musée d'Orsay's façade. He shivered as he trotted down the service stairs into the garage. A ramp led from there to the building's back courtyard. Amy's car was parked around the corner. Frost lay thick across the windows and door handles. The Peugeot protested when Jay turned the key but the engine eventually started, quaking and spitting vapors out of the tailpipe. The windshield wipers scratched at the frost. Jay rubbed out a porthole. He drove with his window down, the air chilling his face and hands. Stoplights blinked at intersections. Jay slowed the car then continued through, heading eastward. In ten minutes he'd crossed the river and followed the Right Bank expressway to the Marais. He cruised down Rue Charlemagne behind the Baroque silhouette of Saint Paul's church and parked nearby.

A few years earlier, Jay's former business partner Bruno had shifted from vintage photography into digital multimedia.

Bruno had always railed against computers and the Internet. He'd been a mediocre paparazzo and at best a journeyman photographer. But he was as good as they came in a darkroom at burning and dodging black-and-white images. From chemicals to pixels, Jay mused.

He walked a circuitous route past boutiques, delicatessens and restored landmark properties. They were dark and quiet now. The whole of the Marais had been transformed from the slum he'd known when growing up into a boutique-crawler's dreamland. It offered the cachet of the antique retrofitted for contemporary luxury. The hitch was, the retrofitting had eliminated half the short cuts and hidden alleyways. They were locked now, with door codes and video surveillance.

He zigzagged southeast through the Saint-Paul antiquarians' quarter, passing under the windows of the auction house where he'd first seen the man in the camelhair coat with Serge Gonflay and the fedora-crowned Georges Henri. Bruno's new office was due east two blocks. Once Jay was sure no one had followed him he stepped into Rue Beautrellis and turned right.

Bruno must have found good backers, Jay reflected. The high-tech bubble had burst years ago but Multimed Services had a tony address. Jay thought of the French Revolution and Daguerre's birthday. He keyed in the door code and climbed a sweeping stone staircase that was probably four hundred years old. He keyed in 1-7-8-9 again on the second-floor landing. With the flat pockmarked key Yves had given him he opened the reinforced steel door.

The media company's offices were in the palatial salons of a Louis XIII townhouse. Faint light came from two emergency exit lamps and made the gold leaf glow on the ceiling beams. Below the painted beams wiring harnesses ran between half a dozen state-of-the-art workstations. Jay reached for a light switch just as someone sat up and turned to face him.

"Boo!" Bruno laughed.

"What are you doing here?"

"When else do I get to see the famous J. Anthony Grant?" Bruno yawned and strode over, offering his hand. "I don't want to know the details," he said. "Whatever happens," he continued, leading Jay to a cubicle at the back of the office, "I didn't see you, you didn't see me and you never used my equipment to do anything, okay?" He handed Jay a box of DVDs. "Copy whatever it is onto these, because the minute you step out the door I'm erasing everything. In fact I'm going to reformat the hard disk, not that that's foolproof." Bruno lifted his sparkling eyeglass frames and massaged the bridge of his nose. It was a big, bent nose. He looked like Gerard Depardieu playing Cyrano de Bergerac.

"You'd better scrub your browser too," Jay said. "I'll need to upload some files onto the Gilford Foundation site just in case."

"In case of what?"

"I'm not sure."

Bruno licked his lips. "Okay. I can always say you had the keys and were here without my knowledge."

"It won't come to that."

Jay settled into a leather swivel chair. He tilted his head back to look at the beams overhead. Early seventeenth century. Maybe life was brutish and short back then, but it hadn't necessarily been ugly. Not for the lucky few. He hesitated before turning to face the computer, the scanner, the DVD burner and the audio and video decks filling the cubicle. He felt unexpectedly exhilarated. He was back in the cockpit of a space ship about to fly into the land of factual fiction.

First Jay scanned the shots of Gonflay walking his terrier. Then came the man in camelhair. He wasn't exactly Central Casting but did look like a high-end French hood. There they stood, Gonflay and the hood, black-and-white cutouts to be reassembled on screen.

The tail of Jay's mouse curled and lashed as he positioned it and clicked in rapid succession, but his mind drifted. The words *photographic truth* floated alongside in a cartoon cloud. Photographic truth? It was something Jay had once believed in, though he wasn't sure why. There had been no reason to, ever. Photography's history was littered with stories of manipulation, fabrication, forgery and technical glitches. For instance, the fact that you could see Quincy Alphonse Louis Thomas having his boots polished that day in 1838 on Boulevard du Temple was the result of a glitch. Jay tried to remember exactly what Samuel B. Morse had written about the image to his brother back in April 1838. Morse had handwritten the letter. He hadn't telegraphed it because, though he'd already invented the telegraph, no transatlantic cable had been built. Morse told his brother that he'd been at Daguerre's side and had witnessed a "latent image" developing on a silver-dipped plate. The man with the boots had been *without body or head*, because he'd inadvertently moved. *Objects moving are not impressed*, Morse had noticed. The boots hadn't moved. But everyone and everything else around them—the carriages, the horses, the men and women trying to avoid them, the thousands of living human beings that spring day in 1838—they were left out. They were ghosts. Ghost images. That mechanical imperfection caused by primitive lenses and slow shutters had scared the bejesus out of the people who'd seen Daguerre's first "sun pictures." It had opened up an uneasy world of scientific and pseudo-scientific suppositions. What was color if it couldn't be impressed on the plate? What was movement? How do we perceive the outside world? Are there other worlds, parallel worlds, in unknown colors we can't see? Can an image steal your soul and leave your boots behind? Is a photograph more than an object, because it captures time in space, light in time?

But all it turned out to be was a technical flaw, an unwitting photographic falsehood.

Falsehoods came in other forms. Desired falsehoods. They reached the state of high art under the Russian spymasters. In the 1920s and '30s they removed unwanted individuals from group portraits of Lenin or Stalin. Not only could you rewrite history, you could also retouch it.

Truth? Truth was a lie. Sometimes you had to lie to preserve the truth, *dixit* William Grant and Nicolò Machiavelli.

In the past, photographs were nearly always clumsily re-touched. An expert could tell. But no longer. The electronic age was the age of the perfect, hermetic falsehood.

Jay's balloon drifted to earth. He clicked on the PhotoShop icon and began working on his electronic gallery. He knew that if he were thorough he would be able to create flawless falsehoods, images of Henri meeting the man in the camelhair coat, images of them pushing Gonflay under the bus and then running away, images of Henri in the car with the killer at the wheel. False images of a truth no one had captured.

Two hours later Jay finished copying his creations onto a photo DVD. He made double backups and watched the prints roll out of the laser printer.

"Insurance," Jay said. Bruno towered over him and handed him a mug of instant coffee. Jay opened his briefcase and pulled out the portraits of the Free Europe Committee. With quick, deft gestures he scanned them onto another DVD and printed out copies of them. Bruno stood behind, watching the computer screen, unable to keep his eyes off the pictures. Jay clicked on the Firefox icon, typed in the FTP address of the Gilford Foundation website, keyed in the code and began up-loading. It took three minutes to upload the images. He signed out, went to his own site, entered the storage folder and up-loaded the images again.

"If anything happens to me or Amy," he said, handing Bruno copies of the DVDs, "you can decide whether you want to give these to someone trustworthy, or direct the right parties to the site and let them into the off-limits area." He wrote out the URLs and access codes. "It's safer than sending a license plate by snail mail."

Bruno handed the original prints back to Jay. "I don't understand what you mean."

"You don't want to." Jay paused. "There's just one more thing." He removed *Knowing Clouds* from his briefcase. Flipping the pages, he found his father's note and the alphanumeric table he'd drawn up in his aunt's attic.

For old times' sake he said aloud. His eyes scanned the words. *Now you have the plates as you always wanted. Dad*

Bruno watched in silence. Jay checked his notes. He'd deciphered the first eight letters of the cipher. M-D-L-B-H-I-N-D. He turned pages, ran his finger down the lines and counted to the right to find the missing letters. M-D-L B-H-I-N-D...

H
E
A
T
R
H
A
T
C
H

Madeleine de Lafayette. Behind the heater hatch.

Jay felt his face burning. His father had been a creature of habit. Behind what heater hatch? What would he find? Another waterproof fishing tackle box?

"Your father?" Bruno asked, his features drawn from fatigue and worry.

Ä

The one-way streets branching off Avenue de Suffren near Madeleine's house were empty. Casing her block seemed useless. Either someone was waiting inside the house or the approach was as clear as it would ever be. Jay circled once for good measure but saw no one. He parked on the corner of Rue Champfleury and Avenue Charles-Floquet a hundred yards from the house.

The flashlight Amy kept under the front seat was rusted shut. Jay remembered that she always bought more cigarette lighters than she needed. He opened the glove compartment and found two. Both were nearly empty. They'd have to do.

The Peugeot's tool kit was stuck to the waterproofing at the bottom of the car's trunk. Jay lifted the tire iron from a pool of oily water and pried the kit free. He took out a pair of pliers and a long screwdriver but hesitated. He weighed the tire iron, deciding to take it instead of the pliers. Fingerprints? His would already be all over the car and why not on the tire iron too, or inside Madeleine's house? He'd ridden in the car for years and had been to Madeleine's a hundred times.

Jay picked up his briefcase and tools and let himself through the gate and up the short flight of stairs to the front landing. Until then he hadn't contemplated the possibility that the keys he'd taken from his aunt's pegboard might no longer work. Now, as he wrestled with the front door, the realization struck him. The lock had been changed. He searched the stone façade for wires or circuit boxes. There was no sign anywhere of an alarm system. Madeleine had never wanted one. Maitre Henri's bonded movers would be arriving any day now to haul away her possessions. Then Maitre Henri would file for a demolition permit, sell the property to developers and cream off his share. To be used for what? Jay still wasn't sure. He glanced up at the Eiffel Tower and was glad to see it standing, the New Year's countdown running.

Jay set the tire iron on the freestone wall along the sidewalk. He vaulted over and dropped into the garden, pulling his briefcase after him. The garden was leafless and provided no cover. He'd be visible to anyone at a window in the high-rise apartment buildings next door. He crouched behind a boxwood shrub then crossed the lawn to the basement door. The second key on his ring fit. He turned it. But the door wouldn't open.

Jay had always hated the cloak-and-dagger aspects of paparazzo work. They reminded him of his father. Yet he'd mastered the tricks of the trade just as Yves, the Legionnaire, had learned the fine art of dislocating joints, thrusting knife blades between ribs and firing point blank into the enemy's face. Jay shuddered. He'd never fired a gun in anger and hoped he never would. He peered through the dark at the basement doorframe and ran his fingers along it. He could feel a padlock and hasp. He twisted and drove the tire iron through the hasp, hung his weight from the iron and jerked. The hasp tore the screws from the door frame. Jay stepped inside and put the padlock on the first free surface he found. Pinching his briefcase between his thighs, he flicked the lighter.

Crates and boxes were piled on both sides of a path across the floor to a wooden staircase. It led up one story. Jay read the packing labels. *Clothes and kitchen utensils. Garden furniture.* This was the wrong part of the house.

The stairs creaked. The door at the top was locked. Jay tried the third key on the ring and the door swung open with a moan.

Light seeped through the kitchen windows from the streetlamps outside. Jay bumped his way between more crates. Heaps of straw and bubble wrap, packing paper and cardboard filled the hallway. Movers always start upstairs, Jay reasoned.

They would bring Madeleine's belongings downstairs to be sorted, catalogued and packed. He glanced around. The parquet was scuffed and dirty. The runner had been pulled off the stairs. Bare bulbs dangled from empty walls.

Jay raised the cigarette lighter to the first stack of crates. He flicked and read. *Bedside table. Two floor lamps. Living-room throw rug.* He crouched and crawled, flicking and reading then pausing to listen. It took him five minutes to work his way along the hall into the sitting room. The first lighter began to run out of gas. He pocketed it and flicked the second lighter. Then he heard a noise.

Darkness enfolded him as he released the gas lever. His blood pulsed. His lips were dry and taut. The scratching sound came again. A locksmith's pick being inserted into the front door. He was sure of it now. Someone had a pick, or the wrong key, the same key he had.

Sitting motionless in the dark he counted to ten. Someone was approaching, scuttling across the room at the end of the hall. Jay stood up and raised the tire iron. He backed over the creaking parquet toward the kitchen, straining his ears and eyes. The scratching became more frenzied. Jay's hair rose into a hog's back on his neck and forearms.

They're waiting, he told himself, waiting for me to make the first move. They've sent someone around to the basement.

He looked out of the kitchen window into the garden. The panes were dusty. He couldn't see clearly. The scratching noise seemed closer now. He felt the presence of someone in the room, somewhere near him. Someone was there.

Scuttling and clawing it rushed at him across the kitchen floor. He fell backwards and dropped the lighter. The attacker changed course and ran toward him in the dark. Jay jumped to his feet and batted his arms shouting. A rat. For chrissakes it's a rat. Calm down. Control yourself. It's just a fucking rat.

Jay mopped at sweat. It stung his eyes. He shuffled in the

dark until his right foot punted the lighter. On hands and knees he felt around, aware the rat might be somewhere nearby. Then his fingers grazed the lighter. He flicked it. His steamy breath gushed from his mouth. He swiped again at the stinging sweat and groped his way into the sitting room. With the lighter's flame running low and his fingers scorched, Jay at last found the stack of wooden crates marked *Miscellaneous Vintage Photographs.*

With the tire iron he popped off the crate's lid. The sight of familiar objects calmed him. He stripped away layers of bubble wrap and brown paper. Here were the cityscapes of a bygone Paris taken by Bayard and Marville. Priceless nineteenth-century celebrity portraits by Nadar stared out—the faces of Victor Hugo and Louis Pasteur. There was a rare Fox Talbot Calotype, probably worth $100,000. It lay on its back, thoughtlessly packed.

Jay struggled against his emotions. He lifted the frames out one by one, his fear gone. The images' fragile beauty, a beauty born of acid and sunlight over a century ago, mesmerized him. He held a Gustave Le Gray seascape up to the feeble light of the streetlamps and then carefully nested it exactly as it had been. Why hadn't they stolen these, he asked himself? Why steal *La Liberté: Study of Schooner Shrouds* but not these? It made no sense.

In the second crate Jay recognized the gilt frame he'd bought years ago at Paris' Porte de Clignancourt flea market. He peeled the packing away and stared at the eerie chiaroscuro composition of shells, vases, coins and a signet ring, arrayed in a glass-fronted curiosity case. "Free," he whispered, his hands unsteady, "I'm free at last."

Jay made room in his briefcase and slipped *Curiosity Case* inside next to the cloud codebook and the Brownie Box camera manual. He repacked the crate, his mind clearly focused.

There was only one way to explain why the thief would

have had taken *La Liberté: Study of Schooner Shrouds.* Madeleine must have had it with her, in her hands, when she died. Whoever had killed her had stolen it. Maybe Serge Gonflay, or the man in the camelhair coat. But why would Madeleine have it with her, unless she'd wanted to send a signal? To someone who'd understand. A message about what? Plates and ratlines? And who would that someone be, now that William Grant was dead?

M-D-L. Behind the heater hatch.

His father's message played itself back to him. He peered through the darkness, trying to remember where he'd seen a heater in Madeleine's house. The logical place would be the kitchen. But in the kitchen, the closets and cupboards stood open and empty. There was no heater. Where else were heaters installed?

The basement.

Jay opened the door from the kitchen and looked down. The basement was a black hole. He couldn't see the treads of the staircase he'd climbed. He flicked the lighter and got a second's worth of flame, enough to show him where the first step was. Jay bit the handle of his briefcase and used both hands to feel his way down. Flicking the lighter again at the bottom he traced the hot water pipes along the ceiling to a wall-mounted heater in a corner of the cellar. Next to it stood an old coal-fired furnace. Like his linotype machine it'd probably been too heavy to move. Jay flicked again and saw in the split second of light that there was a hatch on the side of the furnace. He needed the tire iron to open it. But he'd left the iron upstairs. Cursing, Jay put down his briefcase and felt the sweat starting up, prickling his neck and back.

Outside, a car rolled quietly down the Avenue Floquet. Another followed. Jay checked the glowing hands of his watch. It was too early for garbage trucks or traffic.

Faster than before he felt his way back up the stairs and

through the kitchen door, retracing his path to the crate. On his hands and knees he felt around for the tire iron. He'd laid it down to the left of the crate, if memory served. But it was no longer there. It had to be there. He held his breath and heard the scratching noise from before. The lighter was out of gas. He flicked anyway. The flint provided a spark of light, enough to assure him the tire iron was no longer where he'd laid it.

His fingers ached. He worked at the lid with them and pried it back up. On top of the bubble wrap he made out the iron's unmistakable shape.

Stumbling on the staircase he fell down the last two treads and hit his head on the wall. Jay waited for the dizziness to subside. He felt his way forward to the furnace. The hatch was closed with a cast-iron lug. With cold, stiff fingers Jay aligned the tire iron between the ridges on the lug and unscrewed it counterclockwise. It fell, hitting Jay's briefcase and rolling noisily across the floor. He lifted the hatch out and flicked the lighter. But he couldn't see inside the furnace. With the tire iron he cleared away cobwebs and cautiously reached in, hoping there were no spiders or rats. On a masonry ledge inside the furnace his fingers touched what felt like a small hardback. He pulled it carefully out of the hatch. Unable to read the cover in the darkness, he blew the dust off the book and slipped it into his bomber-jacket pocket. After groping around the base of the furnace, he put the hatch back and the lug and rubbed his hands together to get rid of soot and filth.

It was dark outside but seemed lighter compared to the blackness of the cellar. Streetlamps threw a muted glow along the tree-lined avenue. Jay paused by the basement door long enough to pull out the book and look at the cover. In gold embossed letters it read *Le Prince*.

Smiling wide he set his briefcase and tools on the top of the garden wall and vaulted over, landing in a crouch. As he stood, his own shout of terror took him by surprise.

$\mathbf{\Lambda}$

"Don't even think about running," said a voice Jay recognized. A hand grabbed his left arm below the arm pit and hauled him the rest of the way to his feet. On his right side a man grabbed his other arm and simultaneously pulled the briefcase off the wall.

"No noise," she said. Her voice was hoarse.

Debra Wright's face looked like carved wood, hard and impenetrable. She jerked his arm. "Vlad," she called, "get the tire iron off the wall and put it in the trunk. Make sure there's nothing left on the ground then fall in behind." Debra squeezed Jay's arm with a strength he wouldn't have expected. He felt it through the fleece-lined aviator's jacket. "As long as you're with me they won't touch you," she said. "Step lively, Jay."

He stumbled on something in the gutter and swore as he climbed into the front passenger seat of Debra's high-riding Jeep Grand Cherokee. Think fast, he told himself. With a flick of the wrist and some body English Jay palmed the book from his jacket pocket and slid it under the seat. Debra slammed the driver's door and started the engine. "We're on the way," she said. Jay saw the speakerphone on the dash. Its throbbing red dot signaled automatic voice-activation. He watched the man whose name was Vlad get into the back seat behind him. There were no cars in sight. But Debra put on her turn signal and checked her rearview mirror before pulling into the deserted street. Another set of headlights flicked on and swung into the rearview mirror, aligning themselves behind.

"What do you have in the briefcase, Jay?" Debra Wright's bluegrass lilt was gone.

He stared through the SUV's windshield. A silhouette rose through the predawn sky, a single light at its top warning aircraft of its presence. The Eiffel Tower.

"I have a feeling you know," Jay said. "Who are you any-way?"

She took her hands off the wheel long enough to click on the passenger compartment light and pass him a laminated card. The passport-sized photo of her was followed by the title *Debra Wright, Homeland Security Liaison Officer.*

"Homeland Security in Paris?" Jay said. "I've got one of those phony ID cards." He handed hers back. "They're easy to fake. Where are we going?"

"You'll see," she said. "It's a familiar address."

He turned and looked at Vlad's expressionless, Slavic face and counted the fingers on Vlad's hands. Five and five made ten. "Two's company," Jay said. "What if I decided to step out of here and let you and Vlad ride alone?"

Debra held up her hand—the same gesture she'd made on the plane yesterday. It seemed like another life. "I don't think you know what you've gotten yourself into, Jay. I hope for your sake you don't. But I'm here to help. Believe me you have no idea what dangers you're facing and how valuable your as-sistance can be." She drove north, flashing her high beams at intersections and waiting to make sure the car behind stayed within a hundred yards.

"On one point you're right," Jay said. "I have no idea what's going on. Suddenly I'm getting strange messages from my fa-ther, and everyone's dropping dead or chasing after me." He paused. "How did you know where I was? Wait, let me guess, the shoe check at the airport? Or you stuck a GPS dot on me during the flight over? You put a bug in my briefcase when I went to the bathroom?"

Debra's face morphed. She smiled a brittle smile. "As a mat-ter of fact I did," she said. "But it turned out there was no need. Your satellite phone did the job. You've been in constant touch and plotted to within three feet."

Jay swallowed. "I hope you've enjoyed it."

"It's part of the job," she said. "Ease up, I'm on your side. I'm taking you to meet someone so we can have a little conversation and get to work."

"You people have safe houses in Paris?"

"Nah, our HQ, it's safe enough and there's no time for a trip to the countryside. Everyone knows where we are."

"Everyone?"

"Well, not everyone. At least we hope not, otherwise we, and a lot of innocent people are going to be in trouble instead of drinking champagne at midnight on New Year's. If what we think might happen actually happens, we'll be the first in line."

"This has something to do with my father, doesn't it?"

"Uh, huh," Debra said. "It sure does."

Jay tapped the armrest of his seat, using the heel of his left shoe to keep the book from sliding out. "I figured something in his past would catch up with me."

"Yeah, that can happen when you've got a dad like yours. But Jay, you screwed up too," she said. "All those forged pictures and that weird stuff with these crooked auctioneers and foreign legionnaires and a dead former station chief. We know about that. I'm asking you to help us now, to cooperate, and we in turn can try to help you."

Jay pondered Debra's genteel blackmail. He realized they were driving at the exact equivalent of twenty-five miles per hour. Kidnapping was fine but don't exceed the speed limit.

"Without knowing what you want, or why I'm in danger how am I supposed to help you?"

"I'm not authorized to tell you but I can give you a hint."

Jay waited. "Put it this way, what is it I'm supposed to help you do?"

"I'm not authorized to say. You'll see."

"Debra, you're talking like a robot." They paused at a flashing yellow light on the Pont de la Concorde. Beyond the Egyptian Obelisk of Luxor marking the center of what was now a glorified traffic circle, the American embassy was a few hundred feet to the left. French riot police would be on duty around the clock. There was always a contingent of US Marines and embassy guards. Jay's palms began to sweat. The car rolled past the obelisk. Jay tested the door. It was locked. He flicked the central switch between the passenger seats and released his seatbelt.

"Hey," Vlad grunted. "You move I grab you. They shoot."

"I wouldn't do that," said Debra. "The minute you step out I can't protect you anymore. Europol or the French services will grab you if Vlad doesn't. If you think they can't or won't you're wrong, and their accommodations make Guantánamo look like a vacation spot."

Jay leaned back as Debra accelerated and swung the rest of the way around the Place de la Concorde. Now he knew where they were headed. The Champs-Elysées.

"Who's trying to harm me?"

"That's off limits information, Jay. You don't want to know the details and I can't tell you." Debra nodded to no one then said, "It's okay guys."

"The car's wired," Jay said. "You're probably wired. By now I'm probably stuck like a pineapple with GPS dots and bugs."

Debra laughed and shook her head. "You've got quite an imagination."

"You can't expect me to work with you in the dark."

"That's what you do, isn't it? You work in a darkroom. That's basically what we want you to do for us now. We have something to develop and we think you can help us stop something horrific from happening right here in the heart of Paris, real soon, and we think you've got a few things to share with us. I've seen your father's duty file and I'm convinced that's what he would want you to do."

Jay considered this. "I'd be careful about putting wishes into the heads of dead men." He felt his own head throb.

"How do I know you are who you say you are? Fake IDs are easy to make. A Homeland Security Liaison Officer in Paris with a Jeep and an ex-Soviet thug for a boyfriend?"

Jay felt Vlad pulling the headrest as he scooted forward. "You shut your mouth," Vlad said, sounding like Arnold Schwartzeneggar.

Debra held up her right palm. "Vlad, drop it. I know all about your fake ID, Inspector Langlois of the Brigade Criminelle." She tapped the brakes and slowed then gentled the car to the side of the avenue. "Wait," she ordered. "Ron? You want to talk to this guy?"

After a void of a few seconds a canned, distant voice spoke from a hidden speakerphone.

"Jay?"

"Who is it?"

"Ron." It was a mature man's voice. "L. Ron Errington. I worked with your dad. You and I met."

Jay thought. "Sure Ron. Where did we meet?"

"At your father's funeral."

Jay counted to three. "Where?"

"Marseille."

"When was that, Ron?" Jay heard clicks on a keyboard. Ron whispered to someone. "December 23rd of last year," Ron said. "It was raining."

"That was fog, Ron. Fog from the Corniche overlooking the Mediterranean. When was my father born?"

Jay heard the clicking again. "September 10, 1928," Ron replied. "In Boston. His mother's maiden name was Scribner. He drank Johnny Walker black label, neat." Ron paused. "What else do you want to know?"

"The last four digits of his social security number," Jay said. "And why in hell you let him down."

Jay heard Ron swear. "It's too bad you never wanted to work for us, Jay. You're pretty good."

"It's too bad you let him die," Jay said. "Unless it was you people who killed him."

"Stuff happens," Ron retorted. He covered the microphone on his end and uncovered it a few seconds later. "Four-zero-five-nine."

Jay hung his head. He watched Debra put her left turn signal on and accelerate up the avenue.

Spotlights picked out the Arc de Triomphe at the top of the hill. The sky had begun to lighten. "It'd be a real shame to see all this blown up, Jay," Debra said. "You've got no choice but to help."

Access to the underground parking garage was from Rue Washington. Debra's car spiraled down three floors and drove several hundred yards back toward the Champs-Elysées. A security guard waved them past, a barrier dropping behind. A second guard saluted as they parked. Jay thought about the book under his seat. The man named Vlad was watching him, holding the briefcase on his lap. Jay unbelted and silently let his loft keys slip between the seat and the transmission mound.

Debra waited until Vlad and Jay had stepped out. She locked the car and used a flat, perforated card to call the elevator. No one spoke. The garage stank of diesel oil and French fries.

Jay counted the ticks as the elevator rose. It dipped before stopping. He tried but couldn't guess what floor they were on. Florescent overhead lights behind plastic louvers illuminated the hallway. Halfway down it another tall, Slavic-looking operative awaited.

"No sheepskin indoors?" Jay's tone was provocative. "And I thought they were Russian."

"They are," Debra said. "Things change, Jay. We have Russians and Romanians and former East Germans on our European Team. We even have a Frenchman or two. The new war brings us together."

"The new war?"

Debra signaled him onward. "Over to you guys," she said, waving goodbye.

In a small room without windows the Russian ran a wand over Jay and then frisked him. "Strip," he ordered. "Everything." The words came out as *streep, ehvryting*.

Five minutes later Jay reassembled his shoes. The Russian had pulled the insoles out of them. He put his clothes back on and waited. The Russian returned his signet ring, pocket change and wallet, keeping back the police ID card. Jay knew it was part of the game, the humiliation-and-fright sequence. It was also a convenient way to embed GPS dots and bugs. He'd expected them to put a hood over his head and cuff him, or walk him naked on a leash. This was an improvement.

Jay followed the Russian down another hall into an over-heated conference room overlooking the Champs-Elysées. He guessed they were on the fifth floor. A short, sixty-something man in a brown tweed jacket and badly matched open-collared check shirt turned away from the windows.

"You're not letting us get much sleep these days," he said in a tenor voice with what passed for jovial indulgence. "Ron. Good to see you again, Jay. Thanks so much for agreeing to come in." He stepped forward, his hand out. Jay avoided the handshake.

"Got any coffee?"

Ron picked up a telephone and spoke. He cradled it. "Drip okay? The encryption guys prefer it. If you're hungry we can rustle up something from downstairs. What do the French call an Egg McMuffin anyway?"

"Egg McMuffin," said the Russian.

Jay waved his hand. He sat in an uncomfortable plastic bucket seat. "Coffee is fine. Black. No sugar."

Debra stepped in with Jay's briefcase. "I think we did better than just all right," she said, the Kentucky accent back.

"Oh?" Ron raised a bushy eyebrow.

"A book," she said, unpacking the briefcase, "a manual, a little black package, some snapshots, a pocket camera, an old photo in a fancy frame and two big envelopes. Not bad." She laid them on the conference table then opened the envelopes and aligned the license plate and prints of Maitre Henri so that each item was evenly spaced and clearly visible.

"So, you were right," Ron said, lifting and examining the group snapshots from the 1940s. "Well I'll be, there's Bill with his friends from the Free Europe Committee. I doff my hat to Homeland Security. Debra really is terrific, isn't she?"

"You mind letting me in on the joke?" Jay asked. Vlad handed him a tall paper cup of coffee. He took off the Starbucks lid and sipped, recognizing the aroma and flavor.

"Ron and his people in Langley wanted to pull you in a month ago and ask you to cooperate," Debra said. "I wanted to run you. I figured, with the right stimulus you'd bring in more."

"And maybe get killed."

She shook her head. "You had people watching over you, people picking you up off the sidewalk, giving you a ride home, making sure you got out of a locked cemetery, that kind of thing. I've got to admit you're one tough dude."

"Like his father," Ron said, his gray-blue gums revealed by a bright, toothy smile.

Jay counted to three. "You know I'm not trained for this."

Debra showed Jay her palms in a by-now familiar gesture. "It's over to Ron. I'm just a liaison officer."

"She's far too modest." Ron sat on the edge of an unstylish desk near the windows. He struck a paternal tone. "We understand you feel a certain degree of rancor toward your father's profession and his former employer," Ron began, fanning the snapshots. "But if you know anything that might help us to continue your father's work we would be very appreciative."

Jay forced a smile. "My father supposedly retired years before he died, and if you think he confided in me your intelligence is worse than your coffee."

Ron thrust out his chin. "Okay Jay, touché, we're all aware of the tensions between you and Bill, especially over that old Jim Morrison investigation. That was a long time ago, Jay. You were a boy. The world has changed. Vietnam is ancient history. Your father knew that and I know you're smart enough to move on and do the right thing. I can assure you we're facing a situation of immediate danger. We've prevailed on the French to maintain an orange alert when it should be red or black, but we don't want to show our hand. If we don't find out what we need to know in the next twenty-four hours this will be the bloodiest Paris New Year's in history. So I'm going to ask you straight: do you know if your father had a cache of documents or used a codebook and substitution code to communicate with anyone here in France?"

Jay shook his head. He was unable to hide his disgust. "You wait until he's been dead a year to tell me my father hadn't retired, and whatever sensitive work he was doing may have been accurate, was ignored, and that he was allowed to die as a consequence, and that you, his supposed colleague, don't know whether he was communicating with someone over here?"

Ron and Debra exchanged glances. She lifted the license plate. "Where's the note that went with this?"

Jay waved at the cloud book. "In there."

"You see, the license plate didn't mean anything to us," Ron said. "And neither did the Bonham's catalogue. We wondered why your father mailed them to you just a few days before his accident. We wondered if he meant something else by *plates*, and what the reference to *old times' sake* might mean. Debra was right to have them delivered. They got you from point A to B."

"So what's with the Jaguar license plate?" Debra asked.

Jay cleared his throat. "My father bought that car for my mother on my birthday."

Debra nodded. She read aloud from a printout. "1968 Jaguar XKE, bought new in Boston, sold in California in 1996. It now belongs to an individual in Southern California and is in fair condition. The L.A. team checked it inside and out and found nothing. Only the original tool kit and the manual are missing." She paused. "The manual is missing," she repeated. "Your father bought the vanity license plate in 1978. Ten years later he resigned from active duty. Why do you think he removed the plates from the car, gave one to you to hang on your wall in Paris, kept one back and sent it to you all these years later?"

"Read it," Jay said. He realized someone from Homeland Security or the CIA had been into his attic room. "It's an obvious message. He loved Jags, meaning cars."

"JAG is your nickname, isn't it? Jason Anthony Grant."

"It's an acronym for my name, not my nickname. No one calls me Jag."

"Your dad did."

Ron segued quietly. "Your mother had divorced him and passed away before he bought the vanity plates." He shifted around to face Jay. Now it was Debra's turn to sit on the arm of a cheap-looking plastic armchair. She watched Jay's body language and seemed to be tapping a Morse code on the license plate with her manicured fingertips.

Jay shook his head, using the gesture as a way to spot the cameras and mikes in the soundproofed ceiling. "Why this cat-and-mouse bullshit?" he asked. "You know he sent me ciphers when I was a kid. I assumed it was the same cipher and some kind of joke. If you were watching him and have been spying on me you know that."

Ron nodded. "We need to be thorough, Jay. There's a lot riding on this and we don't have much time. No time at all." He glanced out the windows.

Debra opened *Knowing Clouds* and flipped through the pages until she found the scrap of paper with the alphanumeric table and William Grant's handwritten note. She read it out loud. "For old times' sake. Now you have the plates as you always wanted. Dad." She paused. "Sweet."

Jay swallowed. Anger tinted his cheeks. His father's warning came back to him. *If anyone ever asks you for this Brownie Box manual or any other book of mine don't trust that person. Don't give him the manual and don't tell him about our game, all right?*

Jay reached out. "May I keep this?" He took the note from her fingers and reread it.

Debra wrinkled her lips. "I'm sorry Jay."

He handed the note back. Debra made a show of studying the crude alphanumeric table he'd written in his attic room. She checked the first letters of Jay's transcription against the numbers.

"So, M equals page 20, line 8, letter 5. D is 19-11-25, and L is 1-12-23," she said. "It's got to be page-line-letter because the message is too short to be page-line-word." Her cupid's bow lips moved silently. "M-D-L-B-H-I-N-D-H-E-A-T-R-H-A-T-C-H," she read from Jay's transcription.

"Madeleine de Lafayette, behind the heater hatch," he recited, cutting her short.

Ron spoke with practiced calm. "What was behind the hatch?"

He counted to six. "The manual."

Debra handed the Kodak Brownie Box manual to Ron. "Okay. That's good. A simple substitution cipher but only you knew the protocol and had the cloud codebook, and only you'd know who M-D-L was, and how to get into her house with your aunt's keys and find the hatch." He flipped through the manual as he spoke, smiling, then one by one picked up the black-and-white photos of Gonflay, the man in camelhair and Maitre Henri. "If I hadn't seen your hard disk transcribed," he said, "if I hadn't been reading every email and text message you send and receive, and listening to your conversations, and reading reports on every darn thing you do around the clock, Jay, I'd be pretty suspicious. I'd worry that you and your dad were up to something. All this stuff with the old photos and the French auction houses and this big, international charity foundation with friends in America and Algeria, sending money and medical supplies back and forth. It looks awfully unusual. Those people have some original relationships with people at high levels in countries we classify as supporting terror." He held up a photo of Serge Gonflay dead, wrapped around the bus's back wheel. "It's messy."

Debra segued. Jay began to wonder whether they'd rehearsed. "Luckily for you we know you're on our side."

"I got your message the first time around," Jay said. "I also have a feeling you might want to avoid what they call a diplomatic incident—the son of a dead spook involved with the great and good of France who turn out to be Christian crazies with some kind of Algeria connection." He paused. He didn't want to sound like he knew too much. "What else do you have? My laptop? You're the people who stole my laptop, if you've been reading transcriptions of my files."

"Very quick," Debra said. "I'll bet you can guess what we're after and what the threat is."

"One thing at a time," Ron remonstrated. "That's quite a haul we have. Even though we've been listening and watching you we don't know everything. So you're going to have to help us bring the picture into focus, Jay. Because, as I say, there's no time left. We need your help, Jay. I'm counting on your patriotism."

Debra unzipped a diplomatic pouch on the desk behind Ron. She pulled out two black plastic packages. Each was the size of a deck of cards and was exactly like the one Jay had found at the barbershop. One had been torn open, the other was still sealed. "What do you think these contain?" Debra asked.

"Tarot cards," Jay snapped. "I hear there's not much time to spare."

"Okay wise guy," she snapped back. "I read your lecture-paper off your computer. All that stuff about Daguerre and Morse and this guy having his boots polished. And we talked about it oh-so-romantically on the airplane, when you could barely keep your hands off me even though you're supposed to be getting married to the love of your life. So I know you know more than Google about the cipher and Morse and the code." She tossed him the open package. "It's a copper plate with etched markings. The lab team says it's a daguerreotype. They X-rayed it. The makeup is copper, coated with silver and..."

"An extremely thin layer of light-sensitive silver iodide," Jay cut in. He checked the plate. "Where'd you get it?"

Debra shook her head. "You don't need to know."

Jay turned to Ron. He also shook his head. "No go," Ron confirmed. "I'll tell you why. What if you and your father were being manipulated and didn't know it? *You* don't need to know everything. *We* need to know everything and *you* need to help us." Ron looked back and forth between Debra and Jay. "The tension seems a little more than professional," he remarked, pulling his dyed brush-over into place.

Jay closed his eyes. He counted silently, realizing with sudden clarity that counting had saved his life more than once. "Okay," he said. His Adam's apple stuck in his throat as he counted once more to three. "Okay. So here's my guess. The plate was sensitized with heated iodide fumes then exposed to light then sealed in a darkroom in black plastic to keep it from double exposure." He paused. "Anyone who wasn't supposed to know that would open the package and ruin the plate. So the information on it would be safe." He paused long enough for Ron to cut in.

"Fascinating," Ron said. "What's the background?"

"Morse taught Daguerre his code in Paris in 1838," Debra said, reading off a printout. "In 1839 when Morse was back in America Daguerre wrote out a message in dots and dashes, took a picture of it and wrapped the plate in black paper." She looked at Jay for confirmation.

"Morse developed it and deciphered the message," Jay said. "That's how it got started, the Daguerre Cipher. It's uncontroversial. Google it if you haven't already." Jay was in his element. "Bear in mind that Morse and Daguerre were painters and inventors. They were experimenting with electricity and chemistry. They also knew their inventions had military value."

"Military value?" Ron showed his gray gums and long, bleached teeth.

"Until I read your paper and did some research I didn't even know there'd been a French revolution in 1848," Debra said. "I thought it was 1789. But you say the 1848 uprising is when photographic codes got started."

"Codes and ciphers have been around for thousands of years," Jay said. "It's heliography that was new. Daguerre was friends with King Louis Philippe. At the start of the 1848 Revolution the constitutional government used daguerreotypes to send enciphered messages in a modified Morse code. Things got out of control. The king abdicated. Daguerre died in 1851, a year before Louis Napoleon Bonaparte declared himself Emperor Napoleon III. It's all in my paper. You read it."

"That was another thing," Debra said. "I knew about Emperor Napoleon the little guy with the silly hat. But I didn't know his nephew became emperor in the Second Empire, and I still don't know what happened to Napoleon II. There wasn't anything about him on Wikipedia."

Ron smiled. "There wasn't a Napoleon II. Go on, Jay."

"By the time Napoleon III went to war with Prussia in 1870 photography had evolved." He paused to see if they understood. "It was like micro-processing nowadays. They had all kinds of new techniques, and a guy named Dagron had even come up with what they called microscopic photography. Basically, it was the first spy cameras, with microscope lenses. Dagron figured out how to put huge amounts of information on microfilm, something like 18,000 secret military orders on half a dozen celluloid strips that weighed as much as a feather. He used courier pigeons to carry the messages over the lines."

"Pigeons?" Debra made a face. "What if they flew away or got shot or something?"

"Forget the pigeons for now," Ron said. "So why did the Free Europe Committee revive the Daguerre Cipher and the plates after World War II if they had this newer, better system? The Nazis had micro-dots and radio ciphers by then."

"Not a clue," Jay said. "You worked with my father. I never found out anything from him. Madeleine was the one who told me about the ratlines they ran. She gave me a couple of old plates they'd used but no codebook."

Ron nodded. "We knew that much."

Debra held up her palms and waved the black package. "Let's recap, guys. Your father and Madeleine and Georges Henri used the daguerreotype plates to send messages about the Paris-to-Genoa ratline, and that we know for sure, though we don't know what codebook they used. I'd love to continue the history lesson but we have to get a move on and decipher these."

Jay took the open package from her and flicked it, catching light. "Someone ruined this one."

Debra blinked. "We X-rayed it first and then opened it."

"But not in the dark?"

She shook her head.

"Brilliant. I have no idea what effect radiation has on exposed, undeveloped daguerreotypes. By opening the package the plate has been double exposed. It's just like opening a roll of film. I think the ASA rating would be 1 or 2 but even with film like that in a few minutes the light alters the chemical makeup and that's irreversible. The chances of getting anything off this plate are slim, especially now that you've been handling it."

"Just so you know" Debra said defensively. "The lab boys tried developing it anyway. They scanned and X-rayed it again. They picked up a few lines, probably an alphanumeric cipher like the one your dad used. We crunched it but it's incomplete and was unbreakable without the codebook."

"Unbreakable? I thought nothing was unbreakable."

Ron formed his lips into a circle. "A substitution code based on a unique codebook text is unbreakable," he said, "unless you can use frequency analysis, meaning you have to have a big sample, and it helps if you know what language it's in. The code reference text could be a book. It could be a rare edition for instance, something with enough pages and lines to give the encoder lots of random material." He looked around. "It could be your cloud book or the Brownie Box manual. If you don't have the reference text the permutations of the coded message are pretty much infinite."

"There are exactly," Debra interrupted, glancing at a flashcard, "403,291,461,126,605,635,584,000,000 ways to encrypt the twenty-six letters of the English alphabet and I have no idea how many for other alphabets."

Ron spoke with studied calm. "We have only a few characters inscribed on the plate. Until you supplied the camera manual, we didn't have a reference text. None of the books your father had at the time of his death were used for the encoding. He must've hidden his copy. We figured there was another out there that he'd entrusted to someone."

"That person might not even have been aware of it," Debra added slowly. She let the sentence hang. "Eventually we figured out it was you. But we think you're unaware of what your father was doing. Either that or you're the best operative on the ground I've ever met. And frankly I don't think that's the case."

"We need your help," Ron said, careful to pick up the beat. "We need you to develop the remaining daguerreotypes for us. If you know the protocols your father used we would very much like you to share that information with us and save us time. It might lead us to persons now engaged in preparing terrorist acts, specifically an attack in Paris that could cost the lives of thousands." He waved at the window. "It's a matter of days, Jay, not weeks or months. I can say no more. But if you ask yourself what the possible New Year's Eve targets are I think you'll be able to put it together. Time is of the essence."

Jay stared through the window. Sunlight spilled into the Champs-Elysées. "I'll do what I can," he said. The taste of bad, bitter coffee stuck to his tongue. "What about Maitre Henri?"

Ron dipped his chin. "Tricky business. We'll talk about it. Right now we need those plates decoded."

Debra stood. "I'll call the garage." She slipped the black plastic packages into the diplomatic pouch.

"You mind if I take my camera back?"

Debra's expression was hard to read. "It's empty," she said. "I checked. It's a Minox film camera, not digital."

"I know it well," Ron said. "We all had one." He paused. "Okay."

"I'd also like my Calotype."

"Your what?"

Jay pointed. "It's a Calotype. I made it and gave it to Madeleine. That's why I wanted it back. It's what took me there in the first place." He showed Debra and Ron the signet ring and told them about Bensonhurst. "It was a birthday present, an inside joke."

Ron dipped his chin, allowing Jay to slip the picture into his briefcase. "We knew you'd come through," Ron said. He flipped open a cellphone.

"There's just one thing," Jay said as he shut the briefcase and stepped to the window. "Why can't I imagine your cryptographers in Langley haven't figured out how to deal with daguerreotypes? You've got the plates and the codebooks. Why do you need me?"

Debra waited for Ron to shut his cellphone. "No time, too risky," she said. "If they find out we have the plates and codebook they can change them. Everyone says you're the expert. You have the setup here in Paris."

"I know enough to wonder why anyone would be using a clunky technique from the 1830s to communicate about a plot to blow up the Champs-Elysées on New Year's Eve. If they have codebooks why not use text messaging or email or fax or the telephone?"

"You are quick, Jay. But you're not up on current technology." Ron's voice betrayed satisfaction. "No electronic communications medium is secure and they know it." He shrugged on a beige raincoat. "For banking, targeting instructions and the really secret stuff nothing is safer than a reliable courier and a double analogue firewall."

"Meaning what?"

"Someone enciphers a document with an old program on an old computer and saves it on a 5 1/2-inch floppy disk," Debra said as they walked to the elevator. "A decade goes by. No one has the hardware or the software to read it. Here it's even more secure. Because it's as if the old floppy would self-destruct if you took it out of its box the wrong way. Like we did when we exposed the first plate. The technology these guys are using is a hundred and fifty years old. No one has the equipment or skill anymore. There are half a dozen different ways to prepare a plate—that's what you told me on the airplane. So who has the chemical mixes or the stuff to heat iodide and mercury? If you use the wrong mix or the wrong heat or timing you're in trouble. That's what you wrote in your paper and I confirmed it. Not even the Smithsonian people felt confident enough to tackle the last plate. So maybe that's why your dad used the cipher after the war—it was foolproof. As long as you had the ingredients and the equipment and you knew how to put it together."

Ron laid his hand on Jay's shoulder. "I know what you're thinking. Your father probably had you promise never to cooperate with anyone in a situation like this. That would be standard Company practice. We're supposed to know only what he wanted us to know. So you're suspicious and rightly so." Ron paused. "Jay I'm appealing to your intelligence and your integrity. Your father was onto something. People in high places at the time felt uncomfortable with his findings. The case was reopened at my behest in light of recent events. I can tell you no more."

The Grand Cherokee had been moved. A Chrysler Voyager minivan awaited in the garage, the Russian named Vlad at the wheel.

Jay patted his pockets. "My keys," he said. "To my loft. Either they fell out at Madeleine's or they're in the briefcase." He checked, noticing a razor-slit in the lining big enough for a dot or a bug.

Debra shook her head. "I emptied it. There weren't any keys." The other Russian stepped up. "Boris did you see Mr. Grant's keys?"

"The keys would have made the wand signal like the ring and coins. He had no keys."

Jay checked his aviator jacket and snapped his fingers. "Your Jeep. When I got in I stumbled. They probably fell out."

Debra signaled to the security guard. "You want to get the silver Grand Cherokee please?"

Jay felt sweat beading on his forehead. This was the hard part. If they looked for the keys they'd find the real codebook.

"We can get into your loft without the keys," Ron said. "We've been in before."

"That's nice to know," Jay said. "You guys are naturals at breaking and entering. What about the DST or whatever it's called now? Won't they find it unusual?"

"That's our problem."

"Sure," Jay said. *Think*, he goaded himself, trying to distract them. "By the way," he added, "who's the operative from New York with nine fingers?"

Ron swung his head. Debra also signaled negative. "Not ours," Ron said.

"That's comforting. Then who tried to break into my apartment in Manhattan the night I flew over? And who was driving the car that almost killed me? Not the DST."

Ron's taut smile broke. He flipped opened his cell. "It's called DCRI now, not DST."

"Whatever," Jay segued. "The burglar broke my super's nose, and he tried to run me over, so I guess he's in Paris now."

The guard drove up in Debra's car. Without waiting Jay opened the front passenger door, leaned in and felt around under the seat. He pocketed the book while flipping up the carpet. "Here they are," he said, holding up the keys.

Debra and Ron glanced inside the SUV. "We might as well go in two cars," she said. "In case one of us needs to get back."

Ron nodded. "I can't get a connection in here. We're too far underground. I'll ride with the two of you. I want to know more about this man with nine fingers. Have we checked on him, Debra? What about the DCRI"

She drove across the garage and up the ramp, followed by the minivan. Jay shielded his eyes from the sun in Rue Washington. It bounced off the mirrored windows of the highrises across the street. As the strain subsided, Jay felt dizzy again. Ron's voice modulated as he spoke into the cellphone, querying someone across the Atlantic about the break-in and the nine-fingered assailant.

"You know the way," Jay said to Debra. "I'm shutting my eyes."

"Yeah," she said, yawning. "We could all use some shuteye."

The SUV lumbered through downtown morning traffic. Jay concentrated on progressive relaxation. He relaxed his toes and ankles and knees, moving slowly up to his hips and midsection. He was feeling feverish from lack of sleep. But his mind wouldn't shut down. Instead of letting his navel drift into Zen airspace, his brain began to draw up a checklist of the ingredients he would need to develop the plates. He wondered again what his father had been up to. Had he joined Georges Henri in some lunatic rightwing crusade? *For old times' sake*?

Traffic was thick and the sun through the windshield warm. Jay felt plaster in his head. Debra and Ron's voices merged. A rainbow of colors passed through his eyelids, teasing his optic nerves. A world of black-and-white would be a restful place right now, he told himself. He felt Debra brake and accelerate, brake then stop then accelerate again. The diesel engine and automatic transmission meshed with menacing efficiency.

Maybe that was why the past was so appealing, Jay thought. It was in black-and-white. Photos and movies of the past were.

Sure, it had been full of color and sound for the people alive, the people in Daguerre's world, for instance. That's why Daguerre and just about everyone else who'd followed had tried so hard to color their images. Black-and-white didn't correspond to reality. It was an abstraction, a distillate, the unmoving essence of reality, not a restful but a disturbing place halfway to oblivion. It was the darkness that swallowed colors at night. Black-and-white was day and night, good and evil, life and death. Death expressed in scientific terminology.

When you stopped to think of it, back in the 1830s Daguerre's giant wooden camera obscura and metal plates, the iodine and mercury, were the period's equivalent of cutting-edge digital equipment. They were scientific, astonishing, troubling in an era of pre-Darwinian religious zealotry. The big wooden box and a tripod weighed over a hundred pounds. A laptop was a lot lighter, but a desktop computer was nearly as bulky, and if you added together the weight of the screen and processor, the scanner, burner and printer, plus a digital camera and lenses and tripod, the totals weren't too far off.

Jay's mind labored to convert from the metric system. It reviewed the pound figures and calculated prices. A complete daguerreotype setup cost around three hundred gold francs in the year 1840. He'd read that somewhere. For three hundred gold francs you got a 380mm lens with an f/14 diaphragm or a Petzval f/3.4 lens, but only starting in late 1840, when the technology had improved. The 164 x 216 mm plates were made of copper. You had to coat them yourself with silver. Coat and polish them. Then you had the bottles of nitric acid, the gold chloride, the mercury and iodine. Jay wasn't quite sure how much three hundred gold francs, plus, say another thirty for consumables, worked out to in today's purchasing power equivalent. But it probably wasn't much different than the cost of a high-end digital setup.

An advantage with digital was the lack of acids, corrosive

crystals and volatile heavy metals. You didn't have to breathe in the hot silver iodide, or the bromide and mercury vapors that brought the light-etched images to life. There was no need to dip the exposed plates into a fixative bath of sodium hyposulfite, either, to remove the iodized silver so that the images stopped developing and became permanent works of art. Jay had done it a thousand times, he'd prepared the plates, burnished them, vaporized them at a 45-degree angle in the heart of the wooden box, bathed them like babies in chemicals and hot water as he counted the seconds from under the black canvas hood. It was always a matter of seconds, like cooking. Like baking a chemical soufflé. He'd wondered sometimes if the mercury vapors in particular had affected his mind, as Amy said when she was mad at him.

"Jay?" Debra shook him. "Wake up. We're here."

"Time to do your thing," Ron said. "Why don't you give Vlad your keys and let him go in first? Just in case."

Jay felt himself emerging from a tunnel into blinding light. Drowsy, he dug out the keys. "Does he know the code?"

"I think he does," Debra said. "What is it, just in case?"

Jay recited it, correcting himself once and shaking his head, trying to wake up. "You dial it into the old pulse telephone." He paused. "I need more coffee and some breakfast."

"Don't we all," said Ron. He spoke into his cell. "Boris is going to bring over something to eat."

The loft's chill air made Jay shiver. He switched on the heater and with shaking hands made his biggest pot of espresso. "It's freezing," he said, opening his desk of drawers and rummaging around. He leaned forward and slipped the codebook from his jacket pocket into a stack of folded sweaters. Fumbling, he pulled out a thick woolen one and took off his bomber jacket. Debra watched him put on the sweater and wrestle the jacket back on. "Okay," he said, trying to sound optimistic. "Let's get to work. You can go out and come back in an hour if you want, or sit down and relax and breathe some fumes. Just don't hover around and make me nervous because I'm too tired and might screw up."

"We'll keep you company," Ron said. He perched like a fluffed pigeon on one of the armchairs near the linotype machine.

"Absolutely," Debra said, sitting opposite. "Vlad, you want to look around, check that back courtyard and the roof?"

"Boris is arriving with breakfast," Vlad said, pressing his ear bud.

Boris knocked four times. He set down two paper bags. Debra sighed. "The best bakery in town is a block away and he goes to the golden arches."

"It reminds me of home," Boris said.

Jay was hungry. But the smell of greasy muffins made him sick. He got a box of crackers out of the cupboard. "Help yourselves, and step back—I've got to move the camera." He wheeled the wooden box camera toward the darkroom.

"What's that for?" Debra spoke through a mouthful of fried egg and muffin. "The plates are already exposed."

"I can't give you daguerreotype lessons right now," Jay said, opening the black curtains and pushing the camera inside. "The angle support is built into the back of the box camera and that's where you vaporize the plate with mercury. If you read my paper you should know that." Jay picked up an armload of bottles and cans from a cupboard in the corner and carried them into the darkroom. He reappeared wearing a chemical gasmask. "You sure you don't want to take a walk? This stuff is toxic and I don't have another mask."

The four of them stopped chewing. Vlad chugged his coffee. "I'll check the courtyard," he said.

Debra put down her muffin. "Are you kidding?"

"No shit," Jay said from behind his mask. "Why do you think Nièpce and Daguerre died so young?"

"Okay," Ron said, standing up. He handed Jay the black packages. "Boris and Vlad, I think you two should go into the backcourt and Debra and I will stand out front for a while. How long do the vapors last?"

"I'll put on the ventilator, but you'd better stay out for at least twenty-five minutes." Jay paused. "Don't worry, I'm not going anywhere. We're on the same side. Anyway, how could I get out?"

"Right," Debra said. "I might just sit in the car."

Jay watched the Russians let themselves out and close the door, locking it behind. He slipped into the darkroom, turned the ventilator and infrared light on and reached up to a canary-yellow container on a shelf. Inside was a roll of ultra-sensitive 3200 ASA film. He checked through the curtains to make sure Debra and Ron couldn't see him before popping the film into his Minox and slipping the camera inside his jacket. The front door slammed.

Under the box camera's black hood Jay opened the first black package. He used his fingertips to remove the daguerreo-type plate from its protective plastic mounts. It appeared to be undamaged. Jay set it in the angled support structure, plugged in and adjusted an electric heater and set it under the container of mercury. Counting out loud, he waited for it to climb to 140 degrees Fahrenheit. As he waited, he slipped on rubber gloves and readied a bath of concentrated sodium hypo-sulfite and another bath of hot distilled water. He watched patiently. The mercury began forming a whitish amalgam where the light had transformed the iodine into silver iodide on the plate's surface. Checking the thermometer again he pulled his glove back far enough to read his watch. "Three-one thousand, two-one thousand, one-one thousand," he counted. With a flick of the wrist he lifted the plate by its edges, bathed it in the sodium hypo-sulfite and checked his watch as the seconds passed. At the precise moment he dipped the daguerreotype into the hot water bath and shook it gently until the iodide was gone.

Where the white amalgam had been Jay could see a series of numbers. He set the plate at an angle and opened the curtains a crack to let light in. With his elbows steadied on the counter, he focused the Minox on the plate. Three times three exposures, changing the f-stop and speed each time, and the 3200 ASA film practically guaranteed readable negatives. Snapping shut the black curtain he set the Minox at the back of the top shelf and turned to retrieve the second black package.

"I'm coming in," he heard Ron say in a muffled voice. Ron's head poked through the black curtain. He was wearing an orange gasmask.

"The hell you are," Jay said, pushing him back. "You want to ruin the whole process?"

"I'm staying here," Ron said.

"Suit yourself. Just don't open the curtain again or you'll wreck the next plate. I hope you didn't ruin the first one. For chrissake don't open the curtain."

Jay could hear Ron behind him laboring to breath through the gasmask. "Fuck off, Ron!" he shouted. "You're making me nervous."

Jay waited until he heard Ron shuffle away. He tore open the second black package. Setting it into the support he ran through the steps again, being extra careful that Ron was not looking when it came time to use the Minox. He coughed to cover the sound of the shutter release and decided he could only risk one exposure each this time.

"What's taking so long?" Ron demanded.

"Back off," Jay barked. "I'm almost finished. I told you not to breathe down my neck goddammit."

"Have they come out?"

"If you don't back off I'll make sure they don't come out,"

Jay said. He hid the Minox inside an empty carbolic acid can marked with the skull and crossbones and stepped back through the curtains. "They're drip-drying," Jay said, making no attempt to hide his anger. "Give them five minutes and if they're ruined it's your fault." Jay poured himself a shot of espresso and lifted his gasmask long enough to drink it.

"You okay?"

Jay waited. Diminishing returns, he told himself, breathing deeply to compose himself. "Okay," he said.

"Good." Ron sat in the armchair, his eyes half hidden by the mask. He stared at the half-eaten Egg McMuffin. "Can I take the mask off yet?"

"Frisk him," Ron said as soon as he had the plates in hand. He snapped his fingers at Vlad. "Mind if I use your photocopier?" Ron didn't wait for Jay to answer. He turned on the HP All-In-One in the loft's office area. The floor was littered with fax scrolls from Jay's old machine. Ron smiled. "Next time buy the model incorporating a plain-paper fax," he said. "Save you a lot of grief."

"He's clean," Boris confirmed. He finished frisking Jay down to the ankles and shook his head. "Nothing."

"Check the darkroom."

"For what?"

"Just check it Boris. Make sure he's not holding back something."

"It's nice to be trusted," Jay said. He watched Boris push through the curtains.

"I don't find anything but chemicals and equipment," Boris said, pulling the black curtains together.

Ron finished making the photocopies of the plates and

handed two sheets each to Debra and Vlad. "We've got these copies in case anything happens on the way, God forbid. Jay, you got a box I can put the plates in?"

Jay found a cardboard case. "They scratch easily," he said. "You should wear white cotton gloves when handling them."

"How come it's numbers *and* letters," asked Debra, reading the photocopies.

Ron glanced at the plates, flicking them to better see the images. "Debra's right. The other code had letters only, no numbers."

"I'm a photographer. Call your guys in Langley and ask them. Scan or fax them the plates and the codebook and let them crack the code."

Ron closed the box and slipped it into his raincoat pocket. "Not safe, Jay. If we can monitor their electronic communications they can monitor ours. So now we go back to the office and work on this."

"Back to what office?" Jay stared ahead. He shook his head. "I've done my bit. I've got to sleep for a couple of hours. You have the plates. You have the cloud book and camera manual. Now leave me alone because I've had enough. I'm not your operative."

Debra held up her palms. "He's right, Ron. We could scan the plates and scramble the scan and email it on a safe line." She raised her index finger and huddled with Ron across the loft.

Dazed and mad, Jay stretched on his bed, pulling a blanket around him. He covered his head with a pillow.

"Jay, listen to me." Debra tugged at the pillow. "Ron's going back to the office. We have a couple of code-breakers there and if they have a problem they're going to call. Jay?" He turned on his side and curled into the fetal position. "I'm staying here," Debra said. "Leave me Boris in the backcourt and take Vlad in the Voyager."

The door closed. Debra slid into an armchair and sucked coffee through a plastic straw. "Jay I know you're listening. I know you're pissed off and you just want us to leave you alone but that's not going to happen. You're into this way beyond your handsome little head. Ron wants you to take some of the stuff our pilots take to stay awake, and he wants you to put on a wire and talk to the lawyer who wears the old fedora hat all the time. Jay?"

Jay held the pillow down. "No."

"Ron says if you don't wear the wire we turn you over to the French, and I wouldn't like that to happen. Honest."

Jay moved the pillow and sat up. "Well I'll be goddamned. I'm beyond tired, and I don't take drugs. You may think this sleep-deprivation stuff is effective but I can guarantee it won't work."

Debra sucked her coffee. She walked over and perched on the bed. He could feel the heat of her thighs. "A wire is nothing," she said, looking at him with milky eyes. "Everyone's wired. Think of it as a headset or reality TV."

"Nothing is less real."

"You might save thousands of lives."

Jay counted to six. "I'll have to think about that, and why all those lives are in danger in the first place."

"Too bad you can't ask your father."

Jay stared at her. He felt a rush of hatred mixed with lust. "Never, ever say that again." His voice came out a key lower than usual. "I'm not a spy, I hate your goddamn games. I hate your fucking false piety and the wars you invent to keep busy."

Debra frowned. "Think fast, Jay," she said, crossing her legs to hide her discomfort. "We can make the meeting happen with Henri the lawyer and make sure it comes out the way we want. You call him and say you need to see him about an urgent family matter. He's your aunt's attorney. You show him what you have, including all those nice old snapshots, and you show him a couple of lines of key information we'll have by then from the plates."

Jay rubbed his face. "No. Go ahead and call in the French. Find someone else. I've done my bit. Bug off. That's a polite way of saying leave me the fuck alone."

Debra stood. She paced alongside the bed, her face a darker shade than normal. "Jay, we can't spook the lawyer or he'll tell his people and they might just cut ties with the terror cell, or tell them to speed up the attack. There are too many targets for us to cover—meaning we don't know if they're going to use car bombs, truck bombs, missiles, a helicopter or an airplane. We don't know if they're going to pack the subway with dirty bombs, or if they're going to hit the avenue and the tower or the cathedral all at once. Do you really want to be responsible for not stopping the worst attack since the Twin Towers?"

Jay rubbed his temples harder. He tried to make sense of the situation. "Why are the CIA and Homeland Security interested in what's happening in Paris? Why not let the DST or that other one, the SIS or DCRI, let them handle it? Why me?"

"I can't tell you that."

"Shit," Jay said. "You expect me to keep risking my life? Be real, Debra."

"You have to trust me Jay."

Jay laughed a savage laugh, his anger heightened by the irrational desire to ravish her. "I'll make it easy for you," he said. "Let me tell you what my guess is. First, you can't tell me anything because my father was involved from the start and you people screwed up because you didn't listen to him. So now you're trying to fix things and you think you can blackmail and squeeze me. Second, you're afraid of leaks in the French services somewhere, so you're keeping them out, or trying to. Third, there's a link between the French terror cells and something back home, and maybe in Algeria. That charity has offices everywhere."

"I'm not authorized," Debra started to say.

"I know," Jay interrupted. "You're not authorized to say shit or confirm that all this is going to happen on the Champs-Elysées at approximately midnight on December 31st which means very soon." He fell silent and leaned close to Debra's ear, the one without the bud. He placed his index finger over the miniature microphone on Debra's lapel, letting his lips brush her neck. "You can nod or shake your head," he whispered, watching Debra bat her eyelashes. "They may be listening but no one can see you nod."

Jay waited. Debra eyed him, her lips slightly parted. She licked them but didn't blink for a full ten seconds. Finally she nodded, licked her lips again and raised an eyebrow. "You have no choice but to trust us," she said. Her voice sounded artificial, mechanical.

"I see," Jay said, play-acting along. "You're a real patriot, Debra. You won't even nod your friggin' head." He stretched horizontal again and shut his eyes, feeling the bed spin. "If I could be sure," he said, "that by wearing a wire and entrapping Maitre Henri he'd stand trial for war crimes or terrorism I might do it." He paused. Debra sat closer to him. Their hands touched. Neither pulled back. "But I know exactly what would happen. The guy has half the world by the short-and-curlies. You'd cut a deal with him. He'd retire to some luxury villa on the Riviera. The whole thing would be hushed up. That's probably why my father persisted, and you let him die, like a good rogue."

Debra pressed his hand. Her expression showed exhaustion. "You want this guy to fry, don't you?"

Jay's face flushed. "This time around he's going to pay."

"Even if it means jeopardizing thousands of innocent lives and maybe creating an international incident, bringing down the French government?"

"It won't," Jay said.

"How do you know?"

"Trust me," he said, mocking her earlier tone of voice. "You've got no choice. Let me sleep a couple of hours and have some lunch and we'll talk. Otherwise call your French pals."

Debra stood. She spun around suddenly and dropped into a kneeling stance, her handgun pointed at the entrance hall.

"Freeze," Debra shouted.

Amy's glance shifted from the gun in the kneeling woman's hands to Jay on the rumpled bed. "I didn't know I was interrupting."

"It's not what you think," Debra said, getting to her feet. "How did you get in?"

Amy rattled her keys. "He's my fiancé."

The door to the backcourt flew open and Vlad leaned in, his outsized revolver gripped in both hands.

"Okay, okay," Debra yelled, the veins bulging on her neck. "Put it down, Vlad. Why the hell didn't someone see her coming and keep her out, or at least let me know she was out there?"

Vlad holstered his gun and turned halfway around to finish zipping his pants. He shrugged and spoke cryptically into a mike embedded on his leather lapel. "She moved too fast," Vlad said. "We didn't know she had a key."

Debra held up her hands, one of them still holding the gun. "All right, okay."

"I'll bet you're Debra," Amy said, her face flushed.

"And I'll bet we both know who you are."

"Basically they kidnapped me," Jay said. "Now they're blackmailing me and trying to get me to wear a wire."

Debra holstered her gun. She pressed a hand over the bud in her right ear. "Jay, Ron says you'd better be a little more discreet. You might be endangering your fiancée here by sharing that kind of information."

"Who's involved?" Amy asked, her cheeks red.

"You don't need to know that," Debra said, her back arching. "How dare you?"

"Debra's right, you don't want to know," Jay broke in. "*I* don't want to know. All I want is to sleep for a couple of hours and eat something."

Debra stepped back and spoke at her lapel mike, cupping her hand. "Okay, here's how we're going to play it. Vlad stays in the backcourt. I'm out front in the car. You've got an hour to rest and half an hour to eat something we bring in. Then we're going back to the office."

Amy shook her hair out of the way. "You can't tell us what to do."

"Don't even go down that road," Debra growled.

Jay took Amy's hand. "It's pointless," he said. "I'll wear their fucking wire but I've got to sleep for a while first and eat something. Give me two hours and I'll meet with Henri."

Debra pressed her ear bud. She grimaced. "Okay. You can't get away. You know that." She signaled to Vlad and stepped out.

Jay held his finger to his lips. He rolled off the bed, turned on a radio and tuned it to *France Classique*. He hugged Amy. "The place is bugged and so am I," he whispered into her ear. "I love you. I'm sorry." He kissed her neck, feeling the tension in her muscles. She stifled a sob.

"Bastards."

"They set me up," he whispered, unzipping her purse and searching for the nicotine gum she chewed. "I've got to do a couple of things. Don't ask questions. They can't hold you." He found the gum, chewed it and pinched off a wad, and then found the mini-mike in his aviator jacket. It looked like a button but they'd sewn it on badly. Jay pressed the chewing gum into the pea-sized mike. He pointed around the loft. "They're all over. When I'm done you go home and pack a bag," he whispered. "Call your lawyer and make an appointment but don't tell him what it's about. I'll phone you twice and let it ring five times. That means meet me at the Louvre, under the main pyramid. Okay?"

Amy nodded. He wrote out a series of access codes and handed them to her. His wristwatch read 11:02am. "Go to my website. Go into the restricted area and download the photos and print them out." He gave her a pack of photo paper and pointed at the printer. She nodded again.

Back in the darkroom, Jay reached inside the can with the skull and crossbones. He heard Amy's fingers on the keyboard beyond the curtain. In two minutes the strip of Minox negatives was dripping over the sink. He heard the printer in the corner of the office area jetting ink, reassembling the high-resolution jpegs of Gonflay and the man in camelhair.

From the false bottom of the fireproof filing cabinet Jay took out a fake French National Identity Card. The name on it was Rousseau. Charles Rousseau. He found a credit card to match. The expiration date was a month away. Plenty of time, he told himself. After feeling around in the sweater drawer, he found the codebook. Amy took it.

"*Le Prince?*"

Jay dipped his head. "Copy the whole thing and pray Debra doesn't come in."

"Pray the ink doesn't run out."

Jay pulled the darkroom curtains shut. He turned on a light-box and checked the Minox negatives with a loupe, choosing the best two of each series and making flashcard-sized prints. Sweat trickled down his back. He switched on the blow dryer and opened the black curtains, watching Amy photocopy the book. *Le Prince* filled only one-hundred-twenty-six pages in the 1852 pocket edition. Concise, he thought. At least Machiavelli had that virtue.

Jay's wristwatch read 11:47am. Amy handed him the copies and the book. He slipped *Le Prince* onto the shelf behind the printer, between *Blades of Grass* and Dante's *Inferno*, then he dug out three manila envelopes from a desk drawer and slid the photocopies into one, the digital prints into another. He pointed at Amy's purse. She silently folded them, struggling to make them fit.

The flashcard-sized prints were still tacky. Jay placed them back-to-back in a waxy, nonstick photo folder. He slipped the folder into the third envelope. Coiled, the negative strip fit inside the skull and crossbones can in the darkroom. Jay wiped the sweat out of his eyes and hoped no one would think to check the can.

The telephone rang, startling them. He shook his head. The answering machine kicked in. They stood close.

"Allo? Allo! Rakan speaking. Your spicy crab is ready. We hold your table."

⚑

They stood behind the loft door, readying themselves to face Debra on the sidewalk. Amy knew what she had to do after lunch. Put articles together, photocopy, highlight, finish the job they'd begun last night. Then contact media friends who'd never reveal sources. Jay in the meantime would figure out a way of shaking Debra and Vlad and meeting Amy at the Louvre.

He removed the chewing gum from the button-mike inside his jacket. "Time for lunch. I forgot I'd ordered that crab." He pressed the gum back in and unlocked the front door.

They stepped onto the sidewalk and within seconds Debra was standing by their side. She reached for Jay's arm.

"Going somewhere?"

"You know the place. Thai, down the block, we're having

lunch and no, we wouldn't like your company." He shrugged her off.

Debra signaled. A pair of men responded across the street. Jay hadn't seen them before. Both were Caucasian, one dark-haired, the other sandy. Both wore mid-calf black leather coats. Probably French, Jay guessed. A new set of minders. Debra spoke fast. "What if I said I don't care whether or not you want me to join you?"

"I'd say something you wouldn't like to hear," Amy snapped. "Leave us alone for lunch. Jay is going to cooperate, you heard him, for god's sake be reasonable."

"Lady I don't take orders from you."

Jay stopped and stared Debra down. "You may think you can do whatever you want but the Patriot Act doesn't apply here, and if you keep this up then you can damn well call the French secret services and I'll tell them my story and live with the consequences. It's up to you, Debra. Keep pushing me and you'll be the one risking the lives of thousands."

Debra's face hardened. She pressed her left ear bud. "See those guys?" She jabbed a finger. "They're going to stand outside the restaurant and watch you. Vlad will check if there's a back way out. I'm watching you too. You have your damn spicy crab and then we're going to the office and no more guff." She turned and stalked to the SUV.

"Nice," Amy said. They marched downhill. Rakan opened the doors at Bonjour Siam and glanced at the minders. "You brought your friends this time?"

"They prefer the golden arches," Amy said. She closed the door behind.

Jay silently formed the word *microphones*.

"Your crab has arrived," Rakan said. "Please feel free to freshen your hands and we will serve you." Rakan led them to Jay's usual table. He raised his eyes to the aquarium. "New fish today."

Amy wrinkled her forehead. "Since when does he talk like that? Everyone's gone nuts."

Jay tapped the aquarium, frightening the carp. He used his fingernail to dislodge what looked like a button battery. "I'd feed you to the fish but they'd die from the heavy metals," Jay said into the bug. He dropped it to the floor and ground it under his heel. "They've stuck their dots and bugs everywhere I go."

Amy shivered. "That's outrageous. We should call the police." She caught herself.

"You go to the lady's room then I'll use the gent's," Jay said, lifting the wad of gum off the button-bug sewn onto his aviator jacket.

"But I just went. I mean, yes, I do need to wash my hands." She picked up her bulging purse and crossed the restaurant. The men on the sidewalk tracked her with their eyes. Their faces were hard, angular and expressionless.

Jay saw Amy knock on the bathroom door before stepping inside. He counted to ten and watched her walk back to the table, her purse empty now.

Tables around them filled with Asians. Jay tore open a bag of shrimp chips and began eating them. "I ordered a double serving of rice," he said. "I'm starving." He lifted a bottle of soy sauce and poured it over a shrimp chip. The sauce spilled onto the table, running over his hands. He swore and used a napkin to mop up the sauce.

"Go wash your hands," Amy said.

The men on the sidewalk watched Jay walk to the bathroom wiping his fingers on a paper napkin. He stepped in and locked the door. Yves opened his duffel coat pocket, showing him the envelopes Amy had brought in. Jay washed his hands. He slipped the small envelope out of his bomber jacket pocket and watched Yves nestle it between the others.

Standing on one foot, Jay took off his left shoe, pulled out the inner sole and tugged on a GPS dot, dangling it like a mouse. He opened his jacket and pointed at the button microphone with the gum stuck into it.

Yves lit a cigarette. His pockmarked cheeks vacuumed into convexes. "Kitchen," he whispered as he exhaled. "Eat first."

At the far end of the bathroom hall a door led to an inner courtyard and the kitchen. Jay waited as Yves stepped out of view. He walked back across the restaurant to Amy. A platter of spicy crab sat on the table.

Amy took a deep breath. "I don't know if I can eat anything."

"Try," Jay said. He lifted a crab claw and broke it open. Amy sucked the other claw.

"Beer?" Rakan stood behind them.

"Better not. I'm about to fall asleep."

"Me too," said Amy. "I'll stick to water."

"The chef says bon appétit, he's happy to see you here and says please say hello to him in the kitchen before you leave."

"Thanks. I'll do that."

Amy waited until Rakan had left. "I can't eat."

"Rice," Jay said. "Eat rice. It'll settle your stomach."

Out on the sidewalk, the minders stepped aside to let the luncheon crowd in. Tables filled. The restaurant became animated and noisy. Jay pulled the gum out of the mike. "I'll wear the wire. I'll make sure that bastard fries. You go on home. I've got to hit the men's room again then I'll go back to the loft and get to work with Debra." He plugged the mike again and leaned over the table. "Time for you to leave," he whispered. "They'll follow you but they won't stop you. Stay in public, on the street. Take the *métro* or a bus."

"Jay?"

"Remember. Five rings, twice. The Louvre pyramid." He gave her a kiss and watched her step outside. Amy stalked by the minders. One of them trailed her. She turned to flip him off. The other minder watched Jay ask for the check and head to the bathroom.

A

Steam filled the kitchen. Yves was waiting in a corner, out of view.

"You get bored in Dieppe?"

Yves stood aside as Rakan set down dirty dishes and yelled in Thai. "Not Dieppe," Yves said. "I never went to Dieppe." He coughed. "Given the situation, it seemed like a good idea to have a little chat with d'Arnac." Yves beckoned Jay into the restaurant office and closed the door. "You need to know that a couple of months ago I might've tossed out a few too many details about a daguerreotype I could maybe get at a price, once Quincy Thomas had been discovered." He paused to let the words sink in. "What I'm saying is, some of this is my fault. I was trying to speed things up and get you back on board."

Jay had never heard Yves admit to wrong-doing. "That explains a lot," he said. "I'd like to talk to d'Arnac myself."

Yves unfolded a handkerchief. "The thing is," he hacked, "Claude-Gilles isn't likely to be talking to anyone."

"Meaning?"

"That d'Arnac was in his bathtub when I got there," Yves said. "The water wasn't clean."

"Dead?"

"Extremely." The restaurant's office was piled with half-empty crates and drums of sesame seed oil. "D'Arnac said something to me the other day. I didn't understand. Now I think I know what he meant. He asked where I was planning to be on New Year's Eve and said, 'Not on the Champs-Elysées I hope, because I sure wouldn't be.' He knows I never do New Year's Eve on the Champs-Elysées." Yves paused. "I figured I'd better help you sew this up."

The veins on Jay's temples throbbed. "We've got to get the hell out of here. There's at least one guy on the sidewalk out front, probably one in back by now and the woman."

"I thought this might be a way to spring you. Spicy crab."

Jay started to zip up his bomber jacket. His satellite phone rang. "Debra."

"The American DCRI woman?"

"Homeland Security. She must've heard us talking." He massaged the keypad. A distant, accented voice began shouting.

"...Mister...Jay?...ello? Hello?" The voice crackled and faded. "I been trying all morning. You told me to call if I saw suspicious things."

The maid. Manuela. He'd forgotten about Manuela Santiago. "Where are you?"

"In a booth sir."

"Give me the number." Jay took it down. "Hang up. I'll call you back in fifteen, twenty minutes. Stay near the booth."

Jay took a breath. He folded the phone, thought for a split-second and turned it off. "They've been tracking me with this and a bunch of those GPS dots," he said. "They even said so. You get so used to it you forget."

Rakan waved his hands and pointed at a pair of delivery carts, shouting orders at a group of boys in charge of takeout deliveries. It was chaos. "Go," Rakan said, jabbing his finger at the carts. "The lady on the sidewalk is coming in."

"I hope you're still limber," Yves said. He opened one of the carts and took out the shelves. "Get in. Don't worry. I'm getting in the other one. They'd recognize me out there and pull me in."

Jay hesitated. He fished out the GPS dot from his shoe and dropped it into a white paper takeout bag marked 'Sticky Rice, Thai Embassy.' Then he climbed into the cart. The doors closed behind. The cart rolled up a ramp into the Bonjour Siam delivery truck. A second cart rumbled in. The truck pulled out, bouncing over potholes.

Seconds became minutes. Six went by before the truck rocked to a halt. The rear door opened. Sunlight and air poured in. A Thai teenager helped Jay out and opened the second cart.

"This way," Yves said. He trotted south, beating grains of rice off his duffel coat.

Jay handed the driver a 50-euro bill and ran to catch up, plucking sprigs of coriander from his hair. A glance told him they were at the eastern end of Rue Simon Bolivar. Yves pointed out his rental Citröen subcompact parked nearby, on Boulevard de la Villette.

"Wait at the car." Jay detoured to a telephone booth and slid in a phone card. "Hello? Manuela Santiago?"

A torrent of foreign words came back at him, spoken by a man. The receiver on the other end fell. "Hello? Mister Jay?"

"Thank you for calling, Manuela," Jay said. "What's happened?"

"Madame has not been feeling good," the maid told Jay, her syntax and diction out the panic hatch. "Deezy. Seeing things. Hearing things. With eyestrains, headache. Saying I move things, stealing things... Just like the last dead Madame. I want the police to know, I want you to come see for yourself I'm telling the truth, that someone else is stealing from the French ladies. Come now before another Madame dies," Manuela insisted, her voice choked. "Tonight, before five when I go home to your aunt's house."

Yves' car accelerated north into the nineteenth arrondissement. The broad Canal de la Villette came into view, bordered by housing projects. Jay glanced into his palm where he'd written in blue ballpoint ink the address Manuela Santiago had given him. He imagined Manuela in a pink uniform talking breathlessly into the phone while down the block in her dark, rambling villa Madame Clothilde Perrière-Lafonte rocked slowly in a chair.

He wasn't sure why his mind's eye saw the Parisian dowager sitting in a rocking chair or why her villa should be dark and rambling. The fantasy seemed right, probably because the woman's old-money name was familiar and so was the location, an exclusive neighborhood flanking the Bois de Vincennes parklands. Maybe the explanation was simpler. Maybe he was thinking of Madeleine de Lafayette.

A plan was beginning to form in Jay's mind like a print in a chemical bath. The maid would let him into the villa. Henri or, more likely Henri's men would show up. That might be the way to flush them out, a better way to nail them than wearing a wire. Catch them in flagrante.

Afternoon cross-town traffic made the going slow. Yves tuned into *Radio Nostalgie* and lit another Gauloise from the one he'd smoked to its unfiltered end. Edith Piaf and her 1940s accordion accompaniment wheezed, the musical equivalent of the accordion of bumpers outside. Each bumper was on the verge of slamming into the one just inches ahead, as the slinky-toy accordion slunk forward. Yves gunned the rental car's engine and leaned on the horn. Others began honking. Yves nudged forward, clutching between neutral and first.

"The maid goes home at 5pm so we've got under four hours," Jay said, checking his watch.

"To do what?"

"Decipher those plates and decide whether to share the information with Debra. Decide whether to go out to this old lady's house and try to catch someone in the act."

"The act of what?"

Jay hesitated. "I don't know."

Yves leaned on the horn, barely avoiding the car ahead. He swung out and tailgated a truck down Avenue de Flandre, turning into Rue Riquet. On Quai de la Seine he pulled into an empty parking place. The radio died when Yves cut the engine. They sat in silence.

"What's this about a code and plates?" Yves handed Jay the envelopes he'd taken from Amy in the bathroom at Bonjour Siam. He cracked open his window to let the cigarette smoke out.

"The less you know the better off you are," Jay said. Yves made a face. "It's some crazy thing my father got into and I'm not even sure on which side."

Jay sketched out what had happened, from the license plate to the codebook in Madeleine's cellar and the de-briefing on the Champs-Elysées. "They've been running me, using me." He paused. "I'm not even sure if they're legitimate."

"It's getting better all the time," Yves said. He dropped a second butt through the slitted window. "You think they're running you right now?"

"Maybe."

"Shit. Sure they are." Yves grunted. "Someone is running you. Why else would they let us get away? In delivery carts?"

Jay thought about it. "I agreed to wear a wire to entrap Georges Henri. They might think I'm stupid enough to go back to the loft or Amy's place and they can nab me."

"You really think they want to get Maitre Henri?"

Jay struggled with conflicting scenarios. "Maybe they want me dead."

"Like your father?" Yves asked. "They could've killed you ten times over if that's all they wanted."

"They think they have what they want. The plates and codebook."

Yves cleared his throat. "My guess is, there's more than one secret service involved, and so far that's what's saved your ass. They both want you. All three of them."

"They want the enciphered messages off those plates.

They've probably figured the Brownie Box manual and the cloud book aren't the right books. They know I have the real codebook." Jay paused.

"Where?"

Jay hesitated. "At my loft. On the shelf. I hid it."

Yves exhaled in exasperation. "You think they haven't found it? You think they didn't see you put it there? They probably installed a dozen videocams in the walls while you were in New York."

"One way or the other," Jay said, "I've got to decipher the plates and decide whether to share the information." He handed Yves the envelope of digital prints. "Take a look at those while I try to figure out the protocol."

"What protocol?"

Jay studied the alphanumeric series on the daguerreotype plates. "You'll see."

Yves lit up again and flipped through the digitalized prints Amy had downloaded. He compared them, brushing ashes off as they fell from his cigarette. Grainy and blurred, the shots were the kind a paparazzo or police photographer might take on the fly. The pictures worked together, a comic book sequence. *Click, wham, bam.*

"I like the way you reworked the real ones to make them look like these manipulated images." Yves fingered the crucial manipulated shots. Two frames showed the man in the camel-hair coat heaving Gonflay toward the bus.

Jay smiled inwardly. He'd used PhotoShop on all the pictures, even the authentic ones. They looked uniform.

"Let me guess," Yves continued. "You took the bodies of a couple of bystanders, here, transferred the clothes and the heads to them, and found a few arms somewhere else. I probably wouldn't have known if I hadn't printed the originals myself. The grain and pixels make them look real. It's the high-sensitivy film."

It was nice to be complimented by a pro. "Give me a second," Jay said. He wrote out a crude correspondence table.

A B C D E F G H I J K L M N O P Q R S T U V W X Y Z
26 25 24 23 22 21 20 19 18 17 16 15 14 13 12 11 10 9 8 7 6 5 4 3 2 1

"It looks like the numbers are unciphered and the letters are Z = 1."

"What are you talking about?"

"The numerals haven't been ciphered, just mixed into enciphered letters. Never mind. Take this." He handed Yves the photocopies of *Le Prince*. "I'll read out the page number, the line number and the letter number and we'll see if it makes sense. You find the corresponding page, count down to the line then count over to the letter or word and I'll note them down. Okay, 18, 7, 24."

"Slow down." Yves flipped to page 18 and found line 7. "No letter 24, the line ends at 18."

Jay frowned. "Give me a minute to reverse the order." He crossed out the numbers and reordered them.

A B C D E F G H I J K L M N O P Q R S T U V W X Y Z
1 2 3 4 5 6 7 8 9 10 11 12 13 14 15 16 17 18 19 20 21 22 23 24 25 26

But the new protocol didn't work either. Jay pounded the dashboard.

On the back of the envelope of 1940s photos, Jay drew up another correspondence table. He made M = 1, N = 2, L = 3, O = 4, and worked symmetrically from the center of the alphabet outwards. "2, 17, 6," Jay read out aloud, his pen shuttling back and forth.

A B C D E F G H I J K L M N O P Q R S T U V W X Y Z
25 23 21 19 17 15 13 11 9 7 5 3 1 2 4 6 8 10 12 14 16 18 20 22 24 26

"Okay," Yves said, running his finger down the page. "That works. It's either the letter 'e' or the word 'est' as in 'east' or 'is'."

Jay noted both on the envelope. "Next. We've got a long way to go."

For each enciphered series, Jay noted a corresponding letter or word. Soon, what looked like an IBAN account number and Swift address began to form.

"Debra and Ron may have a secret agenda," Jay said, his pulse throbbing. "But I don't want to be responsible for not stopping a terrorist attack."

"Keep working," Yves said. "Another hour and we'll have both plates decoded. Then if you want I'll drop you on the Champs-Elysées and you can be a hero or a stooge, whichever way it turns out. Or you can do the smart thing and courier the information to them."

"Give me five seconds," Jay said, holding up his hands. "My brain is dead." He stepped out of the car and stood by the canal, breathing in the cold air. The sky had clouded over, choked with nimbus formations. Rain began to fall. A tour boat was about to cast off from Quai de la Seine. Jay wished he could be on that boat, be an innocent tourist in the magical Paris kingdom, worried about the weather, the lines to climb the Eiffel Tower or the Arc de Triomphe.

He walked back, detouring down the sidewalk to check for unmarked police cars. The Eiffel Tower was still on his mind. Rain fell harder. A pile of cigarette butts had grown under Yves' window. What if it's the tower they want? The GIA had tried. The Champs-Elysées would be even worse, ten times worse than blowing up the tower. Half a million people, maybe more, partying on a single street, packed together, with the Arc de Triomphe behind, the symbol of France, of Napoleon Bonaparte's triumphs. It had to be.

Jay got back in. The smoke from Yves' cigarette stung his eyes. He shut them and felt himself falling down a black, spiraling hole. His brain refused to respond. It reran the exchanges he'd had with Yves that afternoon, mixing them with his own unspoken thoughts since the maid had telephoned earlier. *I've got the incriminating Curiosity Case back*, his voice whirred in his head. *Gonflay and d'Arnac are dead. I've got plates and a coded message that probably links a terror cell to Maitre Henri, and Amy has a dossier an inch thick. So why not drop everything into the hands of the French police and media, or let Debra and Ron fight it out? Give up and get out.*

The response was immediate. *Because either they'll screw up*, shouted the voices in his head, *or they'll never get to square one, that's why. The men in gray suits will make sure of it. The guys in unmarked cars, the friendly agents in a parallel world, the disembodied voices at the other end of the telephone line. They'll cut a deal and let Henri go. Listen to the maid.*

"Hey, time to wake up." Yves shook Jay's shoulder again. "You've been talking in your sleep. What's with this maid? What did the maid tell you anyway?"

A

Yves parked outside the big-box electronics store in eastern Paris. Jay followed him to the video department, where he picked out a Camcorder. It was similar, Yves said, to the one he'd used a few years back on assignment in Italy. Jay left him to it, thinking of Amy and what she would say.

Whereas Jay harbored fears of traps and secret agendas, and was tempted to tip off the French authorities rather than go to the villa and meet the maid, Yves' reaction was celebratory. It was a call to arms, the Legionnaire with his finger on the trigger again, an index away from fortune or death.

This time around, Yves' rifle would be a video camera. He would catch Maitre Henri's men on tape. Add the video to Jay's manipulated photographs, the pile of incriminating documents, and the daguerreotype plates, and the evidence against the lawyer might make the case difficult to sandbag, especially if they put everything on the Web and got it circulating in blogs and chat rooms.

Jay didn't need convincing. The plan seemed the only guarantee the story wouldn't wind up DOA, with more flesh-and-blood bodies to follow, their own, maybe. It was time, Jay told himself. Time for Maitre Georges Henri to pay, and for Ron and Debra to learn a lesson about courage and betrayal and trust. They'd betrayed William Grant, the rogue who wasn't a rogue. They were ready to betray his son. For the greater good?

Jay and Yves sheltered under the awning of a café across the street from the electronics discounter. Yves handled a bright red cellphone. "I picked it up with 35 euros credit. You can't use your satellite phone or they'll be on us, right?"

Jay stared at the cellphone. He fought off a wave of exhaustion. "Right," he said, thinking again of Amy. With the new cell he could call her. Soon. No, not soon. Later. They'd be listening on her end. He'd have to wait.

Jay scraped away the plastic coating and read the fourteen-digit code on the back of the phone card. He activated the cell account, listening for confirmation. "Okay," he said.

"Try my number." Seconds later Yves' mobile rang. "Let's go."

Jay mulled over their improvised plan as Yves' rental Citroën merged with the column of cars heading east toward Place Daumesnil and the spot where Serge Gonflay had been run over the day before. Sleet fell steadily. It wasn't even 5 o'clock but the streetlamps were already flickering on. Jay wondered if the motorcycle courier had delivered the package to Bonjour Siam yet. He'd put the photocopies of *Le Prince* and the deciphered daguerreotype plates in with them. The coded message made no sense to him. He'd written Rakan a note: *Give this to the American woman who says I sent her in for spicy crab. Only if she asks for spicy crab. If she doesn't show up, and if I don't phone you, forward the package by courier to Le Monde.*

Insurance, Jay said to himself. Reinsurance. It might be the only way to save myself from Ron and Debra.

Yves drummed the steering wheel. He was pumped up on Legionnaire's adrenaline. "Who killed your father?" Yves blurted.

Jay shook his head. "I don't know." He stared at the frozen lion fountain as they passed the traffic circle heading east to Vincennes.

"Sure you do. Think about it. If his own people didn't protect him they killed him. That's how it works in the Legion. Some people might like it if we had a 9/11 here."

"Why bother? France is already a police state."

"Just wait and see," Yves grunted. "It can get a lot worse."

Jay lifted the Camcorder and looked through the eyepiece with his colorblind eye. He pressed the "review" button and saw a shaky black-and-white version of himself walking toward the car near the electronics warehouse. A test sequence.

"Maybe my father got on the wrong side," Jay said. He stopped the video and erased it then turned the camera on Yves and the traffic and let it run. A minute later he reviewed it with his normal eye. In the darkness there wasn't much difference between black-and-white and color.

"The world isn't black-and-white," Yves said. "It's way more complicated."

"So why do you wear cowboy boots and want to ride to the rescue?"

Yves coughed loudly. "Maybe because I wish it were black-and-white. Maybe I like to fool myself into thinking it could be."

Jay licked his lips. "Okay, here's a best-case scenario. We hide in the villa, film the guy in the camelhair coat, or whoever it is ripping things off from the old ladies. We send the memory chip to *Le Monde* with the rest of the material and guess what?"

Yves coughed again. "What?"

"The lab technicians take a close look and find these test sequences you started shooting." Jay paused. "Even if we've recorded over them or erased them they're still there. You can't get rid of them."

"Who told you that?"

"Bruno," Jay said. "Bruno says the techies do it with hard disks. Now they do it with video memory cards. Nothing is lost anymore." He removed the memory card and with difficulty snapped it in half, dropping the pieces out of the window.

Yves grunted, took his hands off the wheel long enough to pull another memory card from his duffel coat pocket and leaned on the horn. A pedestrian with an umbrella darted between the cars on the six-lane Cours de Vincennes, the main east-west highway to Vincennes. Other pedestrians followed, silhouettes bent against the sleet. The traffic limped toward the beltway and Paris' city limits.

"At least we know the camera works in the dark," Yves said. "Close the window. Everything's getting wet."

Jay shook his head. "Toss that thing out and I'll close it." Yves muttered, took a last drag and flicked his cigarette out. He cranked his window closed and turned up the heater. The noise of the fan, the honking horns and the voices on *Radio Nostalgie* made it hard to think. Jay couldn't hear what Yves was saying about video cellphones permanently linked via satellite to the Web. He tuned out. His mind drifted to Amy, the Gilford Foundation, and New Years' Eve. By turning around in his seat Jay could see the Eiffel Tower's glowing top across town. The luminous countdown was too far away for him to read. Tomorrow, he said to himself. Life will start again tomorrow.

"We're almost there," Yves said. "You ready?"

Manuela Santiago had given Jay vague directions. The house turned out to be an ivy-hung villa on a quiet residential street facing the Bois de Vincennes. Even without GPS Yves found it quickly. Jay felt adrenaline filling the passenger compartment.

It was hard to imagine Greater Paris as a city of almost twelve million spilling beyond Vincennes. The park was an enclave of forests and lakes bounded by the meandering Marne River. Yves drove past the villa and around the block a second time. This time Jay noticed snow drifts caught in old chestnut trees. Ice rimmed a creek across the street from Madame Perrière-Lafonte's mansion. It was rambling and much grander than a house, spreading over two lots. Out front was a wrought-iron gate and two curving, stone-faced wings that formed a horseshoe.

The third time Yves drove by Jay felt sure no one had followed or was waiting for them. Only a few cars were parked along the street. The mansions had garages. It stood to reason that the rusting subcompacts by the curb belonged to servants and handymen. As a precaution Yves parked a hundred yards away facing the main park drive. Once on it, you could turn onto smaller landscaped boulevards or lanes and drive back into town, provided you could remember which were through streets and not dead ends. The Marne River was on the far side of the woods. The A6 freeway onramps were a few minutes farther.

"Let's run through it one more time," Yves said, bundling himself up. "I wait in the garden. You go in, have the maid show you around, then either you let me in the back door or I wait outside. I catch them on video coming in and meet you inside to tape what they're up to. Anything goes seriously wrong we call the gendarmes and hope for the best."

Jay knew it was too dark for Yves to see the apprehension on his face. "Right," he said. "What if there is no back door?

What if Madame Perrière-Lafonte asks for my ID or calls the police?"

Yves shook his head. "Look at the size of the place. There's got to be at least one door other than the front door. Remember the time we took those pictures at that producer's place in Cannes? It was built just like this." Yves began reminiscing. Jay cut him off.

"We'll take it in shifts," Jay said. "It's too cold. I'll figure out how we can come and go. It might take hours."

Yves grunted. "You worry about yourself. I can take the cold." He rattled something in his duffel coat. Jay caught sight of a pair of handcuffs.

"What are you planning to do with those?"

Yves shoved them down and stowed the video camera in another, deeper pocket. "I thought d'Arnac might need persuading, so I took the cuffs along in case." He convulsed in a coughing fit. "Maybe if we get everything we need, and it looks like there's a good opportunity, I can cuff one of the bastards."

Jay held out his hand. "Give them to me," he said. "This isn't the Wild West."

"Never been there."

"Okay, it's not the Algerian desert. Let's just shoot the video and get out."

Yves ignored him. He opened the car door. Jay could hear the handcuffs clink. "You take care of yourself," Yves repeated. He pressed the keys of his cell, hit *memory* and jabbed at the keypad. Jay's phone vibrated. "The miracles of technology."

Something made Jay check his pockets. He found his wallet, the Minox and the two cellphones but not his police ID. Where? Boris. Boris had kept it. He pressed the wad of gum firmly into the button mike and followed Yves down the sidewalk to the mansion.

The night seemed darker than the darkest sepia-washed prints. Every ten yards or so streetlights shone through a freezing mist. Jay counted the steps between the lampposts, keeping a running count and calculating how long it would take to cover the distance at a sprint. A stream of traffic on the main road painted the trees with headlights. Only two cars passed on the frontage road while they walked to the mansion's gate. Neither was a Chrysler minivan or Grand Cherokee, or the lawyer's luxury Renault.

Under a streetlight Jay checked for the door code and punched it in. Timed lights flickered inside the garden court. The gate swung open.

A layer of snow dusted the lawn in the middle of the garden. Box hedges and shrubs surrounded it. Bamboo hid the perimeter walls and neighboring mansions. Yves raised a gloved hand and pointed to a window next door. There were no such things as Neighborhood Watch groups in France. Busybody neighbors did the job without having to express anything like solidarity. Jay took Yves by the arm and counted. One-one thousand, two-one thousand, three…He counted the seconds, puffs of breath billowing. Fifteen, sixteen… twenty seconds. With no movement, the motion-sensor light went out in twenty seconds. The sensor was by the gate, he reasoned. Another one would be by the front door.

Yves forced his way into the bamboo, leaving footprints in the snow. Jay used a broken branch to erase them. He turned to face the house and saw Manuela Santiago at the front door, peering at them, her arms wrapped around her chest.

"Mister Jay sir?"

"Yes." He picked his way across the ice. "A police agent is with me," he said, shaking her hand. "We'll be staking the place out." He realized he'd spoken in French. He spoke again in English and stepped through the door.

"It's cold," Manuela Santiago said, shutting the door. "No matter how long I live in Paris I never get to like that cold."

Jay glanced at the flagstones, Persian throw rugs and oak chests. Beyond stretched a living room. There was no rocking chair in sight and no sign of the mistress of the house. The timed lights went out in the garden. Yves was beyond the motion-sensors' range.

"Madame is in bed," Manuela said. "She was too cold to stay up, sir. I told her not to be worried by noises, that a repairman was here to fix the heater."

"That was smart." Jay raised an eyebrow. "What's wrong with the heater?" He unzipped his jacket, felt the cold and zipped it back up.

"It started yesterday and the house is cold now just like the house of Madame de Lafayette. The repairman didn't come, sir, they never do when they say they will." She turned on lights as they walked from the hall into the living room and from there to the kitchen and pantry, then back around through a sitting room and utility room. Late 1800s, Jay guessed. It was a horseshoe floorplan like his aunt's apartment but on a bigger scale.

The maid pointed out paintings and sculptures and polished antiques. Jay was no expert but he could tell most of it was eighteenth-century and valuable. The house smelled of beeswax, dust caught in hidden recesses, old fabrics and upholstery, leather-bound books and musty rooms whose windows were rarely opened. It reminded him of something. Not just his aunt's. It reminded him of Madeleine's house.

In the living room sat a dry Christmas tree. The fir needles smelled like lemon. Pin-sized lights twinkled. "I should take that away now," Manuela said. She turned to Jay. "Madame never goes into the kitchen ever since her husband died I think, so you can wait there once I'm gone."

Jay nodded. "What's upstairs?"

"Two bedrooms, sir," she said, "and a bathroom and a room where Madame's husband worked."

"An office?"

"That's correct. But Madame never goes up there now. She can still climb up the stairs. Up is not a problem but not down, sir. The rooms have been closed since her husband died."

"And when was that?"

The maid counted. "I think, once she told me, five years ago. Maybe more."

Jay walked back into the living room. "What does your employer say is missing?"

"Some art," she said, waving at a credenza. "Some men and women."

"Sculptures?"

"Yes, sir. Sculptures in metal, sir, and a picture too." In the hall, a rectangle on the wall seemed one shade lighter than its surroundings. "I don't know what picture it was, sir, but it's not here anymore. Madame says the table isn't where it used to be before I came to work for her."

The table stood in a corner of the sitting room. Jay got down on his knees and pulled out a drawer. Even with his limited understanding of Louis XV furniture he could see it was a reproduction. "All right," he said, standing up. "Tell me, if Madame Perrière-Lafonte isn't well, why does she live alone in this unheated mansion?" He motioned at the immensity of it. "She must be able to afford a housekeeper and a nurse."

Manuela smiled. "If you knew how many French ladies live alone, sir," she said. "The money isn't anything. Like Madame Madeleine. They want to be alone, to be independent. They don't like to feel like elderly ladies."

Somehow this wasn't plausible. Jay began to wonder if he'd wandered into a trap, if Maitre Henri, or someone working for him at the agency, had persuaded the maid to call him.

"Besides," Manuela added, finishing her thought. "Madame is taken care of. She has a beeper. I come five times a week for half a day. The nurse comes every two days. She was here this afternoon and gave Madame some medicine and a massage. Soon Madame will get a live-in nurse. Next week, they say. Or maybe she will move to a home."

"Who are they?"

"The agency, sir."

Jay nodded. "Père Labé's agency?"

"Yes, sir."

Jay waited. "What exactly is wrong with Madame Perrière-Lafonte?"

"Oldness," the maid said. "She's almost one hundred years old, sir."

Jay muttered in admiration as the maid led him around to the kitchen and showed him how to lock the back door when he was ready to leave. She wrestled her arms into the purple overcoat he'd seen before. It reached down her calves, covering the pink uniform.

"Don't worry," Jay reassured her. "I'll be in touch with you tomorrow. In the meantime, behave normally, leave at the normal time for work, don't say anything to anyone about this, not my aunt and certainly not anyone at the agency." He paused. "And don't look for the plainclothes policeman in the garden. Close the gate the way you always do." Manuela Santiago bowed. "One more thing," Jay said, checking the screen of the red cellphone. He wrote out the number for her. "In future please call me at this new number."

Jay watched Manuela slip out the door and double-lock it. The garden light snapped on. Twenty seconds later it turned off automatically.

Madame Perrière-Lafonte's kitchen smelled of sour milk, as if a good meal hadn't come out of it since her husband died. Jay found the darkest corner, dragged a chair over and sat. A quarter of an hour later he tried the red cellphone, hitting the memo key and watching the bamboo.

"Nice and warm?"

"No," Jay said. "The heater's broken. You want to come in?"

"I like it out here."

Jay pulled the cellphone away from his ear. A car glided past. "When you come in, use the kitchen door. It's unlocked."

"I'm signing off," Yves said. "I don't want to get picked up by the motion sensor."

The signal went dead. Another quarter hour later Jay began wandering around the house, trying to memorize its topography. He avoided Madame Perrière-Lafonte's bedroom. The Christmas tree winked in the living room. Down the hallway, the bedside light went off. She was hard of hearing, nearly deaf, Manuela had said. He could make noise without bothering her. Anyway, she thought he was the heater repairman.

Jay walked the length of the ground floor over creaking parquet and thick carpets. He tried to clear the cache in his mind. But words, sentences and double-edged thoughts cut through and wouldn't be deleted. Hadn't the maid said something about the old lady taking medicine and being massaged? She was having headaches and nightmares?

Jay stopped pacing. Now he was sure. Every three minutes a car rolled by on the street between the mansion and the park. He'd kept a running count. Headlights from the main road projected shadows of trunks and branches on the living room walls, a magic lantern show. He wondered about Yves in the cold, and his thoughts again turned to Amy. Was she at home, waiting for his call, knowing it was too late to meet at the Louvre? Why had he suggested a place with limited opening hours? He should call her, he told himself. If he talked fast, Debra and Ron wouldn't be able to trace the call or pinpoint him, even if her line was bugged. He could try Amy's work number and leave a message. But what would he say?

He keyed in Amy's landline number but paused. Concentrate, he told himself. Stay calm. Think of those paparazzo days waiting for starlets to appear, for British parliamentarians to put on leather g-strings and spiked collars.

Jay sat in the kitchen corner again, determined to stay alert. The house creaked and groaned and spoke in dead languages. Wood expanded, plaster contracted, mice scurried, a clock ticked in an airless room.

Another half hour and his nerves couldn't take it. Get back in the car and leave the country, he told himself. With Amy. Call Debra and tell her to pick up the deciphered message at Bonjour Siam. It suddenly seemed insane to be sitting there waiting while terrorists were readying an attack. What were the chances someone would come tonight anyway? He'd staked out houses for hours, for days on end, dozens of times. But this was different. This was his life. Panic engulfed him. He counted the criminal offenses he could be charged with. Fraud, forgery, breaking and entering, use of false documents, deception, withholding evidence from law enforcement agencies, endangering innocent lives.

His fingers trembled as he zipped his jacket and started for the kitchen door. Before he could turn the handle the garden light snapped on. Yves? He counted. One-one thousand, two-one thousand...Yves had probably stepped out of the bamboo. Or rustled it...Eight-one thousand...Jay edged toward the window and peered out. Down the brick path came a man in an overcoat. He was wearing an old-fashioned felt hat. It was not a camelhair overcoat. The hat was not a fedora. Ten-one thousand...The man stepped up to the front door, put a key in the lock and turned it. Thirteen-one thousand...

Jay forced himself to inhale. He heard the man step into the hall and close the door. Seventeen, eighteen, nineteen, twenty

...The timed light went out. Jay's head pounded. He cracked open the kitchen door so Yves could get in. One second, two, three seconds passed. Where was Yves? Why hadn't the light come on again if Yves had stepped out of the bamboo? Count right. Count again.

Footsteps neared the kitchen then moved away, over the creaking parquet. But no inside lights came on. The man knew his way around. He must've thought he was alone to be making so much noise, Jay reasoned. Alone with the deaf old woman. Jay waited another three seconds, readied his Minox and tip-toed from the kitchen down the hall. From the sitting room he went into the living room following the carpeted areas.

Where the hell was Yves?

The Christmas tree lights flickered. Jay crouched behind an armchair. The footsteps stopped. He edged to the hallway and looked toward the bedroom, glimpsing furtive movements. A shadow. An arm. An arm raising a pillow. He heard a muffled cry and a thrashing sound. The garden light snapped on. Jay sprinted down the hall, the seconds ticking in his brain. The silhouette lifted the pillow and shook something. Jay realized it was the woman. The man was shaking Madame Perrière-Lafonte. Jay popped the flash, temporarily blinding the intruder.

He watched, unable to stop the man as he jerked Madame Perrière-Lafonte's head. As he rushed into the room the woman's body slid to the floor.

Pop, went the flash, the motor winding. Pop, pop.

The intruder spun around. Jay found himself face to face with a mask, a carnival mask with eye cutouts. He slammed into the man's chest. The hat flew off and the camera fell from Jay's hands as the two of them hit the floor. Jay wrenched him-self free of gloved hands. They clawed at him, at his throat, one hand in front, the other behind.

Wrestling, they rolled out of the bedroom into the hall, scuffling toward the living room. Jay's heel dug into the intruder's stomach. As they fell entwined, he ripped away the mask. Before they hit the floor for the second time Jay caught sight of a face. Her face. Rosalie's. The nurse. Her face was twisted into a grotesque. Gasping, Jay jumped up. But Rosalie moved faster. He heard Yves shouting from the entrance hall and felt Rosalie's knee rammed up between his legs. Falling again, curling into a ball, he caught sight of her running, pulling chairs and side-tables over behind her. He blacked out and seconds later willed himself to his feet in a star-swirled void. Yves hauled at him and leaned him against a wall.

When the stars stopped swarming Jay grabbed his camera and limped out. He was too nauseated to run. He heard a car burn rubber. From the garden gate he watched the taillights of a Renault disappear. He opened his eyes again. Yves skidded to a stop. Jay staggered into the front seat and felt Yves floor it. He saw trees flash by. The car swerved southeast toward the Marne River and the park boulevard back into town.

Breathless. Jay was. And sick. To his stomach. Words tumbled from his mouth one by one. Nurse. Rosalie. Murder. Crazy. Killing old women. Killing them for their money.

Yves gripped the wheel and headed in what Jay guessed was an easterly direction. Toward the freeway, Jay realized. Into the countryside. They could call Amy. Have her meet them. Good. A good plan.

As the pain and nausea subsided Jay raised his eyelids and sat up to a swarming blur of tail and headlights. The car slalomed. He had a sudden perception of speed and jabbed at his seatbelt buckle, trying to resist the car's G-force. Yves always drove like a rally driver. But he was out of control. The Citroën alternated between two wide wet lanes, avoiding commute vehicles. Jay wobbled, a bowling pin in a bumper car. He held tight. In the rear view mirror, a pair of headlights slalomed behind, gaining ground.

Jay twisted backward. The Renault. He swore out loud.

"They were waiting," Yves barked. "They drove around the block while I got the car." He downshifted to third, merged into the left lane, passed a delivery van, jerked to the right and pulled right again at a Y-junction onto a park road and through the woods.

Jay recognized the spot. Amy had forced him to go jogging there years ago. He twisted around again and counted. One one-thousand...two...three...

In his head he began to thank Yves for losing them. Seven one-thousand...nine...The headlights reappeared. "Shit," he shouted. Yves tightened his grip on the wheel. It was another car, Jay told himself. It had to be someone else. "Where does this road come out?"

The Citroën flew behind its own high beams. Yves shook his head. The Renault looked like it was three hundred yards behind. Yves jerked onto a one-lane road into the forest. "Saint Maurice," he blurted. "It comes out there. If they haven't..."

But they had. Half the park's roads were now closed to cars. Jay saw the galvanized barriers a quarter mile ahead reflecting the Citroën's headlights.

Yves killed the lights, hit the brakes and accelerated while winding the steering wheel counterclockwise. The car began a controlled spin. But its back wheels slipped too far and slid off the pavement. Jay heard the front wheels dig in, kicking back mud and gravel. The Renault closed the hundred yards now separating them. It slowed, facing off from the middle of the road, its high beams a wall of light.

Jay shaded his eyes. Yves blinked then gunned the engine, ready to play chicken.

Jay had always hated chase scenes. He braced himself and hoped the Renault would swerve out of the way, hoped this

would be over before it began. In a near out-of-body state he
watched as the big car ahead skidded to a stop and slid sideways
blocking the narrow road. Yves jerked left then right, a futile
confirmation of what Jay could see was inevitable. The shoulder was narrow and tipped up. Jay felt high-speed sequences in
slow-motion. He bucked toward the windshield, held back by
his seatbelt. The Citroën tilted at a 45-degree angle, its front-
end hitting a tangle of shrubs. The ride was over.

There was no time to speak or plan or reason. Jay unbuck-
led and saw the silhouette of a man moving outside. Call the
cops, he told himself, instinctively turning on his satellite cellphone. He pressed a memory button. He knew it didn't matter
what number he called. Debra would pick him up on screen.
But it was too late.

"Drop it," shouted the man.

Jay heard the phone fall between the seats. He held his hands
up. In four decades he'd never had a gun pointed at him. He
stared at Rosalie. The pistol seemed smaller than what he'd
seen in the movies, and she looked ridiculous holding it that
way, gripped with both hands, her knees bent like Debra that
morning at the loft. Rosalie waved the gun. He turned as if in
a dream to speak to Yves for what he realized might be the last
time. Another gun was in motion outside the driver's side, a
revolver held by a hand protruding from a camelhair sleeve.

"Get out I said!" It was Rosalie's voice. Jay pushed open the
car door, forced it up and slid outside. "Go around the front
and push the car back," she ordered. The gun's muzzle tracked
him. "Push the car! Jean-Paul, help him."

Jay was aware of the presence of the man in the camelhair
coat. He stood a yard away from him now. The stick figure was
lit by oblique high beams. As a reflex Jay began to ease out his
camera to steal a shot. But he put his hands in front of him instead and leaned his weight into the Citroën's nose. Someone
camping in his mind observed with detached fascination as the

man named Jean-Paul used a single hand, his left one, to push the car. His right one waved the pistol. Yves was still at the wheel. He revved and rocked the car forward and backward until it was free of the bushes and back on the shoulder. Rosalie pulled open the rear door so Jean-Paul could climb in.

"The bullet will go right through the seat and you," Jean-Paul told Yves. His gloved hand pressed the gun into the back of the driver's seat. The other hand felt its way around. He had a surprisingly high voice. Surprising because he was well over six feet tall, with wide shoulders padded out by the camelhair overcoat. The voice and face made a better match. They were pinched and nasty.

Jean-Paul handed the envelopes and Camcorder out of the window. But Rosalie couldn't hold them while training her gun on Jay. "I'll get the cameras and other things later," she said. "Put the memory card in your pocket." Jean-Paul popped open the Camcorder.

It was the calmness of their manner that scared Jay most. Rosalie's pretty smile and the lilting southern accent were gone. She moved and spoke like a trained SWAT team leader, like a French Debra Wright. The carnival masks were off.

Jay walked in the direction she indicated with the pistol's twitching tip. As they reached the Renault an electric window slid down. A small, gloved hand reached out from the back seat and took the envelopes from Rosalie.

"Get in the other side," said a suave baritone voice. "Move."

Jay had been blinded until then by the cars' headlights. Now he could see the fedora on the man's head. He had to be a short man, Jay reasoned. How else could he be wearing a fedora inside a car?

Rosalie's pistol showed Jay the back way around the car's trunk. He opened the rear door and ducked in.

"Family reunion," said Georges Henri, his face expressionless. The skin was blotched and stretched like a drum over prominent cheekbones. He raised a handgun from under the long blue scarf coiled around his neck.

Jay opened his mouth and instinctively reached forward to protect himself. But Rosalie grabbed his collar from behind and pulled him back to the corner of the seat.

Handcuffed, her mouth sealed with duct tape, Amy stared from the front passenger seat, eyes wide with terror. She clawed at the door latch. But her shoulder belt held tight.

From his corner Georges Henri trained the gun on Jay. "Tell her to stop that, will you? The door is locked. It's pointless."

Henri said nothing until Rosalie sat behind the wheel. She flashed the headlights and revved. Unpinned, her long hair fell around her shoulders. She let the Citroën pass before falling in behind it.

"You always were a troublesome boy," Henri commented. "Troublesome to your mother and your father and your aunt."

Jay cleared his throat. "Take the tape off Amy's mouth."

Maitre Henri considered the request, frowning at Amy. He motioned to Rosalie but spoke to Jay. "Is that any way to address an old family friend? You might say 'please, Georges'." Rosalie hesitated then ripped the duct tape off Amy's mouth. She stuck it to the headrest.

Amy gulped. "Picked me up . . ." she gasped. "Outside the office . . . I . . . ." She tried to turn but Rosalie cuffed her on the temple. "Why?" Amy asked, reeling back. "Why are you doing this?"

Rosalie raised her hand as if to hit Amy again but unstuck the duct-tape instead and slapped it across her mouth. Jay lunged. Henri showed him the gun, waving him back. "She's asking for it," Rosalie snarled.

"We want it to look like an accident," Henri reminded her. "Jean-Paul knows where. Follow him and wait, Rosalie."

The Citroën flashed its lights and turned left off the pavement onto another forest road. Sleet fell. The Renault's wipers swiped at the clotted windshield.

"An accident?" Jay asked. "Like Nicolas de Lafayette? Like Arlette's accident?" He reached forward to touch Amy's cheek.

Henri nodded from his dark corner. "Bravo, you've found the key," he said, savoring his words. "Don't worry. We'll take care of your aunt Jacqueline, won't we Rosalie?"

"Yes, Maitre," she said, the southwestern lilt stealing back.

"With you gone Jacqueline will have no one but Hilary and Rosalie to look after her," Henri added. "And Opus Angeli, of course." He paused again. "We'll wait a few months, won't we Rosalie?"

"Yes, Maitre," she repeated. "Perhaps a year?"

"Perhaps," Henri conceded. "We're both very fond of your aunt," he added. "You've created such a fuss with this business, you and your father. Old photographs and daguerreotypes, who would've imagined such old things would flush out Monsieur Gonflay and that greedy Maitre d'Arnac? And others, too, isn't that right Rosalie? Others who have been meddling with our little project." Rosalie glanced into the rearview mirror and nodded. "Who would have thought you'd create such an awful brouhaha," Henri continued, adjusting his fedora as the car splashed along the pot-holed dirt road. "Your father was like that, always up to something. Way back in the 'Forties he always had to have his say, never could follow orders like the rest of us, and then he betrayed us. He betrayed the cause. He had to go. You do see that, don't you Jay?"

Jay shook his head. His mouth was dry. The words wouldn't come out. "You killed him."

"Unzip your jacket," Henri ordered, waving his pistol. He reached over and felt Jay's pockets, removing the red cellphone. Jay let his hands drop. The Citroën slowed and stopped ahead in a clearing surrounded by fir trees. Jay shifted in his seat, reaching down and removing the wad of gum from the button

microphone in the lining of his jacket. Rosalie turned the car
full circle. She pulled up the parking brake but left the motor
running.

"Why?" Jay asked, picking up Amy's question, his voice
cracking with tension. "Why kill old ladies? They're going to
give you their money anyway."

Rosalie pointed her gun at Jay and waited for orders. Her
eyes moved from him to Amy. Maitre Henri pursed his lips.
They were thin and almost white. "Be careful, Rosalie," he
said. "It has to look like they did it to each other. With a little
help from Jean-Paul." He glanced at the manila envelopes in
his lap as he shook out the contents. "Turn on the inside light,
please." Rosalie obeyed. Henri studied the laser prints, flipping
through them. "Why?" he asked rhetorically. "It would take a
lifetime to explain why." He paused to peer at the prints. "And
why should I bother?" He compared the photographs, his face
expressionless. "Some of our benefactors simply live on and
on." He spoke in a reasonable tone. Jay found himself nod-
ding. "Consider our dear friend and colleague Madeleine," he
added. "Opus waited patiently for her. We waited for years
and years, but she simply wouldn't let go. Madeleine was
a friend but she too turned against us, with your father. She
didn't approve of our methods. And we needed her contribu-
tion to the cause. We needed Madame Perrière-Lafonte's con-
tribution, too, and she's now nearly a hundred."

"She was," Rosalie corrected.

Maitre Henri sighed. "You ask me why? You wouldn't understand why. Your father understood, once upon a time. He
knew the dangers of Communism and we thought he also
saw those of radical Islam. We have five million Moslems now
in France. The enemy is within. But our government is weak,
it doesn't have the will to deport them and purify the nation,
so we must bring about the conditions to make that inevitable."

"It doesn't make sense," Jay blurted. "Père Labé is a good man."

Maitre Henri wagged his head. He held up the pair of prints showing Jean-Paul pushing Serge Gonflay under the bus. "Is this what the accident looked like? Oh my." Henri interrupted himself. He leaned forward again and prodded at Jay's jacket, removing his wallet and a small envelope. "I hadn't thought of it, but you might just be wearing a wire." His voice hardened. "You're rash enough, like your father." He stared at the envelope and seemed unable to resist peering inside. "Take off your jacket and hand it to Rosalie if you please. Slowly."

Jay watched as Henri fished out the digital prints of the Free Europe Committee. Two were black and white, the other a glossy rectangle. Rosalie turned the sleeves of Jay's jacket inside out, feeling along the seams. "Nothing," she said, tossing the jacket back. "No wire."

Maitre Henri seemed lost in thought. He scrutinized the image of himself amid the others in the old group portraits. A grin spread over his dry features.

"Free Europe," Jay said. "You let the Nazis and collaborators go free. You were probably one yourself, weren't you? A mole from the Milice?"

Henri smiled. His skin stretched taut over his cheekbones. "We didn't let them go free," he corrected. "We actively helped them escape, we created new identities for them, we smuggled them out of the country in ships and planes, some of them French and American."

"The ratlines?"

Henri held the snapshots up to the interior light. "Your father and I, with Madeleine and Charles Trichet, and others, of course. Scores of others. Your father was too naïve to realize what he was doing and who was involved, until Genoa, that is. The day we sent Eichmann to Argentina. June 17, 1950." Henri paused to lick his lips. "Those were the good old days, weren't they Rosalie," he added wistfully. "Not that you could possibly know. We still had Indo-China and Algeria. Charles and I were born in Algeria. It was part of France and not just a colony, it was a *département*. We still had the power to keep France French. There were no mosques and minarets yet, no scarves or prayer rugs or Internet, or hamburgers and cellular telephones." He curled his lips at the red cellphone. "Who really won the war? The free world? Our world? Surely not. They did." He raised a finger to the window and pointed toward the suburbs beyond the woods. The gun dropped momentarily. "*You* did, you and your so-called democratic, multi-ethnic culture, *they* and their fundamentalism and their politics of breeding. There are five million of them in France now. Five million."

Jay felt the hair prickle on his arms. Maitre Henri's eyes were glazed. Rosalie started to say something but Henri shushed her. "You drove your poor mother to desperation," he said out of the blue. "Your poor mother who married that idealistic idiot from New England. It was quite a sacrifice for the cause."

Jay flushed. "She married my father instead of you." Jay felt like spitting. "Instead of marrying *you?*" he repeated, shouting. He felt the veins swell in his head.

Henri stiffened. He raised the gun's muzzle. "You've grown into a bothersome man," he said. "You almost spoiled our plans. The Abrahamian Brotherhood will put on a spectacular show for New Year's. Of course they have no idea where the funding comes from and that's the beauty of it. We'll make sure they're caught and killed of course, when the time is right. Rosalie will help and so will your American friends. So clever they are. So American. Go, go, go."

"Let's kill them now," Rosalie interrupted.

Maitre Henri pursed his lips. "Yes, of course you're right, we should." He waved the pistol. "Once you and your Legionnaire friend there started snooping around we had to act. No one can double-cross Opus Angeli. Your friends Gonflay and d'Arnac were trying to do that. But they were clumsy. When I take a percentage of each legacy it's for the cause, not for personal gain, you understand? They were different." He waved the gun. "Gonflay was always a liability. But it still pains me to think that Claude-Gilles would succumb to simple greed. He was so rich, we took such good care of him."

Rosalie shifted in the driver's seat. "What do we do now?"

"Patience," scolded Maitre Henri. "I've known this boy all his life, I may even have given him life, though he never really knew me. And now I'm going to take his life away." He finished poring over the snapshots and slipped them into his pocket. "Such a shame for everyone," he added. "Even your lovely fiancée has to die. She knows too much. You dragged her into this. And besides, once you were gone Jacqueline might have willed your share to Miss Smith. She speaks so highly of Mademoiselle Smith."

Amy thrashed but Rosalie raised the pistol butt. "Don't," Jay pleaded. "For god's sake don't hit her."

"God?" Henri sneered. "What do you know of God? What mission have you in life? We have a mission. We have a reason for what we do." He turned to Rosalie. "Take the tape off her mouth. Gently, Rosalie. I really can't bear to see her like that, and the tape is bound to leave traces."

Amy winced as the tape came off again. "We have a file on you," she spat, her voice vibrating with rage. "We have documents and pictures, and a codebook and plates. *Le Prince.* There are copies of everything already with the authorities."

Jay segued. "I already sent those photos out on CDs. The prints too. And we're being recorded right now, through this." He lifted the button mike. "Where the hell are you, Debra?"

Maitre Henri laughed. He reached over and plucked the miniature mike out of the lining. "It's a button, my boy." He dropped it to the floor. "It's a button and I'm afraid what you say couldn't possibly be true. Even if you aren't bluffing,

whatever you have we'll make sure is interpreted correctly."
Henri glanced over at the Citroën. Jean-Paul lowered his window. "If you believe in the power of the press or the police in
this country or your own you're either fools or delusional. Your
friends will be discredited or silenced. I wouldn't count on the
maid's testimony. She's likely to have an accident herself
tonight, or possibly tomorrow. It's so slippery out there and
she wears those inadequate little shoes."

"And Madame Perrière-Lafonte died in her sleep," Rosalie
added.

Jay met Amy's eyes. He was about to speak when Henri
held up the manila envelope. "What you have here is very
damning photographic evidence of Jean-Paul's misdeeds," he
conceded. "Very damning indeed and I thank you for turning
it over to the authorities if you have, though I don't believe it."
He paused. "It's convenient. Jean-Paul has become a liability,
like Monsieur Gonflay. In fact he was very friendly with Serge,
wasn't he Rosalie?"

"He was on the take," she confirmed. "He skimmed off
plenty."

"A clever thief and a murderer who was fanatical enough to
fund Islamic terrorists to destabilize the republic, using the
auspices of our charity," Henri said. "Couldn't a thief and a
murderer and a terrorist like Jean-Paul kill a pair of second-
rate forgers and an innocent fiancée before succumbing himself? It works out rather nicely. All three of you, all four of you,
actually, in one neat package. Opus Angeli will be delighted to
cooperate with the authorities, and your American friends.
Where are they, by the way? Why is it taking them so long to
arrive? They were most displeased with your father and they're
bound to be even more displeased by you, and I don't believe
they would help you even if they could. Everything can be explained with a little help from the Ministry of the Interior."
Rosalie smiled at Maitre Henri.

"Please," she said. "Let's get going."

"First have Jean-Paul take care of the Legionnaire," Henri instructed. "Then you take care of Jean-Paul." He paused. "I'll keep Mademoiselle Smith and Monsieur Grant company." He lowered his window and dipped his head at Jean-Paul.

$$\mathbb{A}$$

Rosalie stepped around the Renault, wading through the headlights. She hustled Yves out of the Citroën. Jean-Paul followed. It was hard to see through the sleet and misted windows. The three of them looked like Etch-a-Sketch figures. Then Jay heard a shot. He spun to his door latch. Out of the corner of his eye he saw Amy struggling to unbuckle her belt.

"Sit still," Henri shouted. "Both of you." But Amy's fingers found the buckle. Jay heard the belt rewind. He saw Henri raise the gun and heard him swear, then felt his own hands grab Henri's wrist and wrench it up and back, dislocating the shoulder. He twisted and broke joints as Henri screamed in pain.

The gun went off. A bullet whizzed past Jay's ear and blew out the side window. He was aware of sound and light, shots and screams. Amy jumped and ran as Henri's fedora fell off. Jay's legs were spread on the back seat, his right knee on Henri's stomach. His hands banged Henri's broken arm and forced Henri's head against the window. The pistol dropped. The lawyer's head slumped. Jay stepped over him and dragged him out by his overcoat and scarf.

Back-lit by the headlights, two figures wrestled near the other car. A camelhair overcoat landed on the Citroën's hood, and a lanky man turned around to face Rosalie.

Jay felt the scarf being tugged. He glanced down at Henri dangling, clutching at his throat. Jay retrieved Henri's pistol and raised it. He took aim at Rosalie but didn't fire. His hands shook. He jerked Henri by the scarf and shouted for Amy. But the words hardly came out. Impotent, he watched Rosalie run into the woods, chasing someone. A woman. Amy.

His mind was alive with fear. He felt something he'd never felt before. The capacity to kill. He hauled Henri to his feet, peeled the overcoat off him and reeled him in by the scarf.

"What do I do with you?" he yelled. "Yves!"

But Yves didn't answer. Jay could no longer see anyone through the sleet. He wrestled Henri's overcoat on, ripping the lining. The hat. The fedora. Put on the fedora, he told himself. Put on the fedora and call her, call Rosalie.

Before he'd lost the thread he reached back into the Renault and grabbed Henri's hat.

"The woman got away," Yves panted. "She's hunting Amy."

"Amy," Jay shouted. He heard Henri's whimpering and the rumble of the Renault's engine. "Help me put my bomber jacket on the old man," he said. Together they rammed the lawyer's arms through the sleeves. Seconds later branches broke in the trees behind them. Yves pointed and ran into the woods, a pistol in each hand.

"Go around the other way," he yelled back. "I got their guns."

Jay saw blood on his hands, on Henri and the car. Yves had been hit. Or was it Jean-Paul or Rosalie's blood? Why was Yves running if he'd been hit?

Jay shouted for Amy again and jerked at Henri's scarf. With the fedora on his head, he looped the scarf around Henri's face and mouth, gagging him. Twisting the lawyer's unbroken arm behind him he forced him forward, lifting and pushing.

"Rosalie?" Jay called, making his voice sound like Henri's, lowering the timbre to an old man's baritone, bending his knees to a crouch. The name *Rosalie* caught in his throat. "Rosalie, come out," he called, his voice stronger and deeper. "I've got Jay, Rosalie. Leave the woman alone and help me with Jay..."

Henri stopped struggling. Heart attack, Jay thought. He's had a heart attack. "Rosalie," Jay beckoned, trying to sound calm. He drove the pistol into Henri's backbone and propelled him forward into the trees, calling out Rosalie's name. In a flash Rosalie appeared. Her hands seized the neck protruding from the bomber jacket. Jay pushed Henri toward her and let go.

"Yes, Maitre," Rosalie said as she jerked Henri's neck and caught his dead weight. "Yes."

Jay knocked the fedora backward off his head and stood up. He aimed the pistol at Rosalie. She looked from his face to the body in her arms and let out a howl. Cradling the dead man she laid him against a tree and flew back at Jay. He stumbled, aimed and pulled the trigger but didn't feel the pistol buck. Jay stood for what seemed hours, his finger on the trigger, unable to move, unsure if he were firing or not.

A shot rang out. The bullet brought Rosalie down. The gun seemed to have a life of its own now, bucking again and again. The second and third bullets stopped Rosalie's writhing.

Yves stepped out from behind a tree. Through the falling sleet he stared down at Henri and Rosalie. "Get your jacket off him," Yves said. He bent and tugged. "Don't just stand there."

Jay dropped the pistol and ran into the woods, batting back the branches, shouting, tripping as he scrambled.

Amy's hands were still cuffed. They stepped into the clearing together while Yves wiped down the Renault's interior. He hauled Jean-Paul off the Citroën's hood and dumped him facedown in a puddle. Then he wrapped the dead man's stiffening fingers around a pistol.

Yves listed slightly. He said nothing. A trickle of blood ran down his sleeve. "I got the envelopes." He spoke fast. "I said I've got the envelopes. Take off that overcoat and put your jacket back on. Let's get the hell out of here."

Jay moved mechanically. He nudged Amy toward the Citroën.

"What about the keys?" Yves grabbed Henri's overcoat and went through the pockets. "The keys to the cuffs?"

Jay rocked Amy, shook his head and watched Yves limp back into the woods. A minute later Yves limped back. He unlocked Amy's cuffs and handed Jay a bloodstained envelope. "It was in his shirt pocket," Yves said. "I wiped down his gun."

Yves got behind the wheel of the Citroën and jolted back onto the paved road. The blood-smeared envelope sat on Jay's lap. Amy stared with unfocused eyes as Jay wiped away the blood and opened it.

"I pulled the trigger," Yves said. "Just remember that. You hear me? I pulled it, not you."

But Jay wasn't listening. He rubbed away the blood beaded across the glossy surface of the digital color print. Funny, he thought to himself as the Citroën merged with traffic. Funny how Georges Henri's blood had already soaked into the black-and-white pictures, coloring them red.

A police convoy passed, heading in the direction they'd come from, roof lights swirling and sirens screaming. Jay groped around the passenger compartment and found his satellite phone. "Debra," he said. "You there?" Words came back at him. "Shut up and listen," he said. "Go to Bonjour Siam. Tell them I sent you. Tell them you want the spicy crab. Then go to hell." He turned off the phone and closed his eyes.

Paris, December 31, 2007

Jay reached into the ice bucket and raised the magnum of Veuve Cliquot. He refilled Amy's coupe. They stepped onto the wrap-around balcony. Jay could see up and down the Champs-Elysées. Over the rooftops rose the shimmering Eiffel Tower. The countdown to midnight showed less than a minute to go. As the seconds ticked the roar of the crowd below grew. Bottle rockets and firecrackers exploded. The gun barrel of the sharp-shooter on the roof right behind them looked strangely like a TV aerial, Jay thought. The avenue was filled a hundred yards wide and a mile long with cheering, dancing partiers. He glanced at the row of buildings on the other side of the street and wondered if Debra and Ron were watching. On a table near the French windows behind Amy stood *Curiosity Case*. Next to it was a copy of the *International Herald Tribune*. Jay saw Amy's lips move as she read the inch-high headline. *Abrahamian Brotherhood Cell Dismantled—Orange Alert Still in Effect*. Sirens peeled and fireworks lit the sky. A roar rose in waves from below as Jay turned to kiss her. His eyes moved in-stinctively back to the sharpshooter and counted nine fingers.